More Tales of the Zombie

CREDITS

More Tales of the Zombie

Edited by

BILL OLVER

Big Pulp Publications

Black Chaos II: More Tales of the Zombie

ISBN 978-0-9896812-2-3

Visit us online:
www.bigpulp.com
Facebook (Facebook.com/bigpulp)
Twitter (twitter.com/BigPulp)

Distributed by Ingram

Ebook versions available from Amazon
and other online venues

Big Pulp Publications
BILL OLVER Editor/Publisher

Cover illustration by Ken Knudtsen

Also from Big Pulp Publications
Black Chaos: Tales of the Zombie (2014)
The Kennedy Curse (2013)
APESHIT (2013)
Clones, Fairies & Monsters in the Closet (2013)

Periodicals
Big Pulp (all-genre quarterly)
Child of Words (SF&F)
M (horror and mystery)
Thirst (romance)

Table of Contents

WE ALWAYS GET OUR MAN

by R.A. Williamson

Many a dime novel has imagined how Zarahemla Two Crows and I first met, and what prompted such odd bedfellows as us to embark on an adventure that would ultimately save the world from Armageddon. The truth is, Dear Reader, it all began in the late Winter of 1875, when my commanding officer took seriously ill, and attempted to devour my brains.

This, then, is how it really happened.

Having made the trek north to Fort Edmonton in the worst blizzard of the season, we found ourselves half-frozen upon our arrival at the great wooden gates. If the harsh weather were not trial enough, we had lost the greater part of our horses to a raiding party of Blackfeet who, fortunately for us, were more interested in our mounts than our scalps. It was late in the night and exceedingly cold, made all the worse by a driving wind that blasted us relentlessly with blinding snow.

As advertised, the life of a North-West Mounted Policeman is never wont for adventure.

The night watchmen ushered us with great urgency to Rowand House, an impressive three-story structure dominating the center of the courtyard. I ordered water boiled and as many pelts and blankets as they could find. Several of the men were hypothermic and frostbitten, and I was forced to remove two of Sub-Constable Atwood's toes and Sergeant Roark's left ring finger, lest they become gangrenous.

After tending to my duties as surgeon, I took my leave of our commanding officer, Inspector Maclaren, and retired to the gentlemen's mess. The cook's boy had been roused upon our arrival, and was preparing our meal as I sat by the great fireplace in the large hall. By and by, my comrades trickled in, taking their seats at large rough-hewn tables. Soon the air was full with the haze of pipe smoke and the voices of rough men.

I had devoured one bowl of piping hot stew and was making headway into a second when the door flew open in a great gust of wind. To our surprise, a colossal brown bear festooned with icicles and heavy mats of snow ducked in under the lintel. Several of the men began shouting and drew their pistols. Constable Robins, given to a weak constitution, fainted dead away.

Slamming the door shut, the bear threw down the latch and stomped its boots. It glared, unconcerned, at the firearms pointed in its direction, and pulled open its giant maw to reveal the dark, ruddy face of a man with deep-set eyes that glinted like diamonds.

He scratched at his thick, gray-streaked beard, yawned, and tromped down toward the fireplace between rows of nervous troopers.

I daresay I had never seen a larger man, or a more peculiar one for that matter, and I doubt I ever will. From the top of his wild nest of black hair to the bottom of his heavy, nail-studded boots, he cut an imposing figure. His cloak, made from the skin of a grizzly, hung heavy across wide shoulders, and the room shook with every step he took. He passed me by without a glance and stood in front of the fire, warming his hands in silence.

The cook's boy appeared beside him with a tankard of hot water, which the man took with a grunt of thanks. He threw back his cloak, revealing a great belt studded with high caliber brass cartridges and a brace of large revolving pistols, and sat down heavily on a small stool. It groaned in protest. He had singularly striking blue eyes, like glacier ice, set under a heavy outcropping of thick bone and expressive steel wool brows. If one had asked me to wager on the race of his forefathers, I would not have known where to place my bets.

After a minute, the dusky man turned to me and pointed to the star on my lapel. "No disrespect, son, but ain't you young for an Inspector?"

"Surgeon," I replied, somewhat taken aback by the impudence of the man. "Well, assistant surgeon, specifically. I am attached to Inspector Maclaren's troop."

He extended a massive hand and said, "The name's Two Crows. Zarahemla Two Crows."

"Bonhomme," I replied, watching as his hand swallowed mine in a bone-crushing grip. He pumped my arm vigorously, nearly dislocating my shoulder.

"Doctor Emmanuel Bonhomme," I continued, recovering my tenderized appendage. "I've heard of you, Mr. Two Crows. You're a scout for the detachment here, no?"

"On occasion," he replied, pulling a long braid of chicory root out of his breast pocket. He clamped it between his teeth like a cigar. Firelight played across the shadowy creases in his boot-leather skin.

"We received word they had gone missing—that's why we're here. What happened?"

He chewed on the chicory thoughtfully before spitting the juice into the fire, where it sizzled and danced on the glowing grate. "Done gone got themselves kilt, I reckon," he said.

"And you haven't thought to search for them?"

He shot me a look that could have petrified a gorgon, and growled, "I twernt out in that godforsaken weather on a damn constitutional, Doc."

"I apologize."

"Look, son, I've been cutting for sign since before your daddy was sucking on your grandmama's teat. If what took those men could be tracked, I would've found it."

"Whatever sort of mischief our comrades-in-arms befell, we'll suss it out," I said with confidence. "We always get our man."

Two Crows leaned back and laughed so loud that the head of every trooper in the hall turned in our direction. "You're stepping into territory beyond your ken," he finally said, slapping me on the shoulder. "I wish you the best of luck. But if you value your hide, you'll sit this one out."

"We could use a seasoned tracker who knows the land," I proffered.

Two Crows snorted. "Not for all the tea in China."

Huddling deep into my beaver greatcoat, I clenched my jaw to stop the chattering of my teeth. Wind cut through fur and wool like a lance, freezing the very marrow of my bone. As Inspector Maclaren inspected our line of shivering troopers, the dappled mare under me pawed at the snow, her breath thick and heavy in the morning air.

If Maclaren felt the cold, he did not show it.

Satisfied, he waved his arm in a wide circle over his head and we rode out through Fort Edmonton's main gate in single file. Thick fog was rolling up the banks of the mighty North Saskatchewan, enshrouding us as we traveled in silence. For miles all that could be heard was the creak of saddle leather and the jingle of our spurs. It was a ghostly world, beautiful in its serenity, and yet haunting in its stillness. It felt as if time itself were frozen.

The sun burned off the fog as we rode, and by mid-morning we ceased following the river and turned toward Father Lacombe's small mission in the Sturgeon River valley.

It was Maclaren's intention to question the priest about our missing comrades, and I was glad for the excursion, for it meant I could also see to the business of my immortal soul. From what I knew of Zarahemla Two Crows, it was an odd thing indeed for him to turn down any offer of employment. He was a hard old hunter, and had a reputation of reckless boldness. His warnings, which had at first perplexed me, proceeded to gnaw at my mind until I had developed a sense of foreboding that set my spirit on edge.

I am not a praying man by nature, but the West is a land steeped in mystery, and one's faith in rational explanations can be easily shaken.

Bowing my head, I silently called upon Saint George to watch over us. We rode.

By noon we could see the small log chapel and outbuildings scattered among the tall pines. A thick blanket of snow had settled over the mission, and aside from a great flock of magpies flitting to and from the buildings and trees, we discerned no activity. A chorus of high pitched, nasal squawks assaulted the silence as they bickered with one another in agitation. I traced a weak trail of chimney smoke high into the sky, and noticed ravens soaring in a great, lazy circle.

Maclaren saw them too, and gave the order to halt. We brought our horses into a line on a rise overlooking the mission.

"Don't like the look o' it, sir," Sergeant Brown said. He spit into the snow and smoothed his mustache.

Maclaren creased his hawkish eyes as he watched the ravens. "Sergeant, take a man and secure the perimeter."

Brown nodded to Constable Young as he pulled his Snider-Enfield carbine out of its saddle bucket. The two men broke formation and rode off into the trees silently.

"Keep sharp," Maclaren said to the rest of us. He turned in the saddle and looked Constable Robins squarely in the eye. "And don't get twitchy."

I drew my Adams revolver as we started down the hill. Hippocratic Oath or not, our run-in with the whiskey traders at Fort Whoop Up had taught me the value of a serviceable sidearm, and gone were any compunctions I might have had against perforating a man bent on violence toward me. Indeed, I took down one or two of the rascals myself in the skirmish, much to my satisfaction.

We entered the mission grounds at a slow trot, fanning our line out in a wide crescent. Save for the rough chorus of magpies, all was still as death itself as we passed by the shuttered outbuildings. Corporal Franks, riding beside me, gave a low whistle and motioned with a bob of his chin. I followed his gaze to the corpse of a young Métis woman half buried in the snow. The birds had been working on the body for some time now, but something much larger had been at her first. While she was hardly my first cadaver, the young lady was a strong contender for the most gruesome. And she was far from the worst thing I would witness before this day was over.

Robins had dismounted, and was standing beside his horse. He looked at us with panic in his eyes, gagged, and promptly lost his breakfast on his moccasins. Franks laughed and rode past him, around the woodshed and into the church courtyard. I heard him cry out, and spurred my horse forward.

'Massacre' is a flaccid word compared to what met my eyes when I rode into the courtyard.

Franks was wiping the contents of his stomach from his lips with the back of a glove. He swore and looked at me in horror. He was a hard man, and had taken part in more than his share of bloody business, but I understood his terror. It filled me too. This was not the work of men.

The frozen corpses of women and children filled the courtyard, some torn limb from limb, others ripped wide open from neck to navel. Black from the cold, with their faces locked in rictus, mothers and babes stared at us with hollow eyes. Our horses shifted nervously at the smell of so much death.

Maclaren backed up his horse, revealing a white man in a red jacket crouched over a body. His face was soaked in blood, and he looked at us with wild eyes as he sat on his haunches, grasping his victims entrails in fingers stained with gore. In front of him lay the priest, flayed open like a book. The young Mountie snarled.

"Appears we found one of our boys," Maclaren said. He looked at me. "What do you make of this, Doc?"

I dismounted and walked over to them, swallowing the bile in my throat. Years of medical training took over as I surveyed the grizzly scene. To function as a physician, it is necessary to see people as the meat and bone we are, and repress instinctual sympathies.

The crouching Mountie barked at me as I approached. Maclaren was covering him with a carbine, and I cocked my pistol. We stood and watched him for a few minutes. Apparently satisfied that we did not come to steal his meal, the crazed young man resumed feeding on the old priest's bowels.

"Well?" Maclaren asked, hopping out of his saddle.

"I've read of some cases of cannibalistic hysteria," I said, motioning to the bodies littering the courtyard. "But nothing on this scale, or this…violent."

"He couldn't have done it alone," Maclaren said. "You think he found them like this? Maybe bears? This poor devil's crazed with hunger. It's not beyond a starved man to scavenge on the dead."

"Weren't animals," Franks said, riding up to us. "No claw marks, no tracks. This were done with the bare hands of men."

"Men literally tearing woman and children apart?" Maclaren shook his head. "No, there's something else going on here." He put his rifle in the saddle bucket. Walking up beside the young man he said, "What's your name, son?"

A snarl through barred teeth dripping with blood was the young man's reply.

Maclaren bent over and shouted in his face. "I said, what's your name, son?"

The young man pounced suddenly and tackled Maclaren, clawing at his face with broken and bloodied nails. The two slipped on frozen gore and rolled in crimson snow. Maclaren fought him off with one hand while he struggled to draw his pistol. Franks and I circled the melee, trying to get a clear shot, but they were moving too erratically. The young man gnashed his teeth inches from Maclaren's face. The smell of his breath must have been overwhelming. Maclaren retched. He kneed the man in the groin and stomach, but to no apparent effect.

Finally freeing his sidearm, Maclaren shot the young man in the chest repeatedly until they both collapsed. Panting, he sat up and spit into the snow. I rushed over to help him up, but the insane man's eyes flashed open and he dug his teeth deep into Maclaren's arm, tearing away a large chunk of flesh. My superior grunted in pain, and bashed the young man's skull in with the butt of his pistol until it was a featureless mess of brains and splintered bone.

Franks clucked his tongue. "Well, if that don't take the rag off the bush."

"Dodgasted," Maclaren cussed.

"Come on, sir, let's get that arm taken care of," I said, helping him stand.

"And where the in tarnation were you two?" Maclaren barked. "That maniac darn near took my face off."

Franks shrugged and said, "You was rasslin' around like pirooting bobcats. Couldn't get a clear shot."

I pulled out my medical bag. "Let me see to that arm."

Maclaren composed himself as I rolled up his sleeve and tended to his wound. It was a deep, ragged hole in the flesh of his forearm, coloring rapidly with infection. I flushed it with whiskey from my flask and gave the rest to Maclaren to steady his nerves.

"I'll have to sew this up, sir." I said. "It's going to hurt."

He dismissed my warning with a grunt and took a swig from my flask.

The other men were hanging around the edges of the courtyard, jumping at shadows. Maclaren looked up at Franks, "Get a detail to collect all the bodies. Put them in the woodshed. We'll torch it. And search the buildings for survivors."

"You know there ain't no survivors," Franks said.

"Probably not." Maclaren gritted his teeth as my needle and catgut thread snagged on his flesh. "But idle men get twitchy. Best to give them something to do."

Franks flipped a salute off the brim of his fur cap.

"So, what did you call this, Doc?" Maclaren said, looking at the pulverized young Mountie at his feet. "Cannibalistic what?"

"Hysteria."

"That make a man survive multiple forty-five-caliber bullets in the heart at point blank range?"

"Unlikely."

"So what's your prognosis?"

"Sir," I said, "I have no bloody clue."

He frowned and I finished bandaging his arm with iodine gauze. "You'll have to keep that clean," I said. "It's already showing signs of infection."

"Already?"

"We'll just have to keep a close eye on it, sir."

Maclaren looked over my shoulder and nodded. "Looks like Brown found something."

The Sergeant rode into the courtyard with Constable Young; between them was non-other than Zarahemla Two Crows. I nodded to the giant man in the bearskin cloak and he grinned back, spitting chicory juice from between his teeth.

Brown saluted Maclaren and paused, taking in the grizzly scene at the Inspector's feet. "We found more like that, westward of here, sir," he said in a voice as flat and cold as the Alberta prairie.

"You done gone got yourself nibbled on," Two Crows said, motioning to Maclaren's arm.

"Just a scratch," Maclaren said.

"You're a dead man walking, sure as I was born."

"It's hardly a mortal wound," I said.

Two Crows shrugged. "Infected already, innit?"

"I dressed the wound myself, he'll be fine."

"By nightfall you'll be like this 'un," Two Crows said to Maclaren, pointing at the dead Mountie. "Gnawing on your friends like so much raw beef."

"What are you saying?" I asked. "Are you implying this is contagious?"

"Yup."

"Fiddlesticks," Maclaren said. "This is clearly the effects of hypothermia and starvation—resulting in…er…cannibalistic hysterectomy—ain't that right, Doc?"

"Hysteria," I corrected. "That's one hypothesis. There could be other—"

Maclaren cut me off and said to Brown, "Where did you find this crazy old half-breed anyway?"

"A large group left here on foot this morning. He was riding their trail, braining the survivors they left behind with a hatchet."

"It was the only way to be sure," Two Crows added.

"In that case, why isn't this man under arrest, Sergeant?"

"On account of the 'survivors' trying to tear our throats out."

"Bullet 'tween the eyes should work, too," Two Crows mused, "but I reckon it a waste of ammo."

"What in the Sam Hill is going on here?" Maclaren asked no one in particular.

"Recruiting," Two Crows replied, as if that explained everything.

From the way we all stared at him, I guess he figured we didn't catch his meaning. He spit a long stream of chicory juice into the snow and snorted. He looked at us long and hard before saying, "You take any thought to why all the dead are women and children? Where are all the men? Asides from the handful of stragglers what tried to eat your faces, that is."

I can honestly say the thought had not crossed my mind. Maclaren and Brown looked equally perplexed.

"Someone…something…is perverting the menfolk," Two Crows said slowly, like he was talking to stupid children. "Building an army of darkness. Soulless living corpses. The walking dead. Foul creatures fueled by human flesh—"

"Oh, for Pete's sake," Maclaren cut him off. "Save us the melodrama."

Brown looked concerned. "Creatures? What kind of creatures? Like…Wendigo?"

"No," Two Crows said in earnest. "Something much worse."

"He's pulling your leg, Sergeant." Maclaren mounted his horse. He rode up beside Two Crows and said, "Ride back to the Fort, half-breed, and stay out of this. Stop spooking my men with your mystic nonsense. You hear me?"

Two Crows shrugged and gave a lazy salute in reply. He spurred his horse without a word, and as he rode by he shot me a look that was equal parts amused and pitying. I watched him disappear into the forest and shivered, but not from the cold.

We tracked the trail of shuffling footprints westward. Franks estimated that it was made by two score individuals on foot, and at least one on horseback. Our quarry was moving at a rapid pace, and by mid-afternoon we were no closer to overtaking them. The sun, a ruddy disk on the horizon, cast long shadows behind us, for winter nights come early in the northern latitudes. As it sank behind the distant foothills of the Rocky Mountains, a bitter wind grew across the open plains, kicking up flurries of snow that blinded our horses and obscured the path. We were soon forced to stop and make camp.

Inspector Maclaren gave the order to dismount, and Franks grumbled that by morning the snow would hide the tracks. However, there was no going forward, and with the temperature falling so rapidly, any attempt to do so would be suicide. I attempted to helpfully point out that we could not see the trail any longer anyway, as the driving snow had reduced visibility to a few mere yards and nightfall was rapidly closing in around us. Franks repaid my observations with an obscene gesture and a handful of curses.

We dug shelters deep into the leeward side of a snow bank and pitched canvas lean-tos overhead to protect us from the flurries. Sergeant Brown had the foresight to include one of the newfangled "Rob Roy" alcohol stoves in his kit, and proceeded to boil weak coffee for the men. We had no fires, as the largest timber that could be found were twigs perhaps as thick as a man's finger, and so felt ourselves greatly blessed to clasp a warm mug between freezing hands.

After I had seen to thawing myself out, I lit a small hurricane lamp and found Inspector Maclaren huddled in his dugout. He smiled weakly in greeting when I crawled in beside him.

"Fine evening, Doc."

"Beau temps, indeed. Let's have a look at that arm, eh?"

His face was pallid and feverish under the glow of my lantern, and he ground his teeth in pain as I rolled back his sleeve. Black veins spider-webbed out from under the bandage, creeping up the entire length of his arm. I carefully unwrapped the gauze, and was immediately assaulted by the most putrid smell imaginable.

"Well, don't mince words, Doc. How's it look?"

I shook my head and wiped away the oozing asparagus-colored pus while my stomach heaved like a ship at sea. I am not one to become nauseated easily, but the rancid, cloying odor was testing even my limits. "This is bad," I said. His eyes met mine. After a long pause, I added, "I don't think I can save your arm."

"Well, shit."

"We'll have to put a tourniquet on to keep the infection from your heart. At daybreak we return to Edmonton so I can treat you properly."

"You mean so you can lop it off."

"Most likely."

"Goddamn, Doc. You have god-awful bedside manner."

"I don't believe I've heard you blaspheme before," I said, genuinely shocked.

He shrugged and frowned. "Just found out I'm going to lose my arm. Maybe it's a good time to start."

For some reason this struck me as incredibly amusing, and we both laughed until tears were streaming down our faces. It was morbid and unbecoming, but sometimes laughter can be the best medicine. I dried my eyes and finished the unpleasant business of cleaning the festering wound, sprinkling it liberally with phenol and binding it with fresh iodine gauze. After I was done, I gave him a morphine tablet for the pain, and tied off his arm above the bicep to retard the infection.

"Not exactly what you signed up for, is it?" Maclaren said.

"Eh? Sawing bones and treating young men for venereal disease? No, not particularly my dream when I entered the Université Laval."

He laughed. "Tell you what, Doc. Let's find who—or what—did this to our men, and then you can do whatever you want with my blasted arm."

"It would be suicide for you to leave this unattended."

"You know I'm not one to let that stop me."

"Discretion is the better part of valor, is it not?"

"The difference between discretion and cowardice is a matter of perspective," he argued. With a weak smile he added, "And besides, like you're always saying, 'We always get our man!'"

"We will, in due time." I clasped his shoulder firmly. "But first, my friend, you must get well. I'll get my kit, and stay the night with you."

He harrumphed and turned over, wrapping himself tight in his buffalo skin.

Crawling back out in the freezing gale, I finished conducting my rounds. The elements will maim or kill a man as fast as anything, and I was taking no chances that night. We already had several casualties laid up at Fort Edmonton, and I would be damned if I lost any more on my watch.

After I was satisfied that the men were as safe from the elements as could be in our makeshift bivouac, I fetched my haversack and sleeping roll. The horses were huddled together miserably, and, taking pity on the wretched beasts, I detoured to feed them a bag of oats. The harsh wind was finally abating, and the flurries had calmed, revealing a fiery curtain of green and red shimmering in the northern sky like a great dragon stretched across the firmament.

I was thus lost in reverie when I heard the first scream.

The horses started and nearly trampled me in their panic. It was an unearthly howl, unlike anything I had heard before. It was the animal cry of a man torn limb from limb.

Holding my lantern aloft, I stumbled through the heavy snowdrifts. Sergeant Brown's shelter had caught fire from his cook stove, and I watched in horror as he stumbled out covered in flames and holding his throat, which had been quite literally ripped out. Great fountains of blood pulsed from between his fingers, and he fell, writhing in the snow. Inspector Maclaren stumbled out after him, clutching an arm that had been violently separated from its owner. The Inspector was shirtless and awash head to foot in blood. He looked around with wild eyes as he gnawed on the limb.

Corporal Franks burst out of his dugout with his Adams revolver drawn, followed by Young and Robins, both grasping their Snider-Enfields like lifelines. Maclaren saw them and threw his head back, wailing inhumanly. Without hesitation Franks unloaded all five rounds into his chest, and Young hit him squarely in the shoulder, utterly destroying it in a shower of blood and bone fragments. Robins' shot went wild and I heard it whistle past my ear. To this day I cannot fathom how he missed by so wide a margin, for I was coming up behind him.

Maclaren stumbled, moaning, his arm hanging limply at his side.

Franks and Young were scrambling to reload. Robins stood rooted to the ground, paralyzed with fear. I had my carbine, but could not get a clear shot, as they were between our homicidal commander and me.

Shrieking like a banshee, Maclaren charged them. He reached Robins first, and with a swipe of his hand took most the poor boy's face clean off. I could hear the vertebrae snapping from where I stood, and saw Robins collapse, dead on the spot. Franks drew his Bowie knife and lunged, driving it deep into Maclaren's gut, and the two fell to the ground, grasping and stabbing and clawing at one another.

After fumbling several cartridges, Young managed to get one loaded. He stood over the two men, and fired into the both of them in panic.

Franks slid off of Maclaren, clutching the hole in his chest and gasping for air. The Inspector rose slowly, gritting his teeth. Frank's knife had eviscerated him, and his bowels spilled out around his feet. Young fumbled another cartridge, loaded, raised his rifle into Maclaren's face, and fired point blank.

The impact of the .577 caliber round snapped Maclaren's head back, disintegrating one side of his jaw. He cracked his neck like a prizefighter and looked Young straight in the eye. In a blur of motion he caught him by the scalp, and ripped out the young man's jugular with his teeth.

Maclaren tossed him aside and looked at me.

We stood a short ten paces apart, and I didn't fancy my chances of running. He moaned softly. His tongue lolled out from the massive hole in his jaw, dripping with blood and saliva. He ambled toward me.

I braced my rifle and tried to steady my nerves. At that range, one would think it an impossible thing to miss, but straw men and a friend intent on devouring you are vastly different things. There would be no time to reload if I missed. I was shaking from cold and fear. Conditions were not, how would you say, ideal? I sighted on his chest, as we were trained, but as I was about to pull the trigger I remembered what Two Crows had said, and at the last moment I raised my sights between his eyes, and fired.

Inspector Maclaren buckled, and fell.

I skirted around the motionless body carefully, and checked each of my comrades. All were dead. Collapsing in the snow, I stared at the carnage blankly. In retrospect, I know I was slowly freezing to death, but I felt nothing at the time. I truly believe I would have sat there until I perished, if Two Crows had not found me.

"Nice shooting, Doc," he said, walking his horse into our camp. My dappled mare followed behind them.

I nodded, looking at nothing in particular.

"Yup. Got to brain 'em." He held a large lantern up high as he surveyed the camp. Lowering it to look in my face he said, "It's the only way to be sure."

I watched him as he went around to my fallen companions, giving each a solid blow to the brainpan with his hatchet. When he was done he set the lantern on the ground and sat beside me, wiping blood-spatter off his brow with a bandanna.

"So, what's next, Doc?"

"Excuse me?"

"What's your plan?"

"Plan? What plan?"

"Way I see it, you can sit here and freeze to death." He counted off on a massive finger. "Or you can come with me." He counted off another finger. "And catch the son of a bitch who started this whole mess."

I sat beside the old hunter while he chewed on chicory. We sat for a long time, the two of us. Eventually he broke the silence. "Doc, my ass is done near frozen off. Iffin' you pick option number one, I ain't joining you. Just want to be clear about that."

"Merde," I said.

"So you've made up your mind?"

"Putain de merde." I stood up and straitened my crimson Norfolk jacket. "What the hell. Let's go. I am an officer in the North-West Mounted Police, and we always get our man!"

Two Crows heaved himself upright and, handing me my horse's reins, said, "That's the spirit, Doc."

We mounted and looked out to the western horizon. Dawn was breaking, and the sun painted the snowy peaks of the Rocky Mountains a glorious red.

Spurring our horses, we rode toward them with the sunrise at our backs.

THE SHACKLES OF DEATH

by Thomas Canfield

Cavanaugh listened to the somber, muted tone of the bells as they marked the hour, wondering why he had come. It was true he was commanded to act upon his faith, to live it rather than simply to preach it. But he was too honest not to know that it was not faith which motivated him but lack of faith: lack of faith in himself, in his convictions, in the life he had chosen to live and how he had lived it.

Looking out over the lush tropical foliage which spilled down the hills, these doubts were only reinforced. It was an alien landscape still, even after all these years. It was nothing like the simple beauty of Cavanaugh's native Ireland. He paused a moment, feeling weary, but the girl forged on ahead. Cavanaugh came up behind her.

"You're sure you want to go through with this?" It was a question Cavanaugh had asked before.

The girl nodded. "It has to be stopped. It cannot be permitted to go on."

"Suppose that we find nothing. Suppose there is only the grave, undisturbed. Will you be satisfied then?"

The ghost of a smile appeared about the girl's lips. "I am not mistaken. The bocor is there now. You can sense his presence, the sacrilege in which he is engaged. It is woven into the tapestry of the night."

Cavanaugh stood still a moment, letting the silence fill him. For the first time he experienced something he could not account for: an odd sense of disquiet, an underlying current of disharmony. He cocked his head, puzzled. A pale shimmer of headstones hugged the contour of the land, disappearing into the distance. But Cavanaugh could detect nothing sinister or unusual. There was only silence, the unbroken sleep of the dead.

"Which way?" he said at last, brusquely.

"There." The girl indicated the west side of the cemetery. "Past that stand of maleleucas. Then up the hill."

The girl led the way, weaving between the rows of headstones. Neither of them spoke. The night was dark, the sky overhead a black vault filled with stars.

Abruptly, Cavanaugh stopped. He could hear a voice, deep, resonant, chanting something unintelligible. He could not make out the words, could not tell in what language they were couched. The sound seemed to come from all directions at once. The strange acoustics had a peculiarly unsettling effect.

"What is it?" Cavanaugh said, confused, sounding in that one brief instant like a lost child.

"Wait," the girl cautioned him. "We must wait and listen."

The thick, guttural words spilled forth in a rising tide of fury. The air became charged, a heavy, clinging heat displacing the pleasant warmth which had prevailed before. The sting and lash of the words grew sharper but their meaning remained cloaked, the tongue a foreign one. Cavanaugh strove to penetrate the mystery of the syntax but it defeated him.

A flicker of light appeared off to their left, cast an eerie, red glow over a nearby gravesite.

"That's him, Father!" the girl exclaimed, grabbing Cavanaugh's arm. "Oh, sweet Mother of God! Pray that we're not too late."

Cavanaugh stared in mixed fascination and revulsion at the scene before him. A dark figure crouched before a freshly turned pile of earth, dirt staining his hands and trousers. His naked chest was streaked with sweat and bore a series of inscriptions and signs painted in wood ash. The whites of his eyes flashed, sparkled with transcendent savagery: the bocor, the Voodoo sorcerer.

"Father?" Cavanaugh started, realized that he had been standing there, mesmerized. "He must be stopped before the ritual is completed. Only you can do that."

Cavanaugh looked into the young woman's face and dark eyes. Her voice was quiet, calm, assured. No doubts assailed her. Her faith and her conviction were absolute. Cavanaugh advanced out of the shadows into the red glow of the firelight.

The bocor displayed no sign of surprise or panic. Indeed, he seemed almost to be expecting Cavanaugh.

"Welcome, priest!" The bocor's teeth flashed in a sardonic, mocking smile. "Have you come seeking instruction at our feet? Are you prepared to abandon the false god that you worship?"

"You know why I've come." Cavanaugh's eyes flicked down at the open grave. The bocor said something in the foreign tongue and the earth seemed to stir and shift. Cavanaugh took a step back.

"Do you fear the dead, priest? Does the black womb of the earth terrify you?"

"This man must be left in peace." Cavanaugh ignored the baiting tone of the bocor's voice. "You have violated the sanctity of the grave. In doing so, you have committed a sin against God."

The bocor gave a harsh bark of laughter. "Against whose god? Yours? Your god is a god of weakness and conciliation, a feeble, sickly god. My gods are gods of power and strength, of fire."

Cavanaugh could detect movement in the dark well of the grave. He wanted to creep forward and peer down into the depths but did not dare take his attention away from the bocor.

"I repeat: this is hallowed ground. You will not violate this gravesite. Nor will you escape the just condemnation of God."

The bocor rose out of his crouch with the lithe, agile movements of a cat. He passed his hand over the open wound of the grave, palm downward. Then he repeated the procedure, palm facing toward the sky.

"I have dominion over the dead. And over the souls of the dead." The bocor shot a penetrating look at Cavanaugh, a look which was filled with disdain. "You do not possess dominion over yourself even. Nor over your own heart. What manner of god do you serve, priest, that he treats you with such parsimony?" The sound of wood splintering sent a jolt of fear down Cavanaugh's spine. A foul smell emanated from the grave.

"Rise, soulless one," the bocor commanded. "The shackles of death bind you no more. You are zombie, servant of Voodoo."

A groan issued from the confines of the grave. The form and figure of a man, of what had once been a man, emerged from the dark earth. The zombie's face was colorless, wax-like, tainted by foul corruption. Its movements were slack, wooden, yet imbued with a latent fury and menace.

Cavanaugh staggered back, stunned and sickened. He clutched the Bible he carried to his chest.

The bocor's eyes shone with triumph. He advanced, cuffed the zombie roughly. He spit in its face. "Dung," he addressed it. "Lower your head. You are unworthy of beholding the glory of your Master." The zombie stared at the ground. "You see, priest," the bocor taunted. "Do you see? This is how a bocor deals with your dead. This is the esteem in which I hold your god." He cuffed the zombie again.

"This is mad," Cavanaugh protested. "You can't be permitted to do this."

"And who will stop me, priest. You?" The bocor barked out a command. The zombie straightened, swung around to face Cavanaugh. The blank mask of its face was lit by a distant malice, an echo, not really felt but imposed by the will of the bocor.

"You are a straw man, priest, and you worship a straw god. I will destroy you."

Cavanaugh fumbled with his Bible, opened the book and began to read a passage of scripture.

"A straw man," the bocor repeated. "You are enmeshed in weakness. You have adopted it as a doctrine and embraced it as a religion." He barked another command and the zombie began to shuffle forward, the blank, opalescent gleam of its eyes terrifying. Cavanaugh's gaze flitted from the zombie to the passage of scripture and back to the zombie again. His voice faltered. The words were without effect. They fell harmlessly, like an autumn rain, devoid of power. A straw man!

The zombie pawed at the air, flexing its fingers. "Do not despair, priest," the bocor mocked. "Death will not hold you long. I will raise you again on the fifth day, to serve and to obey. This I promise you."

Cavanaugh continued to back up, a cold slick of terror spreading through his body. He could not abide the zombie, could not abide the foul sacrilege of its existence. A wave of nausea washed over Cavanaugh, leaving him dizzy and weak. He could see the zombie's mouth open in a soundless cry of triumph.

Then, from over the crest of the hill, a faint, plaintive, reedy noise penetrated the night. It gathered volume and depth: an eerie, disconcerting sound, at once deeply disturbing yet somehow captivating. Cavanaugh closed the Bible. A faint smile lightened the pallor of his face. He stood a little straighter, seemed to breathe in the rich, resonant skirl of the pipes as though it were sustenance, as though it were strength and heart and fortitude: the Highlander's bagpipes. Cavanaugh had prepared this one subterfuge, should it come to the final extremity.

The zombie halted not five feet away, hands hanging slackly at its sides. Its head was cocked at an angle, as though listening to some distant voice. A second set of pipes joined the first. The little group in the cemetery stood transfixed, listening.

The bocor was the first to stir. "Attack the priest," he commanded. "Drive him through the tombstones. Kill him and let his blood soak the parched earth." The zombie stirred, took one halting step forward and stopped. Again it cocked its head, listening to the skirl of the pipes. The bocor made a harsh, grating sound in his throat.

"Imbecile," he reviled the zombie. "Are your ears awash with nothing but death? I command you to kill." The bocor's voice resonated with venom but now a new note, one of uncertainty, had crept into his tone. They all seemed to sense it.

Cavanaugh advanced a step toward the poisoned earth of the grave. He faced the zombie. "Soggarth Righ, A chara," he said, and the strength and richness of his own voice surprised him. "Sealg Uruisg nan Leitir. Caoine." The words were Gaelic.

The zombie turned, began moving toward the bocor. A glare of rage had kindled in the flat, lustreless surface of its eyes. The bocor stared at it in mute astonishment. Only at the last instant did fear become evident in his face: fear and horror.

"Not me," he pleaded. "I am your Master. You dare not attack me." The skirl of pipes beat down upon the gravesite. The zombie fell upon the bocor in a frenzy of killing and mad revenge.

Cavanaugh watched the slaughter without flinching, the keening wail of the pipes caught in his blood. He had fought fire with fire. The Scots and the Irish had pagan gods of their own: forged not in the blast furnace of the Congo jungle but in the icy, biting winds of the Highlands, in the heaths, the moors, the mist-cloaked lakes and depthless lochs. Cavanaugh lifted his eyes toward the black vault of heaven above. He said a silent prayer of thanksgiving.

Though to which god he addressed this prayer he could not have said.

WHEN IT'S NOT LOVE, IT'S HATE : A PSYCHOBIDDY GOTHIC ZOMBIE LOVE STORY

by Dawn Wilson

The young lady of the Peace house was scheduled to get married and the old flabby tongues around town got to knocking.

They said she had hoodwinked Good Tom. They called her names like vixen and tart and praying mantis and prude and virgin and illustrious. The young lady wasn't well-liked.

She had spent much of her youth away at boarding schools, which maybe had done her swell, but what it did was keep her from mingling with the children of Broken Bow. When you didn't mingle with the children, the children had nothing to tell their elders, and the elders looked askance and suspicious.

The whole Peace family was suspicious, with their big Victorian house and their dressing the children each night for dinner. They had glass in every window and stairs up to their porch and they had flimsy sheer curtains which kept folk from looking in during the day. The Peace family was suspected of putting on airs, and in Broken Bow, if you weren't One of Us, you weren't hugged at Christmas and you barely got a friendly nod in the street.

The Peace folks had put their only daughter in pantyhose long before her thirteenth birthday, and so it came as a surprise that one day the young lady actually was grown up and not just looking it. It was just the thing for a growed-up young lady to return to the family home, wink at a good-looking boy, and marry him the next Sunday.

"They've engraved the invitations," Ludmilla said to Miss June as she handed over a cup of tea without the saucer. "Not just printed, mind you. Those words are so fat the blind folk at the asylum can read them."

Miss June straightened her long floral skirt. "The Peace family's been here as long as anyone, but they still haven't learned to be one of us. They sit up in that house like they watch us with binoculars and make notes."

Ludmilla intoned, "One of these days…"

"Nothing will happen."

"But one of these days…"

"You just like to say that."

"I do. It makes me feel like there is a God. One of these days…"

Miss June wiped away the idle cosmic threat. "Marlena's got bees. She makes local honey. The Peace woman imports hers from up north. Are their bees superior?"

"Aren't they all?"

"When the Church has its fair, does the Peace woman bake a pie?"

"Well, she donates…"

"No. She has her maid bake five pies, as if the quantity will make up for the fact that those are slave pies. She may have bought the ingredients, but it's Lauren who's donating five pies. Lauren, she's the one who's better than everyone in town, that's what I start thinking, when I look at all the charity work she does in Mrs. Peace's name, and all the work she does to keep the house running. And does Lauren complain?"

"No."

"No! Not a word! Doesn't even tell us what it's like inside the upstairs. No one's ever invited upstairs. Guests stop in the parlor and if they're lucky, Lauren makes fresh tea and brings out the special northern honey that the special uppity bees make. Well, Ludmilla, what do you have to say to that?"

"That you don't like the Peace family in its entirety."

"I don't, do I?"

"No, Miss June, you don't. Now, I know we're not all over-the-top sophisticated, but you can't beat us for feeling comfortable around each other."

"And safe."

"And knowing everyone's business so we don't offend them."

"That's true."

"But we offend the Missus Peace something fierce."

"And yet she called me, Ludmilla, and I think she called upon you, too."

"Yes, Miss June, she did call me. How did you know?"

"It takes the both of us to render services, Ludmilla. Normally I would refuse that woman."

"But you didn't?"

"May God have mercy on her cold and frigid heart."

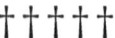

The Peaces had named their daughter Charmaine. They did it right at birth, too, as if there was no doubt in their hearts or their minds. The child was just absolutely destined to be a bitch. Beautiful and pedigreed and hard-hearted and selfish.

The one thing the parents hadn't counted on was that a precocious child with a precocious education would have precocious ideas. Charmaine didn't take so kindly to the fact that she was expected to inherit the Peace house if and only if she could create a couple children and learn to top-lattice a pie. "Mummy? Daddy? You can make me marry some boy and you can train him all you want, but you need to understand that when you kick off, there is no way in hell I'm letting some stranger run your business into the ground when I am twice as educated and four times more capable." Charmaine tossed her coffee cup into the fireplace and flounced out of the room. Her hips spoke as loud as the spurt of flame that bounced out onto the Oriental rug.

There was a reason (five of them) that the Peace family never had guests. Four of them were boys. One of them was beautiful. All of them were disgraceful.

If perchance the Peace family noticed Charmaine's insolent behavior, the only mention passing between them would be a little smile and the words, "Charmaine just needs someone to take care of her so she can be a girl again."

Yes, all she needed was someone to take care of her.

"Soooo, you and Charmaine Peace, huh?" Bad Tom said to Good Tom outside the barbershop where an old-fashioned pole stood.

Bad Tom wore spats over his black dress shoes. He wore three gold watches, one on each wrist and one tucked into his pocket. He wore a red suit with fabric that glittered and a collar that exceeded six inches wide and had ceased to be fashionable many decades before. Bad Tom kept his hair a little too long and slicked it back, and touched people not usually on the hand or shoulder but in ways that made them uncomfortable without quite being downright illegal.

Bad Tom fished for information so he could sell whale stories to the general public for ten bucks a pop or a hundred if it was particularly juicy. Juice he sold to his cousin who owned the printing press that doled out half-truths and sensational lies. No one could resist a sensational outright lie. Bad Tom's own family were some of his best customers; they couldn't resist hearing their own dirt spread far.

But Good Tom was so jovial that no one had ever spit in his face and only Bad Tom had even thought about it. In all his years, only three or four ugly girls had tried to curse Good Tom for not looking past their defects into their glowing hearts. The rest forgave him and took themselves to Heaven via the big willow tree with the one sturdy branch and a tall ladder and a chafing rope.

"When's the big day?" Bad Tom asked.

"On a Sunday, of course!"

Bad Tom had to clamp his hand over Good Tom's mouth to keep him from breaking out into a song. They were standing around the barber pole, after all, and Good Tom was quaint, traditional, and just a bit of an exhibitionist.

"She's a beauty, a real beauty," Good Tom said. "My heart was all a'flutter when Charmaine winked at me. Little old me. Can you imagine why?"

"It's the pretty face."

"I sure hope so."

"You could sink ships."

"That would be terrible."

"Would you do it?"

"In a heartbeat."

Miss June talked Ludmilla into inviting Charmaine Peace for tea. "It's what you do," Miss June explained as Charmaine sat on the edge of the davenport with her legs crossed in a too-sexy pose for tea with two old biddies, as if she expected someone to be illicitly snapping her photograph every moment. "When a young lady gets married, she becomes one of the town elders. You're no longer a child. Now you're one of us."

Charmaine's face retained a sweet look, much practiced and exquisitely feigned.

"A young wife entertains and is entertained in return."

"Oh, you poor dears," Charmaine said. "You actually expect me to come here three months hence and ask you to please tell me why I'm thickening around the middle?"

"Well…"

"I didn't grow up backwards with a tight-lipped nanny and a swooning mother hiding my girlish bodily changes from me. I wasn't lied to every day and, though they may have tried their best to teach me to keep my mouth shut and think not a whit, well certainly you're aware that never happened."

Miss June pursed her lips and glanced at Ludmilla. Ludmilla caught the look and rose from the settee to pull the drapes.

"Mind your elders," Charmaine said, "but what darlings you are, clinging to past tradition. How quaint." Her voice grew cold. "Really, if there's one thing I've grown tired of, it's people shoving dolls into my hands to see if I cradle it nice, to see how far along I am being brainwashed into childcare. I'm tired of men coming up to me at conferences and patting my back just a little too low and saying it was sweet of me to come listen but I must have been bored out of my mind as I couldn't possibly understand the physics, or the biology, or the neuroscience.

"I don't cling to your traditions, you two old sweethearts, and everything you cling to is about to change—or are you too blind to see it? Every last one of you is pressuring me to marry. Someone bland and easily trained with a malleable spirit, so I can appear to become subservient while retaining my own intellectual stability? No, indeed, all you ask is that I marry quickly. You say, Charmaine, dear, marry now and marry all the sooner so you can produce a few heirs and please do attempt to die in childbirth.

"A birthing machine! That is what becomes of a girl with good genetics. The wet nurse will suckle the children and the nanny will raise them and I will spend my entire time breeding and spawning and mating. What woman wouldn't want to die?"

Miss June leaned forward. "That's easily arranged, you know."

Charmaine even had a cold laugh. She obviously suffered the frigidity that women came down with when they were shut away into dark damp dormitories for most of their formative years. "Don't worry. I have other things planned. Marry off the only daughter, but in two days, my first brother is of age. Off to war. A year and then the next. Four in a row, one each year, and you know the Peace family has always been unlucky in war, though patriotic. We are born but to serve as fodder for man's cannons.

"They'll be gone and I'll be seemingly barren…I learned a trick: you stick a sharp piece of metal into the vagina, whereas the man is rendered impotent. Will he try again? It's the most effective birth control. The woman who told me was a shrew. She said do it when the moon is new. As if that matters. It's supposed to induce blood poisoning and sterility in the male. All I care is that he feels a tinge of the pain that he inflicts on me.

"But maybe by the time my brothers are dead, I shall have earned my space in the business and my passions will return. Good Tom may shake in his work boots, but if I beg, I'm sure he'll try again. He'll try again and find it pleasurable, and then he will cry with relief and do me no harm.

"And the wet nurses and nannies and maids and nurses will do the thousand tasks my mother's dark cold eyes wish upon me. You should see her, when she looks at me. The hate and contempt of the woman who did not dare—"

Miss June's eyes narrowed imperceptibly and Ludmilla took her cue. She lunged forward and overturned Charmaine's empty teacup onto a platter. She held her hand over the bottom of the cup, counting silently.

"What are you doing?" Charmaine asked. She looked between the two women and uncrossed her careless legs. A woman, ready to fight.

"There are ways to punish insolence and flights of fancy," Ludmilla said as she finished her count. She raised the teacup and tossed it away so it could never be used again. "Maybe your mother loves you."

"My mother doesn't understand."

"Oh?"

"My mother submitted."

Miss June leaned over and turned the platter to look at the mess of leaves and the dregs of tea. What very special tea. It could not only foretell the future; it could alter it.

"Oh, I see!" Charmaine's voice rose. She turned haughty. "Here I'd hoped you weren't all so backwards. But pooh. Reading tea leaves?"

"I haven't said anything yet," Miss June said. "Don't you want to know? Or perhaps you already do."

"Idle threats! The truth is, tea leaves are just a poor man's Rorschach test, and that, dear ladies, was invented in order to diagnose mental illness, not the future. Go ahead. Say your piece so I'll know just how sick you are."

Miss June covered the leaves with a napkin, paper and cheap. "No need."

"Besides," Ludmilla said, "it's not us who decided to act. You can thank your mother for begging us to heal you from being the thorn in her heart."

Charmaine stormed out, just as her throat started to close up. For a second, she wondered if she was about to cry, though she wasn't sure why she would, but then the tingling started, from her head down. By the time she walked up the hill to her parents' house, she felt as if she was floating. Because that's what it felt like, didn't it, when you had been poisoned and you were about to die? Too bad no one would ever know, as the poison robbed her of her voice just as the convulsions started.

They buried the young lady of the Peace house on a Sunday, in a long red ball gown with a flowing satin skirt, a tiara, and a pearl necklace. The jewels were of no value, as everything of value was passed from one generation to the next, never buried with the disappointment that comes from unused wedding invitations.

The eldest brother in the Peace family was declared 4F for military duty because he was a too-clever lad with a host of parlor tricks.

Even with all his tricks, he did not expect to hear the grave bell ring while he paid his respects. Ting-ting, ting-ting.

He'd stopped by to gloat, as if he was the new daughter, the one the family would dote on and expect little from. Instead, the bell attached by a long string through the dirt into her coffin rang clearly. And no one was around to help him with the shovel.

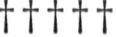

Charmaine Peace, the eldest of the Peace family, and their only daughter, walked slowly into town three days after she had been buried. She leaned heavily on the arm of her brother and she spoke not a word. Her eyes were vacant, as if she had never seen the world before and didn't have any word to describe it. One hand had to lift the long skirt of her ball gown, and her brother occasionally stopped to straighten her tiara. Her hair was limp, but her make-up, now that color was returning to her face, was garish. It wasn't meant to be seen by daylight.

People watched her pass like they would have watched the solemn parade of a funeral. Like it was impolite to get on with their lives, but that they couldn't bear to see their own mortality reflected.

They whispered amongst themselves.

"And there."

"Yes, I see."

"They grew to hate her."

"Yes, all of them."

"So they buried her."

"That's what I heard."

"Not a single person liked her."

Good Tom caught sight of Charmaine as he helped the postman sort some letters, holding fancy ones up to the sunlight, for a peek, just a hint of the vicarious. Good Tom sprang forward, as if thrust by a hope renewed. "Hellooooo, Charmaine! You, you're…not dead." He rushed over and circled her. She slowed her already slow pace as if he were in the way, her eyes unfocused. "Can't help but notice, honey. How are you?"

Her little brother, smeared in dirt, muttered, "I've had a hard day."

"You want me to walk her home?"

He gladly surrendered her.

Charmaine Peace was married on a Sunday. She had not regained the power of speech, but that was overlooked on account of the difficult time she must have had. Every woman deserves a dream wedding and fantasies of a future family and quiet nights spent knitting by the fire. The townsfolk pursued her dreams for her. Once engaged to Good Tom, they made sure she married him in good time.

If you put two knitting needles in Charmaine's hands and threaded the yarn, you would just need to stop her movements before the scarf she created got too long. She woke, she slept, she ate, she breathed, she vacated her bowels, she had sex with orgasms, and sex without. She walked, she dressed, she bathed. All the while with Good Tom at her side. All the while with Good Tom learning a trade from Mr. Peace at his factory. All the while her waist began to grow thick.

Bad Tom said to Good Tom one night at the pub. "How's the old ball and chain?"

"Well, she doesn't seem unhappy." Good Tom laughed.

"And you? How's marriage?"

"Far superior to what I imagined."

"Still not a word from your bride, huh?"

"No. But who needs it, who needs it?"

"I guess it was a shock they got her to do what she'd sworn she never would."

"She's obstinate."

"She's broken."

"She's not!"

"There's nothing left of her."

"There's everything left! Everything important, that is."

Bad Tom snorted. "I never thought I'd see the day we swapped and you became the bad side and me the good."

Good Tom got up from the stool. "Well, maybe, it just depends on who you're talking to at the time."

"Where are you going?"

"Home to my wife. My happy, happy wife."

Ludmilla and Miss June walked slowly to Marlena's for a jar of honey for their homemade herbal tea. Down the street outside the haberdashery, Good Tom's docile wife stood wearing a new feathered hat. "Look, Ludmilla," Miss June said proudly, "her waist is thickening."

"Mmm, she's one of us now, is that it?" Ludmilla asked.

"Well, she's certainly not in a position to put on airs anymore." The women bowed their heads to her and smiled and said, "Hello, Charmaine," and no one ever expected her to answer back, civil or intelligible, because any woman married to Good Tom was in a class all of her own.

SWEET BIRD OF DEATH

by Gary Ives

My grandfather came to Tampa from Cuba as a plant manager for the Hav-a-Tampa Cigar Company where he supervised one hundred cigar rollers, mostly women, for nearly four decades. As a maestro cigarero he was very well paid and enjoyed a degree of social status unusual for the Cubans of that day. His lucrative position at the cigar factory allowed him to invest in land and he established 150 acres of citrus groves on land that then sold for only a few dollars an acre. Consequently, my father and my uncles and aunts grew up more American than Cuban with the benefit of good schools and tutors. My father, the pride of our family, became a Rhodes Scholar and later served as head of Florida's Department of Agriculture. My brother Berto, however, was the black sheep. Berto hated school. He had a problem with authority and stayed in perpetual trouble at school for playing hooky, not completing assignments, and back-talking teachers. Paddlings, detentions, and threats served only to strengthen his hatred of school. But despite this, Grandfather favored Berto and, nonplussed by his recalcitrance, told my father that school was not for everyone. After all, he himself, growing up poor in Havana, had had scarcely any education. "Sometimes, my son, life puts an obstacle in the path. The successful man either goes around or removes that obstacle. Perhaps school is one of those obstacles for him. The boy will find his way around this. Be patient."

So in the ninth grade he'd quit school. Father, realizing the nature of the boy, secured for him a job within the family business. Berto was to accompany our older cousin Rudolfo to learn the business of the groves. Rudolfo, a hot tempered, humorless man, religious and stern in manner, was in fact quite stupid. In a Ford truck, he and Berto picked up sample crates of mixed citrus. These they would drive across to the Atlantic coast to present to hotel managers, many of whom would place orders. Working the coast from Ft. Lauderdale down to Coral Gables, Rudolfo was a competent salesman but Berto, glib Berto, within a couple of months bested him. This infuriated Rudolfo who informed Berto that he, Rudolfo, was the boss and it was he who would do the talking, while Berto must stay to protect the produce in the truck. Berto instead began working the other sides of the street taking orders from barber shops, saloons, and pool halls. Rudolfo complained to my father that the boy was unmanageable. However, Grandfather was impressed with the increased sales and especially with the improvement in Berto's attitude, and therefore nothing was done. Then one day Berto did something that infuriated Rudolfo beyond control. Returning to the truck, he watched Berto passing a large jute sack filled with naval oranges to a prostitute! Learning that on that very afternoon the boy had traded his innocence to a brothel for this! This…this…this bag of fruit! Rudolfo backhanded the boy, knocking him off balance into the street where Rodolfo commenced the kick the boy, breaking a rib in the process. The boy's lung collapsed. An ambulance had to be called to carry him to the hospital.

Now it was father's and grandfather's time for fury. As Rudolfo was family, no legal action would be taken; however his sales job was taken from him and given to Berto. Grandfather's influence secured a driver's license for the 15 year old citrus salesman as well as a new suit and Panama hat. Rudolfo was consigned to work the loading dock at the cold storage shed with my cousin Nestor, who is mute and slow of wit but very strong and a good man who has much pride in the neatness and efficiency of his cold storage shed. On his second day there, Rudolfo tried to assert that he was Nestor's boss until Nestor broke his nose with his fist.

Each morning, the proud, well-dressed young salesman would back up the Ford truck to the cold storage loading dock, infuriating Rudolfo who, like a peon, loaded the crates of citrus onto the truck while father and sometimes grandfather watched. This rubbed salt into the proud man's wound, and he was determined to exact a terrible price from the obstreperous boy. Had not his dignity been assaulted by his spoiled brat of a cousin? He had lost his position and was held in disgrace by his grandfather because of this worm and a common whore. And now this stupid retard had broken his nose and no one cared. Rudolfo knew of a certain Jamaican juju woman who could tell the future and cast spells. He would go to her; he would pay her good money to lay a curse on Berto.

Now the woman's name was Jackie Swift, but her professional name was Shaka Shabazza—Voodoo Queen. Rudolfo sought her out, imploring her to cast a death curse.

"No, mon, no—de death curse is too horrible, not to mention expensive and very complicated. Dat be de most difficult of all juju. Somet'ing very, very bad must have been doin'".

"Yes, something very bad indeed. I will tell you. My life has been ruined. Ruined! And by a snot-nosed spoiled pup. Once I had respect, a future, prospects for fortune. Now—all is gone because of this wicked, whoring whelp. He deserves death, a terrible death, and I am prepared to pay $100 for such a curse."

"Even if I did make dis powerful juju, it would cost $200—but no, no, baby. Besides you not be wantin' to do de act necessary to complete such a powerful curse."

"I would do anything. Anything. And I would pay $150."

"Okay den. Be here tomorrow jus' 'roun midnight. And you gotta promise Shaka you g'wine do whatever is asked, no matter how strange. And you will bring witchoo $175."

"I will do anything!"

"Okay den, don' be forgettin' the $175. In cash, mon."

The next night Rudolfo appeared as arranged and passed the $175 to Shaka Shabazza, who counted the money then led him into her small tent. There before a suspended white sheet on a table was a coop with a large red hen.

"Now den, de bird of death must be engaged by sexual congress while I recite the curse of death. You only gotta touch de bird with your manhood. Dis must be so. No one will watch, but you must connect in such a sexual way wit de bird for this terrible curse to bring death, do you understand?" He dropped his trousers as she gently lifted the hen from the coop passing the bird to Rudolfo.

"Stand here under dis light, and you gonna begin wid de bird as soon as I leave."

Shaka Shabazza disappeared behind a canvas screen and began a low sonorous chant in an unknown tongue.

Two days later, for the sum of $100, Voodoo Queen Shaka Shabazza passed to my grandfather the disgusting grainy black and white photographs of Rudolfo engaged in bestial perversion with a bird. He summoned Rudolfo and told him that my father and my cousin Nestor were taking him to Naples, where he was to dig some root stock from an orchard over there. My father drove, with Nestor and me on the bench beside him. Rudolfo rode in the bed with some shovels and a comic book. Ten miles into the Everglades, Papi turned onto a dirt track leading into the palmettos, driving slow for about a mile alongside a wide canal.

"What's this," Rudolfo shouted, "somebody got to pee?"

"That's right," my Papi said. "We all gonna pee now."

Rudolfo alit from the bed of the pickup truck, walked over to a palmetto plant, turned his back and began to pee. My cousin Nestor approached with a shovel and with two powerful cracks to his head Rudolfo's knees buckled and he collapsed into the little puddle of piss by the palmetto plant.

After Rodolfo was buried, we sat on the tailgate. Papi passed a cigarette to Nestor and then to me from a pack of Old Golds. As we smoked, my father explained, "Sometimes, hombres, life puts an obstacle in the path. Grandfather taught me that the successful man either goes around or removes that obstacle." True, the obstacle was removed and none of us held the least suspicion that the obstacle would ever return.

Some weeks later, however, on a Saturday evening, Jackie Swift, aka Shaka

Shabazza, was conducting a two dollar a head séance for a group of Haitian and Jamaican cane cutters seated on crates around a table prepared with symbols of power: a Holy Bible, a machete, a glass of rum, and photos of a couple of saints framed behind cracked glass. Shaka, knowing the Haitian's ceremonial penchant for chickens, had placed the same red hen in a coop beside the other relics. There was no intention of harming the bird, as this hen was a good layer. Midway through the candle-lit service, a terrible stench permeated the tent.

"Oou, someone here bin eatin' of de cabbage? Boiled eggs? Dis smell too bad, Madame Shaka, you tent, here it smell of shit."

"Non," piped another, "Zombie! Dat smell is de smell of dead zombie. My auntie live by de cemetery and I smell of dead zombie plenty time. Mother of God, save us!"

Shaka knew that she had to regain control of the situation pronto or she'd be refunding the take. "No, no, mes amis, that ain' no zombie, let's all step out of de tent and I'll explain while de air be clearin'." Outside the tent she passed out cigarettes and shots of rum, and thinking quickly, she announced that the smell was her own special powder used to keep zombies away from her séance. "You see, my friends, to summon up dem spirits requires great delicacy. Sometime dead zombie he hear our call, him want to interfere. Now dat powder of zombie dust with such bad smell inform any livin' dead that another zombie already bin dare and gone, so if you smell dat bad smell it mean some zombie was try'n to interfere but de powder done turn him away, dat bad zombie."

To her audience this made sense and soon the group returned to finish the séance. After the cane cutters departed, Jackie turned on the lights and examined every inch of the tent determined to find the source of the sickening stench. As the living dead corpse of Rudolfo stumbled into the tent, she spun around. "Damn, them cane cutters was right!" she exclaimed, picking up the machete from the table of power. "Now get the fuck outta my tent, I ain' got no time for no zombie." She reckoned that Rudolfo had appeared seeking a refund of the $175 he'd paid for the death curse. "You tink Shaka is g'wine to refund yo' money? No baby, dis be wrong. G'wine now, git, else Shaka be cuttin' off limbs from dat stinkin' trunk."

Deprived of the power of speech since his vocal chords had fully decomposed, Rudolfo slowly shook his head no, raised a hand and pointed at the red hen in her coop.

"Ah, now I understand. You want me chicken. Dat chicken! Dat's what you want. You done fell in love wid de bird, dat's plain to see. "

Now the fetid head nodded a slow yes and held out one hand for the caged bird with the other across his rib cage just above the rotted heart.

"Okay, dat bird is yours, Rudolfo, under de conditions dat you gotta promise Shaka Shabazza you ain' neveh to return an' also you gotta be sweet wid de bird. You got that, baby?"

The putrid zombie again nodded yes. Shaka gently lifted the coop with the red hen and placed it in Rudolfo's skeletal hands as the pitiful, love-lorn zombie effected a smile and sidled slowly out of the tent heading into the dark with his true love, the sweet bird of death.

COLD, LIFELESS FINGERS

by James Dorr

It did not matter how—a laxness in security, perhaps—but the Zombie was inside the gated community, shambling listlessly down gently curving tree-shaded avenues, passing between its well-kept houses, occasional guard dogs, short-trimmed bushes beneath alarm-wired, barred front windows, feeling lonely as zombies will sometimes since zombies miss company as much as anyone, when it came upon the sign. It paused and it read, moving its lips as it formed the words, insofar as they still were lips, dropping occasional maggots on the mowed lawn around it as it parsed the message: GEORGE ARMBRUSTER, and, underneath a depiction of crossed American flags: Anyone Who Wants to Take My Gun Will Have to Pry It from My Cold, Lifeless Fingers.

The Zombie did not understand guns very well. It did not even understand fully how it had gotten here, one moment having been laughing, singing, in the market at Port-au-Prince. Then the next moment, pfft! All gone. Stuffed in a box with dirt around it. With free emigration to the United States, of course, which was a nice thing, but shipped as common freight.

And then…it did not know. It seemed to suffer from lapses in memory sometimes, it thought, perhaps a symptom of decaying brain-cells. But then it had never done well in school either.

That is, back when it had been a living person.

And then—it was here! That's all. Parsing a sign, unencrypting its meaning. Zombies at the best of times were slow-witted.

But fingers it knew. It looked at its fingers. It raised them to push its dreadlocks back from the sweat of its rotting brow, and felt a coldness, both in the acted-upon and the acting—the brow and the fingers.

That much it established: its fingers were cold, too. It was beginning to take a liking to this "George Armbruster," though it was not yet entirely sure why, until it began to remember one more thing as well: was it not, too, lifeless?

Alors! Of course! What was the point of being a zombie if one was not life-less? Was that not part of the zombieing process, that one first be dead? Then be put in one's grave?

And only then risen?

That much even a zombie could understand, even one in whom the cock-roaches shared space with worms in the ruin of its brain-pan, twisting and scut-tling among the neurons as thoughts crackled through them. That it and this George Armbruster, he of the "cold, lifeless fingers," were kindred spirits!

And so the Zombie abandoned the sign for the flagstoned front walk and shambled forth until it reached the home's steel front door. It raised up one of its cold, lifeless fingers and pointed it forward. It pushed the doorbell.

A middle aged, bald, mustached man answered, one who, in fact, looked quite well-preserved for one of the Zombie's kind, albeit going to fat at the belly. The Zombie was momentarily jealous, the memory suddenly coming upon it of having once tried to be fat itself, except that the worms ate the soft grayness off it as fast as it was able to produce it. But then, the Zombie thought, that is as water that flows beneath a bridge, as rain-formed rivulets through a graveyard: that is, it is in the past. Zombies, it thought, sometimes have trouble with their sense of time-frame, with past times as separate from the present, perhaps because their "lives," after all, are not in the here-and-now—only their lifelessness—and, hence, are often prone to confusion.

But now it remembered. It saw the middle aged man raise a pistol and, thus prompted, it remembered the sign.

"Georges Armbruster," it croaked from its throat, the words rising up like fetid, Haitian-French accented bubbles from within its deepest parts. "You be ze mon, Georges? He who is of les doigts froids et sans vie?"

To underscore its question, the Zombie cracked one of its own fingers off at the knuckle, then offered it forward, but George Armbruster did not accept le doi-gt. Rather, he uttered a word the Zombie did not understand—that sounded as if he thought the Zombie was from Nigeria, even though it was sure it remembered being from Port-au-Prince—preceded by another word, "Damn," and followed by "Get out!" Then he fired his pistol. And then slammed the front door.

The Zombie sat down hard, having been struck in the heart by the bullet. It had not been killed, of course, zombies being by their nature dead already, or even badly hurt, though it did ooze a green and brown substance onto the sidewalk, one tending to earth tones that blended in with the lawn, parts of it moving, and thought this George Armbruster lacked hospitality. But then it saw that others had come out, not zombies like it was, but regular people, neighbors perhaps respond-ing to the noise—it sighed for a moment recalling its own life, before meeting the Bokor in the market who blew the white zombi powder into its face— and then thought that, non, it must give him one more chance, this George Armbruster, who possibly had shot him only from surprise. So, once again smoothing back its dreadlocks with the four fingers remaining on its left hand, noting the neighbors were crowding around it—but not too closely—joined now as well by uniformed gate guards who had their own pistols, it picked itself up. It regained its feet—that is, except for two toes on the right one which, having been badly stubbed when it fell, remained where they had rolled—and once more shambled forth to the front door.

Once more the Zombie extended its finger, cold and lifeless, to ring the doorbell.

Once more the door opened. Once more the middle aged man appeared, his still-smoking pistol gripped in his hand.

Once more he fired it—but this time the Zombie ducked! Zombies may be slow, but they are not stupid. Not even zombies, like this one, with beetles and spiders within its brain—what was its brain once—but rather it stayed crouched, pressed to the front steps as the door slammed again, hearing the bullet whiz over its head. A scream! from behind it. Now more bullets firing and whizzing above it accompanied by more screams, by ringings as armor-jacketed slugs ricocheted off the steel front door. By crashings and echoings accompanied by soft thuds as bodies piled up behind and around it.

And then…dead silence. It laughed as it thought the pun, zombies not being entirely humorless, and yet it felt a resentment also. It had, after all, reached out to this man—this Américain—twice, had offered its friendship, but what had it received in return? A bullet through the heart. Another one over its head, nearly parting its hair in a way that it was not meant to be parted.

And yet it thought again, as it gazed over the lifeless fingers, not to mention other parts as well, of this George Armbruster's late friends and neighbors, that perhaps it still was nothing more than a misunderstanding. After all, it thought, this George Armbruster was new to zombiehood—had it not noticed itself how well preserved the man's flesh seemed to be? And then, the sign too. Who else but one still unused to his state would think to advertise that his fingers were cold and dead. Cold and lifeless, as stiff as his gun's barrel—one more evidence that rigor mortis was still upon him, that they would actually have to be pried—even if they had seemed to the Zombie supple enough when they had twice pulled the pistol's trigger.

Who indeed? the Zombie thought. Certainly not it, it who, as the memory came, had at best been embarrassed when it had been exhumed from its death-coffin. It would not have thought to have signs painted bragging of what it was. Summoning others.

But then, it thought, it had been only a simple Haitian, no more than a day worker when it had been alive, unambitious, happy-go-lucky, while this…well, this was, after all, America.

And then the rest came to it as well—the cowboy movies it had known in its still-alive childhood—the detective fictions—that, after all, it being America, people did love guns. And so, if people, why not, too, les zombis? What more natural then that this one, new to being a zombie—perhaps confused and embarrassed as well, just as it itself had been so long ago at its Port-au-Prince graveside, but, being an American man, ashamed to admit it—what more natural than to wish to show off instead how fine a gun he owned?

And not just to show it, but to demonstrate it.

Mais oui! It was obvious! This was the way that this George Armbruster proved how much he desired the Zombie's friendship. And so, once again, the Zombie would offer it!

Picking itself up amongst the corpses—these ones dripping red, not green like it did—it once again shambled up to the front door. Once again it extended its finger, it, too, cold and lifeless, when—blam! blam!—the door opened of itself without the Zombie even needing to ring the doorbell and long, twin barrels discharged at point blank range.

This the Zombie was not quick enough to duck. Zombie-parts, most of them still concentrated—most from its middle, the stomach-parts where the white zombi powder still churned and roiled, that portion of powder that, licking its lips reflexively back when it had been living, Bokor had blown straight at its lips and nostrils—these parts sprayed outward, behind and around where the Zombie still stood.

The Zombie itself, however, still stood its ground, having this time gripped the steel door's door-posts, glad in its heart—what was left of its heart!—that its theory had been correct. And more than just correct, for had not George Armbruster this time produced a larger gun to display to the Zombie, a twin-barreled shotgun? To show he desired not just friendship, but love?

And the Zombie loved George Armbruster back. Scarcely noting the subtle change of the dead neighbors' blood from a clotting red to an earth-toned green, the bubbling of flesh and the stirring of body-parts, not at all minding that they now stood up too and shambled forth behind and around it up to the front door, it rang the doorbell. But others pressed, too, against the door itself, pushing against it until it buckled, despite its being made of the best steel, from the sheer weight of them.

Then, with the Zombie still in the forefront, they forced their way inside.

And then a strange thing occurred. George Armbruster unexpectedly—un-understandably—inexplicably—absolutely uncannily dropped the gun that he had been cradling, even though his fingers, as far as the Zombie could tell, had not been even the slightest bit pried. This puzzled the Zombie. It tried to ask him. "Pourquoi…?" it began. But it could not be heard.

And that was one more thing the Zombie did not understand: why it should be that this George Armbruster had all of a sudden begun to scream.

DAVE VS THE ZOMBIE APOCALYPSE

by Angel Luis Colón

This is not how I imagined the zombie apocalypse.

Before I saw those first reports out of Virginia saying that the dead were actually—finally—rising from their graves, I imagined the world grinding to a halt. I imagined man against man as resources became scarce. I imagined myself, well-prepared with a rucksack of weaponry and non-perishables, finally becoming the man I wanted to be—a leader even. People would depend on me—look to me as the guy who could give them a real chance at survival.

All I got was a few days off from school and hourly updates from family members that everything was "okay."

Why the hell did the zombie apocalypse have to be so…boring?

I'm not going to lie; I was very excited.

The news report broke into the latest episode of whatever my roommate Rob watched on Thursday nights. He groaned and flipped the channels to find that every single station—even the paid ones—were broadcasting some kind of emergency alert.

Each reporter said the same thing: the government and FEMA released statements warning residents of the US to stay indoors and to avoid any depositories for corpses—meaning cemeteries, morgues, hospitals and anywhere else a dead body may turn up.

My heart pounded in my chest. This couldn't be true, but they actually said the word—actually displayed it on the screen in bold, white letters: "Zombie." I felt high—the same way I felt whenever Rob smoked his garbage schwag weed and I caught a contact high.

This was it, this was what my dad and I talked about, what we joked and fantasized about. It was finally happening and I would be a survivor.

Rob didn't respond the same way.

He immediately went to call his family and friends, then panicked when the switches were too jammed to get a connection. I ignored his whining and opened my closet to pull out my ruck sack—my "bug-out" bag. Since I was 15, I hoarded extra money from holidays and birthdays and devoted my time to building the ultimate survival pack. I raided army surplus stores during sales, scoured home shopping websites' weaponry selections and bid on multiple movie replica knives and swords on eBay. Everything in this sack was for this moment—the day the world went away.

In the background, I heard the television talk about "confirmed sightings" and multiple witnesses all over Virginia were reporting that the walking dead were converging on residences, assaulting the elderly and eating beloved pets. I wondered when we'd hear about the disease spreading north, towards New York, where we were and wondered when they'd confirm the first risen victim of the zombies—confirmation that they would spread.

"Are you gonna try and call your dad?" Rob asked breathlessly between failed phone calls. This was the first time he'd said a word to me in three weeks. Normally he'd walk into the room with a "'sup?" and hide in the makeshift fort put together with a bunk bed and extra sheets. The dorm room was built for three of us, but we had lucked out and that third person never showed up. There were days I wished it was different, though, since Rob and I had absolutely nothing in common. I think it took us two, three days tops to realize we didn't like each other. After that, it was all "'sup?" and bed forts and bad television.

"Huh?" I hadn't paid an ounce of attention to him, just stared at the TV and played with the zipper of my bug-out bag.

"Your dad? Dave, you gotta call him. Doesn't he live up in the fucking mountains or something? Aren't you worried?" His eyes looked like they were going to burst.

I shook my head and waved the suggestion away. "He'll be fine. He's got guns and food…more than enough know-how to deal with this."

"Oh…okay. Then what are you gonna do?" I think he wanted some form of direction, guidance during the end of all things. That's how it always turns out. People like to think they're better than everyone else and when things get serious, they latch on like a tick.

I smiled and wanted to tell him to go and hide in his little fucking fort for the next few weeks, but that wasn't right—the look on his face told me he needed someone to take the lead. "Well, we should probably hit the dining hall, get as much food as we can, then sit it out here. We live on the third floor, so we'll be straight even if the folks on the first floor get slaughtered." He wasn't going to faze me, I was ready for this.

A wave of relief washed over Rob's face. "Alright, you're the mountain man.

I'll follow your lead."

Damn right, Rob, I thought. I was always ready for this.

"You're fucking with me, right?" I could feel my hands trembling as I stood at the head of the classroom.

Professor Brown stood opposite me with her arms crossed over her chest and a sour frown on her face, "No, I am not, and for using language like that in my classroom, you can leave and not return. You fail the course."

I rolled my eyes, "Oh no, fail? What will I do now?" It was a mistake to have gone to class, but Rob convinced me it was probably the best choice to just get a feel of what the campus was doing about the outbreak. I was stupid to go along with it. We were barely three hours out from the big news and I was too hopped up on adrenaline and day dreams.

The rest of the class watched quietly, a few folks smirking to themselves. I hated this class to begin with—the other students argued against any point I made and the professor whined that I had a 'sleeping problem'. Fuck her. Did it ever dawn on her that maybe she was a boring, old pretentious twat with nothing new to say about a bunch of old books?

I walked over to my desk and snatched my bag and the book we had been discussing for the past week: *Madame Bovary*. I was barely through the first chapter it was so fucking mind-numbing.

I lazily tossed the book at Professor Brown's feet. "You can keep this bullshit. In a year's time, nobody will remember it or your waste of time class—bitch." The drama queen almost jumped three feet in the air.

"Mister Freeman, if you do not leave my classroom now, I'll have campus security remove you themselves." Her eyes were filled with panic and her voice trembled. Seriously? I threw a book and she nearly shit, but a zombie outbreak was ongoing and she was more concerned with 19th century soft-core porn.

Her priorities were clearly screwed up.

I strayed a moment and turned to the class. "Aren't any of you worried about what's going on in Virginia?"

No answer—just stares—judging, asshole stares.

As I walked out, a few of the more pretentious students actually applauded. Any other day and I would have walked back in and given everyone a piece of my mind. Let them call campus security. The head of the department, Bernie Walsh, was a friend of my dad's. He'd make a show of it, but let me off with a slap to the hand. Just like all the other times I was a 'disturbing presence'.

I decided to skip my 10:30 AM class and go back to the dorms. Any time spent in a classroom was time not spent getting ready for hell to start. As I walked through the empty quad, I smirked to myself at the thought of emptying a full clip into zombie Professor Brown's face. I wondered if she would see the irony of a student killing her brain.

Seriously—priorities, man.

I was proud of us—Rob and I.

We set up our water and provisions, shit, even made a spreadsheet to detail the times of day we would eat and drink and how much we'd consume. This was top-notch planning and I was proud that my roommate was so willing to let me take the lead—even in the face of our dick head RA Todd's criticism. He had a way of making me feel nervous, but I wasn't going to let that happen today—not with the beginnings of the end so close to our front door.

"You jackasses realize it's never getting this far north, right?" he asked with the most ridiculous, shit-eating grin. For a Resident Assistant, Todd spent most of his time playing video games or disappearing on the weekends he was supposed to be our, well, assistant. He was handsome to the point of irritation and I always found it difficult to look into his big, hazel eyes.

"How do you know that, Todd? Can you predict how the, um, what was it you said, Dave?" Rob looked to me for an answer. God, I was so lucky to get someone like him as a roommate—ready to listen and follow. This was perfect—nothing better than mending bridges when you had to survive with someone, bed forts be damned.

"The disease pattern, how it'll spread." I answered flatly, "There's no telling how it's going to travel. If it's spread through biting or even just in the air, we can't call whether it goes north, south, east or west. We should still be prepared."

Todd rolled his eyes because he was a dick and that's what dicks did. "What-ever, Dustin Hoffman." I had no idea what the fuck he was talking about. "I'm headed home for the long weekend. Rita's your RA contact while I'm gone." He let a sheet of paper with Rita's information drop to our feet. For a moment my stomach fluttered—it had to be anger, he was always so disrespectful to me—and I tried to ignore him. He could have handed the paper to me like a normal person. We were in this fucking mess together. Now wasn't the time to act all high and mighty—no matter how pronounced his cheekbones are.

"What if she leaves?" Rob's voice snapped me out of what felt like a haze.

Todd smirked, his forehead crinkling the way it always did whenever he want-ed to be anywhere but where he was. "Then I'm sure you and your fearless leader will be able to get through this without help."

Rob lost all the sarcasm in the remark and nodded solemnly. "Well, good luck out there, Todd."

Todd walked away with a half-hearted wave. "Yeah...thanks. Don't go inciting any riots, Dave, and don't get Rob too riled up. I heard about that shit show in

Professor Brown's class."

"Whatever." I muttered as I watched him walk away. I found myself wondering why anyone would wear jeans that fit so tight. Todd was another one of the many that seemed to have a problem with me. Maybe it was my self-confidence or the fact that I rarely took no as an answer—whatever, it didn't matter. What sucked is he really seemed like a cool, interesting dude at first. At our resident initiation we even got to talking about our favorite hunting rifles and he impressed me with his knowledge and claimed he even bagged a nine-point buck a few months back. I mentioned that I'd love to spend some time talking shop—even going out on a trip together and his attitude shifted from friendly to caustic. It didn't matter now. I could see myself having to headshot him out of the blue someday—maybe while I was out hunting for the group.

I kept my gaze on Todd as he disappeared into the stairwell. "Guy's got no fucking concept of how big this is. Assholes like him are the ones that get their damn guts spread like a buffet," I said to myself.

"Like in the movies?" Rob asked.

"I bet it's happening in a farmhouse down South right now. Whole family spread out on a table like some kind of zombie-fucking-Thanksgiving. It's all good, he'll feel stupid when I…we pull his ass out of the fire in the next few days." I thought for a minute. "You know how to handle a gun, Rob?"

Rob shook his head.

"Well, that's a problem we need to remedy."

"How did you get permission to have this on campus?" Rob held my Smith & Wesson Model 64 .38 Special like it was covered in shit.

"Special form you have to fill out. So long as you have a permit, you're good to go," I lied. "Now, hold that fucking thing like you mean it. We don't know if these zombies are runners or walkers."

Rob held the gun like I showed him. He swallowed hard and aimed it over at the makeshift target I built from rocks and a few long sticks. It looked solid enough to take a few rounds, which would be more than enough to get Rob acclimated. A good head start in case shit hit the fan later tonight or tomorrow.

"What does that mean?" he asked.

"Well, what if these zombies are the fast type, like in *28 Days Later*? You hold the gun like it's a fucking handbag and you're done."

Rob nodded and took a deep breath.

"Good, just aim down the sight and pull the trigger. Keep yourself steady… spread your legs apart just a little more." I positioned him just like my dad showed me.

A moment of silence passed and then he pulled the trigger. The target dummy fell apart as soon as a bullet hit and we whooped with excitement.

"That was awesome!" Rob seemed relaxed for the first time all day.

"I told you! You nail this down, man, and we're good to go. Bad-ass mother-fuckers, indeed." I took the gun from him and slipped the safety back on. "Let's get out of here, though."

"How come?" Rob's smile faded.

"That was a little louder than I expected." I said, knowing that campus security was probably on the way.

"But guns are supposed to be loud," he argued.

"Yeah, but I don't want to cause any panic on the campus. You know school shooters are probably the last thing everyone needs on top of this whole zombie thing." I felt like I swallowed a rock.

It dawned on Rob.

"You don't have permission to have that on campus, do you?"

We both beat feet back to the dorm.

Campus security was waiting right by the front entrance of the dorm. I wasn't too scared when I saw it was a group of guys I'd gotten to know pretty well over the past few months.

"Jesus Christ, Dave. I knew you were one of those survivalist types, but a real gun on campus? Are you fucking nuts?" Sergeant Walsh narrowed his eyes at me. He was an alright guy most of the time—even let me fuck around with his back-up pistol once or twice. I honestly didn't think he'd be that upset about the Smith & Wesson.

I shrugged. "Jim, you've seen what's going on down south, I..."

"I don't give a shit about that, son. There's plenty of crazy shit going on every god damned day. The last thing I need is the students panicking because some upstate hick is gonna go trigger happy as soon as he sees someone looking a little off color." He took my bag off my shoulder. "Everything in this bag stays with me, I can't trust you. Next thing I know, you get tossed out of another classroom and it's gonna be hello active shooter and CNN."

"Aw, bullshit..." I began to argue. Rob nudged me hard against the back before I could get started.

"Dave, just...stop. We're getting off easy."

I turned around. "Now you're pussying out, too? This is fucking crazy. There's fucking zombies...zombies coming from down south and we're going to depend on five cops and a few security guards to protect us? You know damn well that at least for our floor, I'm the best hope we got. Besides, let's not get into how you're violating my rights."

One of Walsh's subordinates choked back a laugh. "We got John fucking Mc-Lane on campus." That got a laugh out of Walsh.

My cheeks burned up. "Fine. Take it. I'll come back when shit gets real."

Walsh grabbed my shoulder. "Son, I see your ass pop up near my guard station and you're going to wish whatever the fuck those things down south are ate you toe to balls."

"Zombies." I replied.

"Whatever, Freeman. You get a warning, against my better judgment." Walsh motioned towards the door. "Get out."

Rob pulled me away and into the hall. I jerked away from him. "Fucking traitor. Don't touch me."

We were fucked.

By day five, Rob and I were arguing every ten minutes over the dumbest shit. Here I was, concerned about our safety, and he kept finding the most ridiculous shit to complain about.

"You need to keep your goddamn mouth shut, you fucking wuss. In a few days all the crap you're so worried about won't mean a thing. We'll be back to bartering and stealing," I told him after the third reminder about his lack of funds.

"I'm just saying you owe me for shelling out the cash to get all of this canned food from the commissary," he whined from his bed fort.

Todd sauntered by our open door—some bullshit new policy that seemed to be only for my room. "Any zombie sightings, boys?" He didn't stop, just kept walking. When he was out of view, he let out a low moan, like in the movies. "Braaaaains."

"Fuck you, Todd," I muttered.

The news had no major updates to the original reports. They mentioned that there were multiple sightings, but most folks were containing the outbreak to within a ten-mile radius. Any bodies that hadn't risen were being cremated on a 24-hour cycle. They were even getting back to focusing on local bullshit, like muggings and new bullshit phones. What good was any of that going to be once our entire infrastructure was destroyed by this disaster? Was I the only one who cared?

Sooner or later someone was going to fuck up and get bit, or maybe one of the walkers would slip by unnoticed. Washington D.C. would probably go down in hours and then it would spread up north and be in our neck in the woods within days.

I didn't have a single item to defend myself and others except for a broomstick I managed to steal from the bathroom.

Fucking Rob the rat in his bed fort.

I tried calling my dad, but got his answering machine. Apparently he was off on some bullshit hunting trip in Canada. Probably saw the writing on the wall and ditched the States. He always reminded me that when things went down, we'd all be on our own. He told me that when I chose to go to a college closer to the city, but I ignored him.

I regretted not listening.

That special report graphic interrupted another talk show, but it was just some bullshit update on riots breaking out at cemeteries and funeral homes. People were taking any dead bodies they could find and burning them in huge bonfires. The news people just wanted to remind everyone to remain calm and leave body disposal to the proper authorities. I spent the rest of the evening watching TV and flipping my broomstick around.

May as well get some practice in.

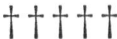

A full two weeks and nothing.

Nada.

Fucking zip.

Rob put in paperwork to transfer rooms. He hasn't said a word to me in days and he even took all of the food we bought together. Didn't even leave me the shit he made girl faces at like the beef stew or deviled ham. Then Todd informed me that there was a formal review into my "objectionable property," whatever that means. I told him that campus security violated my rights in taking away my personal property, but he just laughed.

On the news, all they talk about are the heroes in the army reserve and police forces that kept the peace in Virginia. They keep showing interviews with all these slack-jawed assholes who say it wasn't such a big deal and that cremation of corpses would probably be the best deterrent to future outbreaks.

Awesome, the only fallout of this entire "crisis" was the death of the funeral home industry.

What a load of shit.

I decided a few days ago that I would get the hell out of here anyway. I hate my classes and I hate these people. I'd rather be in the compound with dad hunting and fixing trucks. He told me he could get me a job at his buddy Earl's garage, so I guess it's better than nothing. I should have been more proactive—should have gotten out there on my own. The most action I saw, well, I didn't even see. Some freshman told us how he saw a dog with a severed arm walking down his street, but he wasn't sure if it was from an actual zombie or from one of the corpse bonfires popping up all over.

Dad always said the outside world was full of disappointment.

I finish packing my bags and check by my bed for any loose items when I glance out the window and spot someone walking out at the edge of the woods about a quarter mile from campus. Nothing weird about that, most folks go out there to smoke weed or write. That's about the same place where Rob and I went to practice with my Smith & Wesson. I go back to packing up, but something doesn't sit right with me. This time I take a good, long look out the window and watch the guy. It's wandering around aimlessly and slowly—maybe too slow—I swear it's limping.

My suspicions are confirmed when the person stumbles over nothing and can't stand back up.

I fucking knew it.

I drop my bags and grab the only weapon I have left—that broomstick—and bolt out of my room. I pass Todd, who yells something at me, but I can't hear him past the sound of my heart pounding in my ears. Fuck him, he had his chance. Downstairs, I nearly plow into one of the security guards. He screams my name and tries to grab me, but shove my shoulder into his gut and send his sprawling. Fuck him, too.

I told them this would happen—told them that we needed to stay alert and vigilant, but they took away my weapons and made fun of me. What would they have done if I hadn't noticed that guy out there, shuffling towards the campus and hungry for their warm, wet insides? My dad always said that the greatest heroes, the very greatest patriots were never believed during their time. It was only after their sacrifice and the dust cleared did everyone who doubted got on their knees and praised.

Finally, this is it.

I get out to the clearing and manage to find it in myself to sprint even faster. That man-shaped blotch is getting closer and I can see that he's disheveled and completely out of it. It's not walking like a normal person, it's doesn't even look up at me—probably can't hear too well. In a few more seconds, I'm only a feet away and I raise the broomstick over my head. There's this feeling inside me—happiness or something more. I can't hold it in and I let out this warrior's roar. That seems to get the attention of the trespasser and it jerks its head up sharply, its eyes sunken and glazed over.

It raises a hand open and slowly opens his mouth, "Wha…"

I swing the broomstick in a wide arc, connecting it to its jaw with a loud crack. He drops in a heap and I stand over him catching my breath. I can't wipe the smile off my face.

That's when I hear the sirens.

by Gabriel Valjan

He was found in an abandoned housing project over on Sixth Street on a morning colder than a politician's heart in November.

The ramshackle disaster was popular with the kids who wanted to hang out, play music, skateboard, smoke weed, and drink booze. Mildew and an unidentified stench were wall-to-wall. Spent cigarettes and condoms littered the floor. In a word: a real sty. The police radio said, '187.' Code for homicide. A car was sent over to the scene.

Limbo, the town's lost soul, so named because he had gotten lost in life's shuffle and because he was missing a few cards in his deck, had called 911 from the Piggly Wiggly. He was giving his frantic statement to an officer. Limbo looked as if he could use a Valium to slow him down.

"Jesus," Sheriff said, and not just because he knew the 'vic.'

Coach Simmons, the victim, a scarecrow of a man at seventy-five, was sitting upright on a dilapidated sofa, ashen except at the neck, which was ringed red in an awful shade of lipstick. Old age had whittled the former substitute teacher down to a walking stick. Coach's mind had faded out into shadows a few years back; but the worst thing about this was that Coach had no head. At least not where it should be.

"It's on the floor, Sheriff," Daniel Teague said at the entrance of the apartment with no door. He was technically a deputy but, unofficially, the city's only homicide detective. "I've never seen anything quite like this." Red lights splashed across the wall. The ambulance had arrived.

"What have you got for me, Danny?"

"Only preliminaries."

"I'll take what I can get. Let's hear it."

Before Danny could answer, they were whistled at from inside. Eamon from forensics wanted to show them something.

"Let's go have a look," Sheriff said.

Eamon Farrell was finishing up. He said, "Hope you've got a strong stomach." His words were smooth Irish whiskey about to explain something wicked. Nobody could avoid the obvious: Coach's face looked up at them from the floor, jaw had been hinged open in a silent scream and the eyes had rolled back. The tongue flopped out, gnarled like beef jerky. Flies were abuzz in a chaotic swarm of curiosity.

Sheriff said, "I hope Dave can fix him right. His wife shouldn't see him like that." Dave Yurch was the town mortician.

Grand Isle was rural, but the police department did have a crack forensics technician in Eamon, who had worked crime scenes in Boston and Philly. Marriage had persuaded him to move to Vermont. 'Change of pace' didn't quite cover it. Crime in Grand Isle was normally limited to the misuse of beer and a shotgun during turkey season, or a fight at the nursing home. Old men on Viagra were as ornery as roosters at sunrise. Murders were rare, whereas geriatric STDs were not.

"You're not going to believe what killed Coach," Eamon said to Sheriff.

"The man's head there on the floor tells me it wasn't natural causes."

"Actually, it was."

"Come again."

Eamon had that queer smile that forensic guys on television got when they sprayed too much luminol and found semen on the ceiling. This crime scene excited Eamon and Sheriff could forgive that. This wasn't the usual routine of ponchos and buckshot.

Sheriff Jack Daniels—and yes, he did ask his parents why but he suspected that the drink was what had inspired his conception—stood there humorless. Eamon held up a vial with gloved fingers.

"A maggot," the Sheriff said as he took the small glass vial and rolled it in front of his eyes. The unborn inside it writhed, twisted and turned, helpless and pathetic. Disgusting. "Time of death?" he asked, as he handed it back to Eamon.

"Six to eight hours ago, but this isn't any ordinary fly."

"So, Coach wandered about in the middle of the night. That's consistent," Sheriff said, hands on his hips, as he eyed the room. "Wait? What's weird about that grub?"

Danny overheard them and interrupted: "What's consistent?"

Sheriff looked down his right shoulder at his detective. "Coach was a wanderer. The missus reported him missing a day ago."

"And?"

The sheriff tapped his temple. "Alzheimer's. Folks with it go in and out of the fog during the day and they wander off at night. Sundowning is what they call it."

"Poor bastard. Hadn't known that. Coach coached me and lettered me. Who would want to kill him?"

"About that fly, Eamon?" Sheriff asked.

The medics wheeled in the stretcher. They got the okay from Eamon to bag the body. There was a moment of silence as they watched the body being placed inside the black bag. Shrunken Coach looked as if he could swim forever inside a garment bag. The medic glanced up when he saw the head. Eamon told them, "Separate bag, please." Grotesque request outside of a grocery store. Eamon turned his attention to Sheriff and Danny.

He said, "Only an autopsy proves Alzheimer's."

"Don't you think that's the least of our worries, Eamon? I'd like to know how the man lost his head. Find me a murder weapon and Danny and I will do the rest. Now, about that fly."

Eamon held up the vial again. "Phoridae."

Danny jacketed his notebook and squinted. His face winced in confusion. "Fluoride?"

Sheriff said, "Haven't got all day, Eamon. Dial down the nerd-speak, and please use the KISS method for us laymen here." He pointed at the vial. "That there grub marks the clock for us, but tell me what killed Coach."

Eamon wiggled the vial. "This fly did." He pinched the vial between two fingers. Upright, the creature inside the glass sank to the bottom and curled and bucked like an angry pea. "This larva will mature into a fly that parasitizes ants and—"

"Excuse me," Danny said. "The vic was a man, remember? Not an ant."

"Let him finish," Sheriff said as he scratched his shirt.

Eamon had that geek smile. "This particular fly lays eggs inside the ant and they crawl their way from the stomach up to the head, where they decapitate the ant."

"Gross," Danny said.

"Here's the thing, though," Eamon said, vial up again as proof. "Pseudacteon is indigenous to South America."

"Vermont isn't Rio," Sheriff said. "Too early in the morning for one mystery too many."

The wheels of the gurney creaked by with the frail remains of Coach Simmons in one bag, his head in another. Bowling ball came to mind. A patrolman outside the front door stepped aside, his cover off out of respect for the deceased. He called out to Sheriff for 'a word.'

"Excuse me."

The rookie said, "We've got another body."

Sheriff was thinking postcards: cocaine and illegal aliens came from South America—not some murderous bug. "Another body? Jesus. Who?"

"Mr. Owens, the beekeeper. And get this, witnesses said he walked around, screaming about something eating him from the inside out, and he said that he needed to get warm, but that's not the worst of it."

"It's not?" Sheriff asked.

"Nope. Man's head came right off."

"Off, you say?"

"Actually, he pulled it off. It wasn't pretty. Wife fainted, the other witness puked."

"Thanks," Sheriff said. He called Danny over and said, "You and me are riding together, and Eamon?"

"Yeah."

"Meet us over at the Owens house pronto after you see the body to the coroner."

"Why don't I just join you and Danny?"

"Because I want you to tell Doctor Russell not to release the body or have Mrs. Simmons view it. Tell him to call Dave and have him work his mortuary magic first. She can't see him like that."

"Sure thing."

"Contact me if you do hear anything, but call me on my cell or tell me in person. I don't want any of this on the scanner. Got it?"

Eamon nodded and left. It was twenty-one degrees outside, minus four with the wind. The sun, if it wasn't cowardly, might warm Grand Isle up to one degree. The Owens farmstead was twenty minutes north.

William Owens, Esquire was the closest thing the town had to a celebrity. More than half of Grand Isle hadn't had any idea what an apiarist did, let alone what apiculture was until Bill's honeybees had gotten him on talk shows. The Culinary School in Exeter reserved some hives for exclusive wildflower honey. Bill had produced signature lines of honey the way celebrities came out with perfumes. Très-chic restaurants in Boston wanted honey; the tony boutiques asked for beeswax and royal jelly. Universities around the country would ask him to educate students about beekeeping, pollination strategies, and the professional organization, the ABF, gave him its highest award for improving Jenter kits, which were a fast-track way of getting queen bees. Last Sheriff had heard was 'Busy Bee Bill' had delivered a paper on some renegade mites that were harmful to hives.

Five minutes into the ride, Danny was spouting theories with the enthusiasm of a Boy Scout hot for a merit badge. Sheriff listened, his right hand on the wheel while his left ironed the worry lines in his forehead. Nothing made sense, but Danny had his own MO on working a crime scene. Sheriff said he'd never interfere with a man's modus operandi, especially when working on a homicide. Insect larvae gave him the creeps. Eamon was into forensic entomology the way some men loved woodworking or others restored cars with all original parts. Headless Coach and now headless Bill.

Vultures were one thing, but carrion flies? Eamon could recite passages in which Shakespeare mentioned the blowfly, the coroner's best friend for pinpointing time of death, outside of a liver temp. Eamon had once told Sheriff that flies were royalty in forensics because they were essential when decomposition set in. Sheriff appreciated answers, but could do without the details. Everything in God's universe had a timeline, from the Big Bang to ashes to ashes, dust to dust; the problem was the 'food for worms' part. What did it matter once you're dead, Sheriff told himself, but 'Coach' had buggers gnawing their way northward to eat his brain until the only relief was to rip his head off his shoulders.

"Sheriff?"

He heard it again. "Sorry, I was thinking."

"I could tell."

"Sorry, Danny. I was thinking about Coach. Hell of a way for him to go, and now Bill."

"Think they're related? I mean, other than the headless part."

Sheriff said nothing. His cell phone's text tone had gone off. He groped inside his jacket and read the text. Eamon was en route. Second line said something about pictures off to a bug friend who worked at the CDC in Atlanta. SOP. Shit, Sheriff thought, but the way he had tossed his phone into the tray betrayed him.

"Something wrong?"

"Eamon sent pictures to the Centers for Disease Control. Says it's Standard Operating Procedure."

"What is?"

"Verifying the bug, I guess."

"Last thing we need before we've got a handle on this is the Feds. Damn."

"Eamon did the right thing. I just wish that he had told me." Sheriff smacked the wheel.

He edged the nose of the car into the Owens driveway. One of his men waved him through the gate. Clyde wasn't one of Grand Isle's brightest. Sheriff wondered about that name and whether Clyde should have a sidearm. The expression 'a country mile' was apt for the Owens house since it sat on a hill a full mile from the gate. Bill had done well, between the land his people had left him and what he had purchased with the profits from his honeybees. An attorney by trade, Bill was so bad at it that he couldn't beat a parking ticket if dirt had jammed up the meter and the hands on the Town Hall clock fell off, but put Bill in a bee-suit, a veil over his head, and he was the maestro of thousands. Sheriff put the car in park. Numerous square boxes stippled the landscape in front of them. Hives.

The paramedics were waiting for Eamon. The body, Sheriff was told, was inside and, yes, covered. A grief counselor was with Mrs. Owens in the kitchen. One of the officers gave Sheriff his notebook so that he could read the statements he had taken down. The winter air and the sight of Bill tearing off his own head had aggravated a guest's asthma after she had lost her breakfast. What her inhaler hadn't done for her lungs, some oxygen out of a green tank in the ambulance did. She was home recovering her dignity. Sheriff was thinking he might need some O2 himself after he climbed the steps.

The body was in the living room. One white sheet, two lumps. Sick thought that the bean doesn't fall far from the body passed through Sheriff's mind. He lifted a corner up. Bill was business casual. Everything was neat except for the obvious part. From the looks of the sinews and tendons, the uprooting was like a very violent twist-and-turn of a stubborn wine cork. Sheriff crouched. He looked but didn't touch. There was no visible post-mortem life. Much too soon for that, Eamon would tell him, and being indoors was a definite factor.

The head. The scream was there, but the eyes stared back. The paramedics hadn't closed them because Eamon had to photograph everything. Bill looked pale, but otherwise he was fresh as fallen snow. His lower lip suggested that he had been a brooder. Something else had caught Sheriff's attention: a bee.

A honeybee crawled out from under the ragged margin of Bill's neck. The honeybee staggered. This was no waggle dance, no figure-eight jig. Bill had told him once bees danced as a form of communication; there was considerable organic chemistry behind the choreography. Not this plump fellow. He was drunk. He fell on his side, struggled to get on his legs, staggered some more. He stopped. He seemed to vibrate, almost shook as if he wanted to vomit. He collapsed again. Sheriff peeked closer. The head exploded larvae. Sheriff tried to jump back but he fell on his butt, and crabbed backwards on his hands.

"You alright?" Eamon said at the door.

"Yeah, I think so." Sheriff dusted off his bottom and the front of his legs, fixed his belt. "I'm good."

Eamon's head nudged. "Is it as bad as Coach?"

"Ssh," Sheriff said. He tilted his head. "Kitchen."

"I'll get to work, and let you know when it's good to come out."

"Okay, but bag the bee." He pointed at the head. "And send pictures to the CDC."

"Bee? What bee?" Eamon glanced down at the floor. "About that, Sheriff, I—"

"Forget it, just do it. I'll be in the kitchen, and remember all this has to be bagged and tagged before she comes out of that kitchen." He thumbed in the direction of the kitchen. Sheriff and Eamon knew the house from holidays past. Sheriff and the wife had already RSVP'd for the New Year's Eve party. He walked slowly but loudly enough to announce his arrival. He knocked on the wood of the doorframe.

"Dorothy?"

"Jack? Thank you for coming," the hours-old widow said. Sheriff embraced Dorothy Owens, pecked her cheek, and gave the thumbs-up to the counselor behind the woman's back. The counselor made a diplomatic exit, card on the table.

"It was terrible, Jack."

"I can only imagine. I read your statement so we don't have to talk about that right now. Please, sit down." Sheriff let his hand guide Dorothy to the chair. He saw the quarter-full brandy snifter. Dorothy noticed that he had noticed it. She was an accountant and could spot a misaligned column and a weak decimal point at twenty-five paces.

"I apologize. I needed the drink."

"No need to apologize; this is your house."

"It was horrible, Jack. Horrible. At first I had thought he had an awful migraine. Rare for Bill, but when he had them they were dreadful."

"My wife gets them on occasion. I know how they can be."

"How is Marjorie?"

"She's well, thank you." Manners under duress, Jack thought. Impressive. He unbuttoned his breast pocket and pulled out his little notebook. The thing had more creases and wrinkles than Methuselah. He unsheathed the pen on the right side of it, and rested his left hand on the table. "Walk me through what Bill was doing, before, you know…"

"I'll try," she said. She picked up the snifter and let it rest between the palms of her hands. Rolling it as if warming the liquor meant that she was thinking. "Bill had made some calls. Confirming details with the caterers for the holidays, you know. I can't do all that cooking anymore."

Sheriff offered a smile. "You still make the best lasagna in Grand Isle."

She reached out with her hand and placed it over his left hand. "Don't let Marjorie hear you." She tapped his hand. He felt her warmth, the slide of her fingers across his knuckles. "What was I going to say? Oh, yes. Bill had made some calls. He'd rambled something about finishing one of his papers, but I can't for the life of me tell you what it was about. You know how Bill is about his bees." She took a small sip. 'Is' instead of 'was' said the reality hadn't sunken in.

"I know. About those bees—"

Her hand slapped the table. The snifter trembled and the brandy shimmered. "Now I remember it—his paper was on CCD."

"Catechism? That doesn't make sense."

"No, silly. Bill drafted a paper on Colony Collapse Disorder; it's his latest obsession."

Sheriff made a note. "About what time was that?"

Dorothy rubbed the side of her neck as if she thought that the massage and time stamp would arrive with the blood to her head. "He called the caterers after nine. He went out to his hives, back in around ten. That sounds about right because he was agitated and that got him obsessive about his paper."

Sheriff inked in the times. "Upset about what?"

"The hives, of course."

"Not sure I follow, Dorothy."

"A lot of his hives are dying off."

Sheriff wondered what bees did for the winter. He stopped writing. "I hadn't known about that. He never mentioned it."

"Why would he? It would harm his reputation."

"Can you tell me his theory? This CCD thing and why they were dying?"

Dorothy glanced over at the counter. Her eyes swept over it, from left to right and then right to left along the space. "There's a copy of it somewhere." She got up and sorted through some papers. She found it. "You can borrow it."

"Thank you." Sheriff rubbed his temples in thought. He read his shorthand in his notepad, signposts for short-term memory, but later he would have to draft a complete narrative. "So he was agitated, came in from outside. Anything else before he…?"

Dorothy sighed. "I can't believe I forgot this, but yes, there was something else. When Bill was worked up this morning, he kept scratching at himself. He said his belly and chest itched like hell and then later, he said the oddest thing."

"Odd, how?"

"He said something was moving inside him and that it burned." Dorothy finished off her brandy. Sheriff got up and looked for the bottle. She said it was in the closet next to the refrigerator. He found it and uncorked it, and poured her a generous splash.

"Inside him, huh? Tell me more."

"All he said was that it burned, and that he was cold." She eyed the amber liquid but didn't drink. "I'll admit I thought upset stomach at first or acid reflux, but Bill had an iron stomach. As for his feeling cold, I figured he had just come in from outside." Her hand was deciding on the snifter. "Way to lay Bill low was with a headache, which is why I paid more attention to the migraine. That concerned me, Jack. Married as long as we are, you'd know the difference between a complaint and a serious ailment."

He choked a laugh. "Marjorie is all gut. I'm the head case."

"Then you understand." Dorothy downed her brandy in one gulp. She scowled through the burn. "Damn, that hurts so good."

"Go easy, Dorothy. I know this is hard, but one last question." He put the pen down. Their eyes met. "Those bees of his. They ever get inside the house?"

Dorothy cocked her head, glanced outside the window at the hives. "Hadn't thought of it, but yeah, of course they did. Near impossible for them not to when you live with a beekeeper, but bees never bothered me." She raised a finger. "Funny thing happened the other day. I came across one and wouldn't you know it: damn thing was wobbly and disoriented. I got a paper towel and managed to escort the thing outside, but I don't think it stood a chance. Winter, you know."

"Disoriented and wobbly, huh?"

"The thing couldn't walk a straight line. I blame it on the weather. Not like bees get mad cow disease. I'd just assumed it was old, ready for AARP and Medicare." She laughed. He didn't.

Eamon's knock on the doorframe signaled the end of their conversation.

"We're good, Dorothy. If you don't mind, I'll have Dave take care of Bill."

"Why would I mind? Dave's got Grand Isle sewn up." Her hand touched her forehead. "That's an awful joke about a mortician."

Sheriff leaned down and kissed her head. "Thanks. Call me or Marjorie if you need anything, you hear?"

"Thank you," she said and embraced him. She was holding back tears. Dorothy was good people to Sheriff. She had an awful burden. A man might not want to die alone, but no man would want his wife to witness a wrenching demise. Bill, not in his right mind, had done the unthinkable in front of her. Coach's wife had been spared that agony.

Sheriff walked down the brief hallway. Wood flooring and white trim reminded him of a New England winter landscape. Bill's body and head had been trucked off to the coroner. Bagged, tagged, and photographed, the scene was now ready for analysis downtown.

Sheriff and Eamon were walking to the car. Eamon said to him in a hushed voice, "That bee you mentioned?" Eamon held out his cell phone. "I took a picture of it and sent it off to the CDC."

"One of Bill's honeybees. What of it?"

"Not the bee, but the larvae."

"Pseudo-whatever you said earlier. Ant-killer."

Eamon's hand pulled at Sheriff's elbow. They stopped walking. "Not Pseudacteon. This is Apocephalus borealis."

"Northern lights? We got the fly, and we'll wait to see what Doc Russell has to say. Here, read this." Sheriff handed Eamon Bill's incomplete paper.

"Thanks." The hand touched the elbow again. Sheriff looked down.

"What is it?"

"You don't understand, Sheriff. This borealis is serious. Different fly altogether."

"Oh, for Christ's sake, Eamon. One fly or two flies but same headless result. Is there a nuance I'm missing here?"

"Yeah, South American parasite versus a species that turns bees into zombies."

"Zombies? Stephen King lives in Maine. This is Vermont, Eamon. What the hell are you talking about?"

"Borealis does the same thing as the ant-killer, but the difference here is that Borealis has selected bees as their host."

"And they kill people, according to you."

"It's more than that, Sheriff. Once bees become zombies, they die. Worker bees stop collecting pollen. Do you understand the consequences that has on the world's food supply?"

"I think you're getting ahead of yourself, Eamon. Stick to two deaths." Sheriff pointed at the earth. "Here in Grand Isle." Sheriff took a few steps away, but Eamon hadn't followed him. He asked, "What? Is there more?"

"Yeah, I spoke to Dr. Russell about Coach and—"

"And what did he say?"

"Coach was infested with Pseudacteon."

"Should we be surprised?"

"The thing about Pseudacteon is that it has a humped back, and Coach had a humped back."

Quasimodo fly. Sheriff waved Eamon off. "The man was seventy-five years old. Do you expect a man his age to have perfect posture? Listen to yourself. The man was not turning into a fly. Now get in the car and tell me what you know about this borealis fly."

Eamon opened the unlocked door. The two got in and put their seatbelts on. Sheriff turned the engine. Eamon texted Clyde and asked him to drive his car back to the station.

Sheriff put the car in reverse, k-turned, and headed for the gate, for the main road. He felt itchy. Marjorie had used too much bleach. He was wearing a white shirt. They turned onto the main road into town. Eamon was well into lecture-mode.

"Bees taken over by Apocephalus borealis seek the light. Nobody knows why. My theory is they seek heat so the larvae can hatch. Most of the body's heat escapes through the head. Did you know that?"

Sheriff shook his head. "Hatch? You've got a way with words, Eamon. My mother always did tell me to wear a hat during the winter. Sorry, I didn't mean to interrupt."

"The worker bees abandon the hive. The queen can't do a thing. Without workers, the hive dies."

"Colony Collapse Disorder," Sheriff said. He thought of the drunken bee, the lost bee that Dorothy had found. A headache was coming on. He felt chilled so he flipped the switch for the heater. Had to be the stress, the coffee without breakfast. Damn heartburn. Eamon was talking nonsense. Zombie bees. Zombees.

"This could be worldwide," Eamon said as he angled himself in his seat, away from the vent.

"I told you: don't get ahead of yourself. We have two autopsies. Even your CDC isn't going to rush to judgment until those reports come in."

Sheriff had tears in his eyes, but he blamed it on the cold winter air when Eamon asked whether he was okay. He said nothing as he increased the heat while they drove into town. Ten minutes into Grand Isle, population of six thousand. The sun was out and it was warm.

"I need to pull over, Eamon. I think I'm gonna be sick."

IN THE STORM
THEY CAME

by Sean Ealy

"The air is poisoned," the lady with the missing tooth hissed.

She stood hunched over a gnarly cane at the edge of their lawn, next to the leaning mail box. Introducing herself as a neighbor, she had asked what brought them to Palo Verde.

"To escape my asthma," Leslie had answered, which was true enough. It was also true that Eric had been waiting for a chance to photograph the desert for a long time. But neither had seriously considered making the move until Leslie's doctor mentioned the dry heat would help her lungs.

Now Eric stared at the old woman, considering her response.

"What do you mean?" he asked.

The old lady cocked her jaw. "Just what I said."

"How can the air be poisoned?" Leslie asked.

"It's the dust," the old lady said. Her sallow eyes moved from Eric to Leslie.

Eric nodded. "See, Leslie, it's the dust."

"Oh, don't be coy, Eric," Leslie said, slugging his shoulder. "We had mold coming out of the walls in Oregon. You can't tell me that this place is worse than that."

Eric turned to the old lady. "Is it all dust or just Palo Verde dust?" He emphasized his sarcasm by leaning in and raising his brows.

The old lady lifted a hand in the air. "You should see it when the wind blows." She cackled.

Eric remembered looking out the little airplane window when they flew into Phoenix. The air was brown, but not like it was in Los Angeles. This wasn't smog but dirt.

"Well, I'm sure that we'll be fine," Leslie said. She gave Eric a look that said it was time for this old lady to move along.

Eric wasn't yet ready to let it go. There was humor in this, he thought, and he was going to squeeze it for all it was worth.

"So what causes the dirt to be dangerous?" Eric asked.

The old lady coughed, wet, phlegmy, and then spit something green onto the sidewalk. "Gets worse when the wind blows. Things die when it blows. You'll see."

Eric felt Leslie tugging at his shirt.

"Well," he said, "I guess we better get back to unpacking."

The old lady scowled.

"What the hell was that?" Leslie asked. Her arm slipped around his waist as they watched the old lady hobble down the sidewalk.

"That was our new neighbor." Eric grinned.

"Can't wait to meet the rest of them."

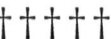

"It's called a haboob."

"It's a what?" Leslie looked up from the color samples she had brought back from Home Depot.

"A haboob. The dust storms the old lady was talking about are called haboobs."

Leslie smiled. "You like saying that word don't you?"

"Yes, I do." He spun his Mac Book around so that Leslie could see the picture on the screen. "These things look awesome. Take a look."

She leaned across the table. "My god, it's a wall of dirt."

"That's exactly what it is. It says these things can be over two thousand feet tall and spread for miles."

"How common are they?"

Eric turned the computer back around. "They're not uncommon. Looks like Phoenix was hit by one just a year ago. Covered the whole city."

"I still don't see how that can be as bad as she made it out to be."

Eric closed the computer and stood. "No, of course not. She was off her rocker." He smiled. "But still badass, right? I'd love to get some pics of one of those."

He reached for his camera bag.

"Wait," Leslie said. "I need help with these colors."

"Ah babe, you choose the colors and I'll paint." He winked at her. "Got a call this morning from a lady getting married in August. Wants to talk about wedding packages. I told her I'd meet her this afternoon."

"You're really not going to help me with the paint?"

Eric kissed her on the forehead. "I trust your divine sense of color coordination."

"You're incorrigible," Leslie said.

"You love me!" Eric called down the hall.

You're a haboob, she thought, and went back to her paint samples.

Later that evening, when Eric pulled up to the house, he saw that Leslie was waiting for him in the window. The translucent sheers fell back in place when she saw him, and she was out the door and down the deck stairs before he was even out of the truck.

"What's up?" Eric asked.

"We moved to the Twilight Zone. That's what's up."

Eric shut the truck door. He tried on a smile, slinging his camera bag over a shoulder, but she was having none of it.

"What happened?"

She stabbed the air with a finger, pointing across the street. "That old, nasty, smelly man across the street. He came to see me today."

"Dear God, the nerve of him."

"Don't be such a dick! He gave me the creeps."

Eric reached out to give her a hug, but she pushed him away.

"Eric, I didn't even hear him walk across the yard. I was working in the flower beds and he just came up behind me and put his hand on my shoulder. I damn near jumped ten feet! I turn around and he's just standing there watching me. The guy wasn't wearing any clothes!"

"Okay, that's weird. What did he say?"

"He said we were going to die."

"What?"

"You heard me right."

"Leslie, that's absurd. He's a crazy old man."

"What if all of these people are like that? What if they're all fucking insane?"

Eric looked down the driveway, across the street, at the house staring back at them. It was smaller than theirs, a single story ranch with neutral colored stucco walls and narrow windows. A beat up old Ford Taurus was parked under a leaning carport, cardboard boxes stacked on either side of it. The front lawn was nothing but dirt, littered with all kinds of debris, old paper and plastic bags. Eric thought he saw someone in one of the windows, watching them, but couldn't be sure.

He turned back to Leslie. "Let's go inside."

She wiped at her eyes. "No, Eric. I want you to talk to him."

"Come on, Leslie, what do you want me to say to him? This is ridiculous."

"I want you to look in his face and see what I saw today. I want you to see that I'm not crazy."

"I don't think you're crazy, Leslie."

She crossed her arms. "I can see it in your face, Eric. You think this is funny."

"No, I don't."

"Then go see for yourself."

"Fine. If that will end this whole thing, I'll go talk to him." He handed her his camera bag. "If he even answers the door."

Leslie said nothing.

"Fine." He started down the driveway. "Probably just a crazy old coot."

He walked across the battered road. The neighborhood was quiet, the air still-born. The heat lingered miserably, even though the sun was now only a thin line of molten metal along the horizon.

This place sucks, he thought. Two days in and I already want to bug out.

They had come from a real neighborhood, where kids played in the street, where neighbors mowed their lawns and took out their garbage every Thursday. This wasn't a neighborhood. This was four houses and an old decrepit trailer sitting at the end of the road.

He glanced back at Leslie, who was now standing on the deck underneath the porch light. He smiled and she flipped him the bird.

He climbed the concrete steps rising up to the cheap metal door and knocked, listening for any sound of movement inside. He knocked again. Nothing. Then he turned, showed Leslie his hands and shrugged.

Half way down the drive and the door opened.

"Hello?" A woman's voice.

Eric stiffened, as if caught in the act of something dirty. He turned around to see a wide woman standing in the narrow door frame. She wore a pink blouse, unbuttoned at top and hanging loose underneath her broad belly. Her black hair fell over her massive shoulders, wet as if she had just gotten out of the shower, still sticking to her fleshy cheeks.

"Look, if you're a sales guy coming around selling sumthin, I ain't got no money." She frowned, her eyes two black buttons immersed in a thousand yards of flesh. "Well, say sumthin, wouldya?"

Eric tried to swallow the goat in his throat. "No, I'm from across the street. We just moved in a couple days ago."

Her face suddenly brightened, her pouty lips curling into a smile. "Oh my god, of course. I seen you guys moving in there. You had a big truck."

"Yeah, sure. The movers."

"Took up damn near all the road, it was so big."

"Yeah, sorry about that."

"Don't you worry 'bout it. You must have a big ol' family to have so many things to fill up a truck like that."

"No, just me and my wife. I'm Eric and that mean old lady across the street is Leslie."

The big woman stepped out onto the porch. "I guess that makes us neighbors. My name's Ellery. Ellery Jane Pearl. What can I do for Eric?"

"Actually, this whole thing is just silly. My wife thought she met somebody today who lived here. An older man."

Ellery's eyes went wide. "Oh, you must mean Daddy."

"I'm sorry?"

"Daddy likes to get wanderin' when I'm not looking. Gets all lonesome, I think." She nodded her head enthusiastically. "He's harmless."

"I'm sure this whole thing is just a misunderstanding."

Her smile faded. "What do you mean?"

Eric slid his hands into his pockets, not quite sure why this whole thing was making him nervous. The wind picked up a little, and a smell from the carport hit his nose. Sour milk and dirty diapers. "My wife got a little spooked by your dad today, that's all. Maybe something he said?"

"He's an old man. I'm sorry he gave your pretty little wife over there a scare." The inflection in her voice changed.

"It's really not a big deal," Eric said. He held up his hands. "I'm sorry for bothering you."

He turned toward the street.

"What did he say?"

"What?" Eric turned back around and saw Ellery was now at the edge of porch. Her eyes were hard and her hands were balled into chubby fists at her sides.

"What did Daddy say to your wife?"

"She thought he said that we were going to die."

A long moment passed between them before she finally said, "Well, you are."

"What?"

"Both you and your pretty little slut wife. You're gonna die."

A shock of laughter bubbled out of her throat like a lunatic, her whole body shaking with it.

"It's going to get you when it comes," Ellery Jane Pearl yelled from her front step. She raised her meaty arms into the air, the flabby flesh jiggling as she shook her fists. "When it comes you'll die, just like the others did. YOU'RE BOTH GONNA FUCKING DIE!"

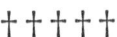

"What was that all about?"

Eric went straight to the fridge for a beer, ignoring the question. He drank half of it in one gulp and then he set it on the counter.

"Let's get out of here, Leslie," he finally said. "I mean it. What the hell are we even doing here anyway?"

"Eric, we just moved here."

He looked at her then, really looked at her, like he was trying to see deep down into her soul.

"You said it yourself," he said. "Something's not right with these people. This place. I just have a bad feeling about it all."

"Did you see the old man?"

"No, but I met his daughter. She had a message for us."

"Tell me what she said to you."

"She said we're going to die."

They barely spoke for the rest of the evening, but they did make love on the couch. It was a needy, eager act and there was something sweet and safe about being in each other's arm. For a little while Eric forgot all about the woman across the street. For a little while it was almost as if none of that had even happened.

"I think she was watching us last night."

Leslie sat on the edge of the bed, watching Eric as he got dressed.

"You mean on the couch?"

She nodded. "The curtains were open, remember? I swear I saw her standing there on her porch, in the dark."

Eric grinned and continued buttoning his shirt. "She got a good show then."

"Gross." She threw a pillow at him. "Why would she just be standing there watching?"

"You are pretty hot, darling." He got up and kissed her on the cheek. "I'm late. Let's talk about all of this when I get back this afternoon."

"Great, just leave me here all alone with the freaks."

But he was already running down the stairs.

Leslie frowned at her reflection in the mirror.

She stood up and went to the window. As Eric pulled away a knot formed in her chest.

She went downstairs to boil some water for tea. When the doorbell rang, she almost dropped the kettle on the floor.

It's her, she thought. It's the fat lady and her daddy.

But the woman standing on the welcome rug was more mouse than ogre. She was thin, had short blonde hair and tiny round eyes behind gray frames. She wrung her hands and flinched when Leslie opened the door.

"I'm sorry to bother you," the woman said. She realized what she was doing with her hands and stuffed them into her pockets. "I'm from next door."

Of course you are, Leslie thought.

The woman smiled nervously. "I'm Brenda Davis. Maybe this is a bad time?"

"No, no." Leslie realized she was clenching the door and forced herself to relax. "I'm sorry. I'm just not used to having guests yet. My head's not in the right place. Would you like to come in?"

"I'd like that," Brenda said.

"I was just getting ready to make some tea. Would you like some?"

"That would be wonderful."

Leslie went into the kitchen. "Make yourself at home," she called, but when she came back out a couple minutes later with two cups of Earl Grey in her hand, she found Brenda still standing.

"It's a nice house," Brenda said, taking the tea from Leslie. "I always liked this house."

Leslie sat on the couch. "How long have you lived on the street, Brenda?"

Brenda took a quick look out the window before sitting down.

"Six years," she said. She held her cup as if it might break just from touching her lips to it. "My husband and I moved here from Iowa right before the housing thing happened, and I've been stuck here since."

"Does your husband work in the city?"

Brenda's eyes darted toward the window.

"He did," she said.

"I'm sorry." Leslie had the sense that she had asked a wrong question.

"It's alright," Brenda said, switching the tea cup to her other hand. "My husband died about a year ago."

"Oh my god! I feel like such an ass."

"You didn't know." She softly blew on the tea and took a small sip. "Have you met any of the other neighbors?"

Leslie sighed. "I met the woman and the old man from across the street yesterday. Well, I didn't actually meet the woman, but my husband did."

"I hate that woman," Brenda whispered. She leaned in closer to Leslie as if sharing a secret. "She scares me. They're not right, her and her daddy."

"I'm glad to hear I'm not the only one who thinks so."

Brenda nodded. "They're all crazy. It's from living in the desert, I think."

Leslie liked Brenda. It was good to be able to talk to someone else about this, actually. It felt nice.

"I told my husband that I wanted to leave," Brenda said. "I wanted to go back to Des Moines, where my sister and her husband still live. But he said we couldn't sell our house on account of the economy being bad and all. He said that we owed too much, and that we had to stay until people started buying again. Now he's gone and I'm still here."

"How did your husband pass away?"

"That disgusting fat woman…" Brenda said. She stared at the window, tears spilling down her face.

Finally she shook her head. "The desert took him. I saw it with my own eyes."

Brenda wiped at her wet cheeks with the back of her small hand.

"What?" Leslie said. The tea cup in her hand had begun to tremble.

"The desert took my husband."

The storm moved slowly northwest, stretching out across the Mexican desert like a dark, smothering curtain, boiling with rage. Lightning danced across the surface of the clouds, like wicked skeletal fingers reaching for heaven and for the earth below, and in each momentary flash the ground shimmered.

Winds blowing from the east collided with the storm, creating a downward vacuum of pressure that picked at the surface of the earth. Dust began to rise, filling and staining the dark air, thicker than smoke. As the storm continued to drive forward, the wall of dust rose higher and higher until the storm itself was enveloped, becoming a flashing, rumbling force of fury, consuming everything in its way.

Among the dust walked the dead. Shrouded by the storm and never leaving its boundary, they were part of its chaos, animated by it, and would expire only when the storm itself was spent.

It was visible by early morning light. Eric saw it through the bedroom window while tucking in his shirt.

"Whoa, Leslie. You have to see this!"

"What is it?" she asked from the bathroom.

"I don't know," he said. "A storm maybe."

She came to the window, still drying her hair in a towel, and didn't immediately see the storm. What she saw was Ellery across the street, standing in her front yard.

"That woman," she growled.

"What?" Eric looked again. "Forget about sasquatch. Check out that storm on the horizon."

It took up the whole southern sky, dark and ominous, like someone was smothering the earth with fleece. She turned to her husband and saw the twinkle in his eye. "Don't even think about it."

His grin was all teeth. "Are you kidding? This thing is killer. I've got to get closer."

She opened her mouth to say something, but he was already out the bedroom door. Within minutes he was shuffling across the front lawn, his camera bag in his hand and his tripod stuffed underneath an arm.

He couldn't take his eyes off it. The thing was huge, and it was coming right at them.

Eric jogged down the street. He didn't acknowledge Ellery, didn't want to deal with that right now. As he passed her by, he could feel her eyes digging into him.

The road continued past Ellery's house for a quarter of a mile and then ended abruptly at a dirt driveway winding up to an old abandoned trailer. Eric went up the driveway and skirted around the worn and leaning wooden fence that partially separated the land the trailer occupied from the open desert behind it.

Wind licked at his face, like warm breath. The air smelled of alkaline and old dirt. The storm was moving quickly, and for a moment he could only stand there in awe of its presence.

The entire sky was darkened. It reminded him of pictures he had seen once of an atomic bomb being tested in the desert somewhere. It was as if the sky itself were collapsing.

Approaching the storm felt wrong to him somehow. It was like coming upon a wild animal, unpredictable and banal, but he had to get closer. He had his 300mm lens but the wanted as much detail of the storm as possible.

When he dared go no further, he positioned his tripod and locked his camera in place.

Something moved at the corner of his vision. An old man walked passed him, his long white hair blowing wildly in the wind. Thin, tanned arms hung motionless at his sides and his face was twisted in an idiot grin, tongue out, eyes bulging.

Ellery's daddy.

Eric watched the geezer stumble across the desert floor, his feet leaving trails of blowing dust with each step. He was naked from the waist up, wearing only an old pair of stained boxers and a pair of striped gym socks pulled up to his knees.

"Crazy old coot!" Eric yelled, but the wind snatched away his words.

Leaning into the camera, he pressed the shutter button down halfway, engaging the auto-focus.

The old man walked right past his field of vision.

Eric cursed. The old man almost fell, tripping over his own feet.

Lightning flashed, deep within the belly of the cloud. In its momentary charge, Eric thought he saw movement at the base of the storm. He leaned into his camera, zooming in all the way, and at first he only saw shifting patterns within the storm, like shadows. He waited for another flash of lightning, and then he saw them. Horrible, stumbling figures, moving together as an army might march, some of them only animated bones. Walkers. Hundreds of them.

The old man was running now. His arms were raised over his head and he flung them back and forth wildly, heading right into the storm.

Eric put his hands to his head. The wind was like a train in his ears now. He opened his mouth to yell at the old man, but he was no longer there.

The desert had taken him.

"Go back in the house!" Eric yelled.

Leslie stood on the front deck, but her eyes were on the storm.

He dashed past Ellery, who was now marching in circles in front of her house, fists in the air. She was mumbling something Eric couldn't hear over the wind.

"Get back in the house, Leslie!" he yelled.

She looked at him then, her face the color of cold stone.

"What?"

He rounded the driveway and took the steps two at a time. Grabbing her by the arm, he pulled her inside the door.

"Eric, you're hurting me."

He locked the door, turned the dead bolt. Then he went to the window. Outside, the fat woman marched and marched, yelling at the sky.

"We've got to get out of here."

"You're scaring me, Eric."

He shook his head. "No, no. We can't leave. It's too close. We have to hide." He turned back to her, and grabbed her by the shoulders. "We have to hide."

Leslie saw the terror in her husband's face and a sudden weightlessness washed over her. It was like stepping out over the edge of a cliff, knowing that there was nothing below you but miles of air. It was impossible to breathe.

Something thudded against the side of the house. Eric jumped. He let go of Leslie's shoulders and went back to the window.

"It's coming," he said.

Outside the wind had risen to a furious force. Trees bent at their boughs. A red lawn chair tumbled end over end across the sidewalk. A garbage can rolled across the road and slammed into the back of his truck. The sky had completely washed away, the light of the sun blotted out by the polluted air.

In his mind, he saw the walkers. They were dead, he was sure of that now. Dead men walking in the eye of the storm. And it suddenly all made sense. Everything these people had been telling them. It was the storm they were talking about, and whatever it was that lived inside the storm.

Dead things, he thought. Dead things walking.

"Eric!" Leslie snapped at him. She was trembling.

"Help me," Eric said. He went to the other side of the couch and began to push.

"What are you doing?"

"Blocking the door." After the couch he moved the coffee table.

But that wouldn't be good enough. In his mind's eye he saw the old man disappearing into the desert, over and over again, like an old horror movie.

Something pulled him in. You saw that, didn't you? Something reached out of the storm and pulled him in.

And on the edge of that: Dead things walking.

"The garage," he said. He grabbed her by the hand, but she refused to go. "We have to go to the garage. I think it's the safest place."

"You tell me what's going on right now! What did you see out there?"

He took a breath and tasted his own sweat. When he closed his eyes and saw the walkers. Wicked faces and twisted, unnatural bodies. Jaws snapping open and shut, open and shut.

"I don't know what I saw," he said.

"I don't believe you."

"The storm isn't right. It's dangerous, Leslie. I think that's what everyone here has been trying to tell us since we moved in, in their own weird way. This whole place is wrong somehow, but it's the storm that makes it wrong, you see? It's the storm and the desert."

Something in his words made her know he was telling the truth, but she just didn't want to believe it. Couldn't believe it.

"What do you want to do?" she asked.

"I don't know what to do." Outside the light was fading. The house creaked and moaned against the wailing wind. "I think we should go to the garage."

"Okay."

He smiled, and for a moment he found hope. They could make it through this if they stuck together.

Leslie's face screwed into a silent scream. When he turned he saw it. Standing at the window, with one hand pressed against the glass, was a rotted corpse. One arm had been torn completely off at the shoulder. Half of its scalp was covered with matted hair that hung in long clumps, the other half ripped away to reveal a muted bone underneath. Its eyes were filled with a green fire that danced in the darkness of its gaze.

"We need to go," Eric said. The corpse hit the window pane. Its jaw hinged open and what remained of its tongue moved over its broken teeth.

He took her hand and they cut through the living room. The window shattered behind them, and the howl of the wind amplified through the house.

"Don't look!" Eric yelled.

But she did look. There were more of them than she wanted to see, each one fighting the other to get through the window and into the house.

"Eric," she moaned. "Eric, they're coming!"

He turned the knob but it wouldn't move. His hand was sweaty and stupid with fear. He tried again before realizing it was locked.

"Shit!" He turned the lock with his thumb and the door opened into darkness. He let Leslie in first and slammed the door behind him. Still holding onto the door knob, he felt along the wall for the light switch, found it, flipped it. Nothing happened. "Shit!"

"Turn on the lights, Eric."

"They're out," he said. "We have no lights."

There was a crash from inside the house. A sound of splintering wood and groaning metal. They had made it through the front door.

"What are they?" Leslie whispered. She was standing next to him now. "What the hell are they?"

Down the hall he could hear shuffling footsteps. They were coming. Oh god, they were coming.

"I don't know," Eric said. His ear was against the door, listening.

Outside, the wind howled and shrieked, punishing the house from all sides. There were other sounds too. Sand and bone and clicking teeth.

He felt Leslie's hand on his waist and he thought she was crying. He wished he could see her face, wanted to look into her eyes.

"I love you," he said, but it came out no more than a whisper, barely heard.

More glass breaking. Something falling over upstairs. On the other side of the door, the shuffling footsteps drew closer, closer, and when they finally stopped there was a period of intense quiet, like the inhalation of breath before a scream.

Eric braced his arms, palms now flat against the door. He could hear them, their snapping jaws, the clicking in their throats. What were they waiting for?

Dead things. Dead things walking.

When the dead men hit the door, Eric closed his eyes. They should have left when they had time. Now it was too late.

"I love you," he said again, leaning his forehead into the door.

Outside the storm raged. It was alive, and it would never end. It would never stop coming.

Like the dead men pounding on the door.

THE ZOMBIE'S LAMENT

by Steven E. Belanger

David Pearson's memories come in bits and pieces.

He was drunk on beer and Dewar's. At someone's house. A party.

Something bad had happened.

He stumbled out of a side door and vomited. People laughed, but kept drinking and doing their own thing.

Now he lay on his back in the soft, dewy grass, happy in his deep sadness.

He sees a pair of old brown shoes with dried bloodstains on them, caked to the laces. Thick, hairy legs. Ripped jeans. Blue and red plaid shirt. Sleeves rolled up to the elbows. Palms and hands dripping blood.

He wants to move but he's paralyzed in his sad drunkenness and the grass feels so cold, so refreshing.

So good.

So peaceful.

The misshapen, red- and purple-splotched face leering over Dave's drips bloody drool and saliva and a red piece of somebody's something onto his lips and cheeks. Before he can scream, the man's bloodied beard and flesh-covered teeth fill his vision. A suffocating stench of rotting meat. A scorching pain as the thing bites into his neck and shoulder and then there's no more.

For awhile.

He thinks.

Then there's the bend of Main Street and the fire station on his right. It's nighttime now and he's stumbling.

A darkness.

Then the frozen, white-topped cove is on his left. Very distantly he remembers the burned and crumbling barge that had been there, before it sank forever into the deep, cold water.

Darkness.

He's climbing the wide slabs of stone, steps from the street to his house. It's an effort to take his key out as he's shambling up the front stairs. After many moments he realizes how cold he is, colder even than he should be, without a coat and walking for about an hour on a winter night. He's inside. The staircase is almost insurmountable. He knows he's dying. He wonders how much blood he's lost. He wonders if he's already dead.

He falls into his bed and he sleeps.

Sort of.

They say your life flashes before your eyes as you die, but for Dave it's a View-Master of images of the past few weeks. Each scene comes with a surge of sadness and regret that hurt more than his shoulder, head and neck.

And it's all very slow, slower than death.

The first: a writer's group. Familiar faces of bald and sophisticated Kenny; thin and sad and sultry Sheila; the cute and smiling Emma.

And Suzie.

First and last, always Suzie.

Her pale skin. Freckles that prettied her face like artsy dots of a Jackson Pollock. Strawberry blonde hair and a shy, knowing smile.

And then nothing.

But are there voices outside his front door?

He remembers the piece they'd critiqued at the long, rectangular table. It had been a good and terrible story as only a talented amateur can write, full of misogyny and author intrusion and great imagery. But Suzie was so beautiful, and they'd looked at each other all meeting long like in some bad soap opera, and he'd wondered why a girl so pretty would ever look at him like that.

The surge of happiness he feels is crushed by the wave of despair that crashes upon him: Where had they gone wrong? All the yelling, all the anger and anxiety—Where had all that come from?

As if from a great distance, Dave sees the white etched swirls of his bedroom's ceiling. Superimposed upon that, an image: He's standing beside her, both of them in front of the huge flat-screen that still hangs on the living room wall beside the front door.

He says: "If you don't leave tonight, I'll just change the locks."

And her soft reply: "You won't have to do that."

And then she's gone.

Silence. The white ceiling paint. The deep, cavernous swirls in the ceiling. No more pain in his shoulder. His neck. His head.

Some time later, he senses someone standing beside him. He's curious, but heavily apathetic.

And he's getting angry.

He suddenly sees, as if he's just opened his eyes, but they must have been already open because the cop he sees staring at his face doesn't act surprised.

The uniformed policeman rolls up the left sleeve of Dave's red and blue Sox shirt and feels his wrist for a pulse. Does the same to the side of his neck that's not destroyed.

His body had started to rigor. From that angle, lying on his back, his left arm looked like it stretched forever in front of him.

Dave tries to move but the stiffness is too strong. Another tide of sadness and regret brings some sensation with it. He feels his swollen neck. Distended belly and face. Settled blood in his back and buttocks from lying in the bed so long. A whiff of vomit from the wooden floorboards of his bedroom, from small dried puddles on his shirt and blue jeans. Urine and waste beneath his butt and upper thighs on the bedsheets.

His mouth is hanging open.

The policeman leans over him again. He's about twenty-five, clean-shaven but with a dark five o'clock, his hair black and cut very short, his eyes as dark as his hair. These eyes are opened wide, his upper lip raised in slight distaste, his nostrils flaring at the smell.

I may be his first corpse, Dave thinks.

The policeman places his hat in the crook of his left arm as he leans further and gently closes Dave's eyes.

Both are startled when his lids spring open again.

He stands straight, rattled, and looks down at Dave for a moment. When he sighs, the room gets darker, an unquiet dark that's not like night. It fills Dave with so much sadness that he wants to cry out—

But the cop sighs again and leaves the room.

And Dave remembers:

He'd been drinking and eating too much, and sleeping too little, since Suzie left.

Joe calls. Says he's throwing a party. Says Suzie will be there.

"Now's your chance to patch it up," Joe says to him on his cell.

Except she frowns at him, at his sloppy appearance and his bloodshot eyes. He's already half in the bag from hours of drinking over many days.

He had more during Joe Nuxhall's party. In his depressed drunkenness he screwed Dawn Reynolds in Joe's spare bedroom.

Where Suzie and Joe opened the door and found them later that night, drunk and as naked as newborns.

"He's all yours, Joe Nuxhall," Suzie says, standing beside Joe in the doorway, pretty in her white buttoned-shirt and blue jeans, in another image pasted to the ceiling swirls. She flips her hair over her shoulders and looks at everybody, disgusted but not surprised.

He struggles to say something as he puts on his Sox shirt, but his mouth is dry and his brain is heavy. So he just stands beside the bed, still drunk and with a throbbing headache, as Dawn fumbles for her pink panties, white frilly top, and jeans.

Suzie's driving away as he staggers out that side door of Joe's house. Her old Ford Escort almost clips a man walking drunkenly in the road.

Dave sees himself seeing this, and then watches himself sink to the cold, welcoming grass.

And get bitten by this shambling man, who later bites old Mrs. O'Grady down the street, and seventeen-year old Jennifer Potter as she tries to sneak back into her parents' house at three a.m.

Dave stares at the ceiling as The Shambling Man—as Dave now refers to him—tries to cross the ice over Old Mill Cove, falls through a thin spot, and flows very slowly, so peacefully slow, under the ice, into the bay, into the ocean.

The images disappear.

He drifts...

Until he hears the cop say, "Were you in any condition to drive at the time, sir?" to somebody downstairs.

He's wide awake again.

And angry.

He sees Suzie crying, her pretty face just leaking tears. Of all the horrible things she's done to him, of all the terrible things she's said to him, the one comment he remembers now most from their fights is when he said—

But he can't remember it.

He doesn't want to see it. The shame of it—the rage engulfs him and he wills it away. She'd been hurtful to him at the end. She'd probably cheated on him, and they never would've worked out anyway—but the shame of how he'd let it end, the regret of his wasted relationship, his wasted life...

Startled, Dave realizes his shame and anger are keeping him alive. That, and a certain thirst, a hunger, that feeds upon his anger and shame.

If it all has to end, he thinks, I don't want it to end like this.

He hears, as if from far away, the cop talking to his friend Joe, downstairs. Joe, whose party he'd gone to. Joe, who stood there with a leering smile, eyeing Dawn Reynolds as she scurried to hide her nakedness.

Joe, and Bobby, and Stevie, and all those guys who he got drunk with, who he'd always gotten drunk with, ever since high school. Ever since he dropped out of college because he'd rather drink than learn.

The self-hatred. The anger.

The rage.

It will not end like this.

He lifts his head. The room swims.

A few minutes pass.

His limbs don't want to obey, but he finally gets his elbows beneath him. He slowly pushes them against the bed and sits up.

Everything goes grey.

Her crying face.

"You know what I'm most sorry about?" he remembers her saying to him a few days before she left. "I'm sorry I couldn't get you to care more about your life. You could've done more with yourself. You're not dumb."

Dave sits upright in his bed, his fury building. The more Suzie sobs, and the more Joe talks, the angrier he gets.

I will swing my legs over, he thinks, and I will stand.

The officer says something he can't make out.

"Yeah, that's Dave," Joe says. "All hammer and nails and beer, just like me and a few other guys. He could always nail down a deck. But he could never nail down a permanent job. Or a girl."

He stands.

And turns.

Stiff as a board, as they say, but he grasps for the doorknob.

The door swings open and he steps into the hallway.

"Any idea what bit him?" Joe asks. He sits on the couch, facing the cop, who's standing in front of him, holding open a little pad and writing on it with a blue Bic.

"Might be a rabid fox, or a wolf," the cop says. "If you have any small pets, I'd be careful when I let them out."

"Okay. Suzie's got a cat. I'll let her know."

The cop folded his pad and closed his pen. "If I need to get in touch with her about this man she says she saw when she drove away, I can reach her at your place?"

"You bet, officer."

"And you're sure he didn't know that she'd been staying with you since they broke up?"

"Absolutely," David Pearson hears Joe Nuxhall, his friend, say with fake solemnity. "I know how it looks, officer. But I didn't do anything to him. Suzie kept saying she wanted to go back to him. That she missed him, and loved him, and all that. So I just wanted her to see how he was. How he gets when he drinks. I hate to speak ill of the dead, but I always told her he cheated on her. She just needed to see it herself."

Dave's jawbone splinters on both sides of his face when he opens his mouth.

Both men listen to the stillness of the house. The officer turns toward the stairs. His eyes widen as he drops pad and pen and reaches for his gun. Joe stands and looks up in surprise, inexplicably taking out his cellphone, maybe to call for the police.

Dave separates from the darkness of the upstairs hallway and stands beneath the light of the small, round ceiling fixture above him.

Green and white growths pepper Dave's face and neck. The skin of his back and butt sag like a bag of water, and his chin rests on his collarbone like Jacob Marley's ghost. Both feet flop as he walks, like they dangle from broken ankles.

Pieces of muscle and bone protrude from his shoulder and neck like something had burst out of him. Jaw muscles shred and vocal cords snap as a deep, guttural growl comes from a voicebox that no longer works:

"I...heard...you..."

Dave jumps down the steps. The landing jars every bone in his body, breaking several. The orbital socket of his right eye cracks and the eye bulges like an egg from the side, almost slipping out.

He brushes the cop out of the way.

Joe's screams are cut off as Dave takes the cellphone with his right hand and Joe's neck with his left.

He dials a number he knows well as he feels bullets penetrate his back. Popping sounds from far away.

Suzie's phone rings and Joe's neck snaps.

Dave holds on.

Joe's chin hits his rigored hand, his body a limp doll, his feet dragging on the floor.

Dave swings his body in front of him like a shield, and it takes a few bullets in the back and out the stomach.

"Hello?" Suzie says.

He forces out a low, sandpaper voice that shreds his larynx and throat. Blood flows into his chest and out of the left corner of his mouth and down his long chin to his collarbone.

"Suzie? It's Dave. I'm so sorry I said that, baby. I'm so sorry I said that about the bus—"

The cop circles around him.

The next bullet enters Dave's heart through his back. He hears a paper-tearing rip as it exits his upper chest. Black, sludgy blood trickles from both wounds.

He releases Joe's neck. The body hits the floor like a heavy load. But he still holds the phone.

Suzie's cries echo in the room.

The next shot blows away his sagging chin and much of his neck in a spray of black blood and brittle bone. He falls to the floor and he remembers:

It was the ugly end. All they shared was anger. Bitterness. Hatred.

Suzie paces in the small hallway outside their bedroom door, her arms flailing in exasperation, calling him an idiot for how he was about to lose her. He stands in front of her, facing her, his right hand on the doorknob, recalling she had once told him she'd been in special ed. in high school after her parents divorced, because she'd been depressed and just shut down. She'd had to take the small yellow bus for two weeks until a meeting with the school psychologist exited her from the program.

"Me?" he says. "Me? I'm not the idiot. I'm not the one who had to take the retard bus to school. That just proves how stupid you are—how stupid you've always been."

His mouth freezes on the last word, not believing what he's heard himself say.

She just stands there, shaking, her pretty face wet with tears.

"Look," she pleads. "That didn't really happen, okay? I was just kidding when I said that. So you don't have to mention it anymore, okay? Okay?"

The cop puts the muzzle against his skull. And shoots.

A mushy spot mushrooms and then explodes on the right side of his head, beneath his close-cut, thinning brown hair. Blood, bone and a black and milky-yellow substance splatter the floor and leak down his face. This river swims with little black flies he hadn't noticed before.

He rolls over and lays on his back on the floor, feeling his life, his blood and his brains spilling onto the wood. Still, somehow, he clutches the phone.

He hears the cop's voice calling for backup, his frantic footsteps close to his face. He hears static from the walkie-talkie, something about biting, and a panic. He couldn't see anything, and all noise was fading to a permanent nothing.

"You weren't stupid," he whispers to Suzie's cries. "I was stupid. I was."

He drifts in the cold water of the cove, peacefully beneath the ice.

Before he dies again, this time for good, he hears Suzie say, "That's okay, baby. That's okay."

The front door opens. There's screaming and snarling and more shots fired.

But David Pearson flows peacefully in the freezing water, his face pressed against the solid ice, a smile on his face. He lets the soothing, cold water carry him, slowly and with ease, into the bay, into the ocean, into the beyond.

DADDY'S HOME

by Bo Balder

Nobody had counted on Doug's return. I am sure of this, because we'd buried him four months ago. Doug hadn't wanted to be cremated, because he liked the idea of the children putting flowers on top of him. A legitimate wish, although I prefer cremation.

When I came home, the nest fragrance of the house was tainted with a strong earthy smell. Someone must be visiting. I listened to a man's voice reverberate in between the children's chatter. It sounded like Doug's voice, although it couldn't be. I geared up for a rebuke. They weren't allowed to let in strangers when I wasn't home.

"Mummy!" my daughter called while she ran up to me. "Daddy's home!"

Someone sat in Doug's favorite chair, which was now mine, because he always had a nose for the warmest, most comfortable spot in a room. Wearing Doug's burial suit. The man snapped the newspaper back into place exactly like Doug.

His body strained oddly in the buttoned-up jacket. The funeral center slit it in the back for the coffin.

When the newspaper sagged down, the face above it was bloated and taut, as if fluid would spurt out if you pricked it. It was gooseberry colored, but the way he growled a welcome was vintage Doug. Taylor jumped onto the couch for the Winx reruns. Zach didn't even look up from his *MAD* magazine.

I knew I should say something, but Taylor whined for a cookie. I went to the kitchen to get the cookie and stayed to cook dinner. I could talk to him afterwards.

Doug grunted and shuffled to his usual spot. Zach had laid a place for him. Kids are so flexible. Doug heaped his plate and started eating straightaway. Taylor was about to rebuke him for it, because they've taught her impeccable manners at daycare, but I lifted my finger to my lips and shook my head. After a mouthful or so, Doug shifted his fork to his right hand and began mashing the food. Exactly the way his father used to eat. It had taken me years to wean him from this habit.

That, and maybe the smell, were the only signs that something had changed.

After dinner, Doug fell back into his chair and snapped the newspaper to its former position. When the children went to bed, I became a little nervous. We watched the news together, silently, and then a cop show. I had still no idea what I was going to say. Sorry, Doug, but you're dead so it's time for you to leave? Honey, I'm so glad you're home? Somewhere in between, maybe.

I worried about the mortgage, because I now owned half of the house outright. If Doug was declared alive, I couldn't afford the payments on my own. Maybe Doug could get his old job back. At ten o'clock, I went to my bedroom.

I heard nothing from downstairs. I stripped rapidly, because the idea of Doug catching me in the nude gave me the shivers. After a perfunctory tooth-brushing, I slipped into bed.

The stairs creaked. The bathroom door opened and closed. My electric toothbrush buzzed. The toilet seat clattered but there was no flushing. I suppose zombies don't have to pee.

The bedroom door opened and a sweetish rotten fragrance wafted into the room. Mushy feet shuffled to the other side of the bed and a weight dipped the mattress.

Doug scooted up against me and put his clammy hand on my breast. I froze and contemplated pushing him off, but the hand slid down and I changed my mind. Doug wanting to make love was so rare that I didn't want to pass up the opportunity. Goose bumps raced back and forth over my body, but it was actually kind of exciting. When his soft broad finger slid inside me, I had to suppress a groan.

It was late, and my body needed a lot of time to heat up, but Doug gave no sign of impatience. He used to ask every two minutes if I'd finished already and I was pleasantly surprised that he had left that habit in the grave. I came long and hard and pushed my hand dutifully into his pajama pants. My hand groped in sticky pubic hair. The flesh between his thighs was spongy, making sucking little sounds against my fingertips, and I had to really force myself to root around further. After a while, I gave up. Nothing there anymore. Well, that was a relief.

"Goodnight, hon," I mumbled and fell asleep.

The next morning the bed was empty. Doug was making the kids breakfast. The kid weren't eating and looked white and strained.

"Mom!" Taylor hissed and held out something to me. It was about three inches long and three quarters of an inch wide, a peculiar lead gray in color. I couldn't figure out what it was for the longest time. Suddenly my brain shifted gears and it was Doug's index finger.

"Where did you find it?"

Taylor pointed to her bowl.

"Don't eat that, honey."

I got out a piece of Quick Clean and folded the finger inside before I put it in the trash.

I walked the kids to the school bus stop. "We have to be kind to Daddy, because he might not be able to keep it together for that long, okay?"

The kids nodded.

"No wrestling, huh?" Zack said.

I knew it was hard to give that up, because it had been his main mode of communication with Doug. "Better not, sweetie."

So here we are, for however long it lasts. He watches the shopping channel all night, because I never allowed him into my bed after that one time. Even if his endurance has increased enormously, I still prefer my Rabbit to that moist, spongy hand.

I wouldn't want him to strain the digits, and, you know, leave something behind inside me.

THE DEAD OF SUMMER

by Wayne Laufert

It's quiet up here. No traffic, no television, no conversations. The steel mill whirs, bangs, belches, grinds and hisses all day long, but those noises don't make it this far up the mountain. Instead, a hum comes from no place in particular. Day and night, it's all around, the hum of creation. And you can't really hear it. You feel it.

So I knew something was wrong when the door slammed. I thought I heard a creak right before, too. A truck door. Out back I saw the gravedigger standing behind his old pick-up, its red paint faded to a flat terra cotta and the frame outlined with crumbling brown rust. The truck and its driver should not have been there. This was in February, and as usual at that time of year no one had been up here in several months and no one was expected for several more. The ground was hard and coated with snow, and more was falling at that moment. There was nothing for the man to do.

As he reached into the back of the pick-up, I asked him why he was here, and he said nothing. Had he heard me? I called to him again. Still nothing. He took a shovel from the truck bed and went up a small incline toward a corner of the cemetery. I followed. By the time I neared the corner to which he had walked, I lost sight of him. Not much was back there. Even so, I couldn't find him, and the rapidly falling snow had covered our footprints. The truck was gone, too. It had left no tracks.

I went back inside, into a four-room rancher with a small office in front.

The gravedigger I'd just seen was not the one whose services I had used in the summer past. I could swear my unexpected visitor was a laborer who had died two years earlier. My parents, long dead, had first employed him many years ago.

Back in my parents' time and even recently, townspeople occasionally took Sunday drives up the mountain and laid flowers and baskets on their loved ones' graves during the three months out of the year when the temperature up here is bearable. Then they followed the road beyond my family's property to their real destination, a camp that was popular with hunters. On the way back down the mountain, they drove past the graveyard, reaching town in a couple hours.

The only other people we saw up here were gravediggers. I kept hiring the same man to do all the digging. That was the man who showed up in the truck later, after his death.

I wondered why he wouldn't talk to me. Maybe he mistakenly believed it was his fault when, more and more often during the warmer months, the bodies he had interred failed to stay in the ground. Thankfully, my parents did not rise up. They had been buried long ago, and I never saw them again.

When my parents were alive, it was mostly my mother who ran the yard, as we called it. Over the years, the lots filled up and our family's income dwindled. Father, who realized at a young age that the cemetery would not sustain us for long, owned the small steel mill in town right by the rail line. By the time my sister and I were orphaned well into our adulthood, everything was settled. She had a head for commerce, so she took the mill, or rather she and her husband did. They lived in town and raised a family. The husband died, she died, and my niece and nephews inherited the mill. They still run it.

Recently they got town officials to authorize the mill's expansion, and its resurgence is made evident by a steelmaking byproduct I hadn't seen in many years: fine silvery particles that form a glittery film over the ground and settle onto the vast covering of snow.

We get numerous storms between mid-September and early May, each one adding several inches of frozen white thickness to the grounds. The road up here is often blocked except for the few somewhat moderate weeks. Most of the kin of the yard's inhabitants moved away when work in the mill and elsewhere in town dried up. Now, even with the mill bustling again, the ones who stayed or came back are too busy to make a day of trekking up and down the mountainside. They use a cemetery down there instead.

I'd begun thinking about what might happen when I'm too old to drive into town for provisions. Call on the gravedigger for help, I guess, because apparently he's still around.

Folks in town, once the long cold season has finally broken, embrace their newly green, pleasant surroundings. Up here it's different. The headstones have to be topped with snow. The ground must crackle under your feet. The air must numb your flesh and rattle your teeth. If not, there's trouble. When the ground is soft, the ones underneath it can escape.

Most of them have been taken care of. Still, some occasionally emerge. Once in a while the gravedigger helped me return them to their holes. In fact, he did that with my brother-in-law. No one else even knew he'd gotten out.

Their time of awakening grows longer. Summertime heat used to rise up past the mountain, but it's trapped now, I'm convinced, by soot and other gunk from the revitalized smokestacks that darken the sky. The first few used to make their way to the surface around the Fourth of July. Now, the walking season begins as early as Memorial Day.

Typically they're the ones who were in the cheap boxes, which are easier to break through after being softened by the melting heaps of snow. Also, they tend to be more recently dead, within a couple years, say, so they're more intact. The yard is small and rather flat and open. I can see them soon after they've sprouted, a couple per week until about Labor Day. Putting them down is easy. I keep a hunting rifle with plenty of bullets in the office. No one's around to hear even when I have to fire more than once. I try to get them the first time, though. I mean, it isn't target practice. Sometimes they come apart when they fall, so I put the bones back and leave the viscera to decompose.

I did not shoot my sister when she showed up at the office door fifteen months after she died. I let her in. Sitting on a couch that was originally intended for customers, she looked rather well-preserved. The color was a bit off. Paler, of course. But her skin was only a little blotchy and her body only somewhat bloated. The embalmer in town is very good, and the below-freezing temperatures help keep corpses fresher up here than they would be down there. Her faded pink dress and brown shoes were soiled from the walk but remained intact. All in all, a very good likeness.

"Why'd you bury me up here?" was her question. I reminded her of our family plot, where even her husband had been laid to rest. She found that response insufficient. "Was that supposed to keep us together for eternity?"

She spoke more slowly than I remembered. Her tongue, vocal cords and other internal parts must have been in bad shape.

"I didn't realize," I said. Her prepaid funeral plan, it turns out, did not represent her true wishes.

Mainly my sister wanted her children to give up the steel mill.

"It's filthy," she said. "It makes the whole town dirty."

But the mill always passed inspection, as far as I knew, and anyway she'd already begun to transfer ownership to her children while she was alive. Did those instructions, I asked, also fail to convey her intentions?

"I don't care what those papers say," she declared. "It's just legal mumbo jumbo."

I hadn't dealt much with papers like that, so I couldn't argue the point. It's too late to change anything, I thought to myself. I told her I'd see what I could do.

"Wonderful," she said, still capable of sarcasm. And with that she shambled out the door. I stared at the couch for a while, feeling nothing except the ebbing hum.

Her visit had not occurred in the summertime, but in early December. The ground was muddy.

I didn't even ask her what becomes of someone who has died.

One of my nephews called after they'd brought him the tattered dress that belonged to his mother. He drove it up to me. I confirmed that it was the one she'd been buried in but didn't say that I recognized it from a couple days earlier. I felt it prudent not to let even my relatives know about the resurrections. My nephew certainly would not have understood why I shot his father in the head.

"You know we're not going to be buried up here," my nephew said, referring to himself and his brother and sister.

"Pretty sure I've heard that, yes," I said.

Dress in hand, my nephew went to his mother's plot to try and piece together an explanation. The dress should have been buried with her. She should have stayed underground. The cemetery lawn should have been frozen. Nothing was the way it should have been. The emptied grave made my nephew furious.

"What happened? Why'd you dig her up?" he bellowed, waving the handful of rags that used to be the pink dress. "How did this end up near the bottom of the mountain?"

That wasn't all that ended up there. By then everyone had heard: Not just my sister's dress but also her head and her right arm and shoulder within the dress had been found inching down the winding road just outside town. A motorist on his way to a hiking trail way down there had made the discovery. He turned around and reported to the sheriff, who was disbelieving but curious enough to send a deputy. At the scene was the dress but no body parts. They were found, immobile, along the edge of a forest a few feet from the road.

Where was the rest? Somewhere between that point and the cemetery, I suppose, in piles of buzzard bait. Probably indistinguishable from the ground, or simply disintegrated.

What did it matter? She was dead. She'd told me herself.

There was no explaining the unearthed corpses, the scattered body parts, the bullet-speckled headstones. It was the easiest thing in the world for the townspeople to accuse me of desecration. What they can't explain is the long journey the dress and the mobile remnants of my sister apparently took.

Although I could not have prevented my sister from joining the legion of the unburied, I could have avoided it. I could have hung a No Vacancy sign on the gate and left the yard behind. My sister and brother-in-law, and later my niece and nephews, had offered to give me a job and find me a place to stay. They didn't care about me. They just wanted to get the crazy man off the mountain. I would not have had to work hard, just sit in an office all day, much like I've done up here. No need to shoot anything, either.

I would not have survived. Being the crazy man on the mountain at least got me this far.

The hum of creation—the unbroken bass note that had been inside of me and all around me throughout my life—is gone. But this morning the gravedigger returned. I noticed he'd hauled up something in his truck bed, so I had a question.

"That for me?"

He looked at me grimly and placed his hand on the casket.

I went inside for my rifle.

WHITE LIGHT, WHITE HEAT

by W.P. Johnson

As the rest of the city fell to infection, Zack and Katy holed up in Chris's North Philadelphia apartment, drinking PBR and snorting lines of Adderall. It was Chris's prescription, but Zack crushed up the pills, boasting that his method was the best for making lines.

"Trick is," he said, "you have to crush them under a dollar bill with a credit card." Lumps were smashed under his thumb before he raked a card over it. After lifting the dollar, he scraped the remaining powder onto the table and divided it into three thick lines. They were clumpy from the humidity.

"Damn it." He chopped again, trying to get the chunks out. A yawn left Chris, having finished his fifth beer. Katy punched his arm.

"That's contagious."

"Sorry," Chris said, "I'm just getting tired is all."

"Well, this will straighten you out." Zack held the tray up to Chris' face, his own nose already blue and crusty.

"I don't know…"

"Dude, it's your prescription."

"Yeah, come on Chris," Katy said, taking the tray. She snorted one of the lines. "Whole world is ending. If that isn't a reason to get fucked up, I don't know what is."

Chris stared at the tray and the remaining line. Another yawn hit him. They started shouting snort, snort, snort, so he leaned in and snorted.

He could taste the line in the back of his throat. It tasted of Sweet'N Low, which made him think of his mother who was still in Lancaster and had tried to lose weight a dozen different times. She threw out all of their junk food and his childhood was a bland series of salad and steamed chicken. Chocolate bars and Doritos were hoarded above a ceiling tile in his bedroom, prompting mysterious outbreaks of acne all throughout high school. After graduation, she begged him to go to a local college instead of moving to Philadelphia.

Adderall had a way of shocking the tangled mess of wires in his head. Too many thoughts at once.

He wondered who else had bothered staying in the city. He wondered how many people were roaming the streets right now, rabid, foaming at the mouth. He wondered if the government would cut their losses and bomb the entire city. When Baltimore was quarantined, they waited it out, tried gassing them with vaccines. Eventually they just let the virus run its course.

Chris was good with numbers. He could sort out the odds of how long they had. Figured on a month, give or take a few days. They'd either live through it or they'd wake up to a bright light that burned their shadows into whatever walls stood after the bombs dropped.

He should have bailed on college and gambled instead, became a bookie, but he didn't know any sports. When he was a kid he tried baseball and took a pitch to the face, cried a whole lot, he cried a lot in school, he had asthma, his mother bought him air purifiers and neti pots, he wondered if Katy would fuck him if she knew this and Zack wasn't here right now. If only Zack was out of the picture and he had a month alone with Katy. If only.

He got up and put *Evil Dead* on.

"Dude, good call," Zack said, cutting up another line.

Katy added, "I looove this movie." She smiled and Chris turned pink.

"Yeah." He cracked opened another beer and drank half of it, hoping it would loosen the tension in his jaw. Zack snorted a line and paced around the room. An old David Bowie tee shirt frosted with sweat stains was the only clothes he brought.

They all snorted another line.

He didn't know she was dating anyone. When he told Katy to come over and bring whatever food she could carry in one trip, Zack came with her, bringing nothing but the clothes on his back and four cases of beer that he carried up the stairs without breaking a sweat. He used to play football, lift weights, biked everywhere, knew everyone and everything in Philadelphia before it became the country's third city to fall to infection, after Baltimore and DC.

Zack stopped his pacing and snapped his fingers to an idea. "Top ten bands from New York City. One, The Velvet Underground." He pointed at Katy.

"Lou Reed." She looked at Chris. Thoughts piled up and he started to sweat.

"Wait...wasn't Lou Reed in The Velvet Underground?" Zack pointed out.

"Yes," Katy exclaimed, as if having completely forgotten this.

Zack snorted another line and closed his eyes so tight they formed two crude gashes.

"Alright, I got it, The Velvet Underground, The Ramones, Television, The New York Dolls, The Talking Heads, Cro-mags, Suicide, Anthrax, Wu Tang Clan, and Sonic Youth."

Katy waved a hand, dismissing the list. "Wu Tang Clan isn't a band. You're one band short."

Chris nodded in agreement. "Yeah dude, rap isn't music."

"Well," Katy said, sneering, "I didn't mean that."

Chris blushed and sank into the couch.

Zack waved his hands at them, frantic. "Whatever, they're awesome, now come on, we still need another band."

"The Strokes are from New York," Chris said. Their faces both asked if he was serious. Digging further into the couch, he wished he hadn't said a thing, wanting to somehow shrink until he fell through the fabric of the couch and lived inside of its filling like the incredible shrinking man.

Daylight stared to peek through the bedroom window. They were on an east-west street and the sun trickled in slowly instead of pouring out when it finally peaked the skyline. Empty bottles piled up in the kitchen and they took to throwing them out onto Girard Ave, peppering the streets with broken glass, filling in the small grooves of trolley track already half filled with trash. It was a neighborhood on the fringe of Temple University, choked of resources while the locals were priced out by trust fund kids.

"I mean," Katy said randomly, "The Strokes were pretty good." A bottle was pitched from her hand, bursting over a closed up Check Cashing place and spitting out brown confetti.

"I was gonna say Interpol, too," Chris said, aiming for the same spot. Zack chucked one at a Quick Mart, shattering it against the caged glass. He grabbed Katy's head and started sucking on her lips, stretching them into his mouth like a chunk of taffy.

Chris backed away, closing the bedroom door and laying down on the couch. The ceiling panels were all he had to stare at as the numbers ran through his head again, numbers of food and water, numbers that were pushed aside whenever Katy's hoarse voice shouted that Zack fuck her harder.

The bathtub could hold X amount of gallons of water, and the generator would last X amount of days if the power failed and the President would lose X amount of points on his approval rating if he dropped the bomb.

When he was sixteen and his acne was at its worse, mother bought him a solar light in hopes that it would help dry out his skin. It was blinding, the kind of light that bled through your eyelids, and he would lay under it, eyes closed, imagining that he was lying in a pit of fire, or a brightly lit womb.

Assuming she was alive, he wrote down the top ten things his mother probably assumed about his life in Philadelphia.

Number one, he decided, was the assumption that her son was dead.

A week passed before the moaning reached North Philadelphia.

They watched from the bedroom window. Their skin looked rotten, their eyes gray. They opened their mouths to moan, showing what teeth they had left. It was like they were always smiling. There weren't many. Maybe thirty. Chris guessed that there was nearly twenty thousand in the city.

"I wonder if they're able to understand each other…"

Zack laughed. "Yeah, they're just hanging out, having some laughs. They probably want us to come outside and crack open a couple of beers."

Chris grinned to this. It made the whole thing easier to joke about it. "Think they're just saying 'chug, chug, chug, chug'?"

Katy peeked through the blinds. "They can't get in, right?"

"The front door has three locks on it," Chris said. "And it's super thick." He held his hand out over her shoulder, hesitating to his own nervousness before setting it down. When she gave a neutral look to this touch, he smiled and patted her shoulder. "Don't worry," he said, blushing.

"They're not getting up here, babe," Zack said. "Plus they can't reach the window."

They watched for nearly an hour. Zack turned the oven on to cook a pizza. They had decided to use up whatever had to be cooked, since the gas might go out any day. There were eight pizzas left.

"Anyone want to watch the *Nightmare on Elm Street* box set again?" Chris asked. It was a Christmas gift from several years ago. The flu kept him up all night, dizzy with fever and he watched the entire box set. It was another gesture from his mother to get him to stay home. Now he was in Philadelphia with a thousand horror DVDs.

They walked back to the couch as Chris put the first disc on. Zack grabbed another round of beers. As the movie played, Katy turned the volume up until it drowned out the moaning that came from Girard.

"Hey, Katy," Zack shouted, "top ten horror movies that actually scared you."

There was a loud scream.

It jolted Chris awake. He had been on the couch, watching a movie and going in and out of sleep. When he rolled over and looked at the TV, the menu options for *Hellraiser* were displayed.

The scream came again.

Chris went into the bedroom, finding Zack already at the window with the blinds drawn. He was naked, peeking through a single slat. He glanced at Chris and waved him over. Katy remained at the end of the bed with the covers up to her nose. Her eyes were wet and filled with panic.

"Some girl is out there," Zack said. He spoke quietly, like he thought the girl would somehow hear him and beg for help.

She was Asian, with a torn muscle tee and filthy jeans. Her bones looked thick under the tightness of her skin. As she stumbled south, she ran down the east side, coming upon a small group of infected. She doubled back, deciding to run west.

"Shit, look at that." Zack pointed west. A small group roamed about with gaps of space she could weave in and out of. As she got closer, they spread out, forming a line. She doubled back, deciding to run south on Eighth Street instead. Another group of infected blocked her.

She started spinning around, searching for another way out. They closed in.

"Someone please help me!"

Katy raised the sheet up over her head. "You guys have to do something."

Chris broke out in a sweat. "Do what?"

Her words were muffled under the blanket. "I don't know. It's not right…just watching."

"Anyone please!"

"Looks like we're not the only ones." Zack pointed at the apartment across the street. In the third floor, a man stood at his window, openly nude while smoking a cigarette. As the Asian girl fell to the ground, he started touching himself.

"Jeez," Chris said, growing pale.

"Help me please!"

They closed in and her screaming dwindled down to the inflection of a high school girl reading a book report. When the first one reached her, it grabbed her arm and peeled the skin away. The others laid her down, pulling off the rest of her skin. Her face was the only untouched part of her. It looked confused, half asleep.

The naked man across the street frowned, lifting his hand away from his dick and walking out of view. Other windows glimmered with movement. Chris wondered if people were watching them and if someone stood in a window to the right or left of their apartment, openly naked, touching himself as the Asian girl was killed.

None of them slept that night without getting drunk first.

Two weeks passed before the power went out. The gas still came on, but there wasn't anything left to cook. They plugged the TV into the generator and watched all four *Die Hard* movies back to back.

"Beef jerky anyone?" Zack passed the bag around and they made sandwiches out of beef jerky and potato chips.

click, click, click

The sound came from Katy's mouth. They both looked at her and she blushed.

"Sorry, it's my jaw." She smacked a mosquito that landed on her leg. A plastic jug of Vladmir was passed around.

"I'm having a real bad fucking day here!"

"Drink."

Every time John McClane complained about being hung over, they drank.

"Jesus," Katy piped, swatting her arm. A mosquito lay dead, its tiny parts sticking to the palm of her hand while its hair-sized mouth remained on her arm. A pepper dash of blood marked the bite.

"So…how about…" Zack stopped in mid-thought over their next top ten. They had drawn up nearly a hundred of them, using the Temple University notebooks that Chris would never fill up. Top ten westerns, top ten TV dads, top ten Danzig albums.

"Top ten fast food restaurants?" Chris suggested.

"No," Zack said, flipping through one of the notebooks. "We wrote that up a few days ago."

There was the sound of glass breaking from the TV.

"Drink."

Every time there was broken glass in a *Die Hard* movie, they drank.

"What the fuck!" Katy swatted another mosquito, missing it. It had been the tenth one since they started watching *Die Hard III*. She looked around herself, finding the blood suckers hovering near her face in a blurry cloud. She waved them away, spitting air at them.

"How about," Zack said, "top ten white singers that sound black."

"Michael Jackson," Chris said. He alone laughed at the joke.

"Ever listen to Steve Marriot? Katy, you have any Humble Pie on your iPad? Look up '30 Days in the Hole'."

She played the track and Steve Marriot sang the title lyric in an outtake that they used to intro the song. A finger snap kept the beat as they repeated the line four times before guitars kicked in. Katy nodded her head, a subtle smile forming on her lips. Chris shrugged his shoulders, admitting, "Yeah, I guess he sounds black."

"You don't like this?" Katy asked.

"I mean…it's, I don't know."

"Jesus!" Another smack. Katy got up and stepped away from the couch. The small cloud of mosquitoes hovered where she sat, filling in the empty space. The swarm migrated towards Zack and Chris. They stood up and stumbled over their own feet, falling to the ground. Zack burst into laughing and Chris felt the room spinning as he stared at the ceiling tiles.

"How much did you two drink?"

"The *Die Hard* drinking game really kicked my ass," Zack said.

Chris leaned up, propping himself on his elbows. Red bumps covered his arms and legs. In a drunken haze he tried to brush them off, thinking they'd fall to the ground like confetti.

He wanted to be home. He wanted to be with Katy without Zack. He wanted it to be years ago when he first came to Philadelphia. He couldn't decide, couldn't choose a thought. He wanted to be naked, lying under a solar light with his eyes closed, dreaming that he slept in a lake of fire.

Katy helped him back onto the couch, spending the rest of the night fighting off the mosquitoes with unused notebooks.

"Yippee Ki-yay, mother—"

"Drink," Zack said, giggling.

The next day Chris turned the water faucet on. It chortled in response and several drops spit out over his hand. He went to the bathtub, hoping to wash his face and clean the taste of cheap vodka out of his mouth.

A thick layer of mosquito eggs floated on the top of the water.

The bites on his body flared up. It was like someone had covered him in gasoline and threw a match. He counted the bites, wishing he had a hundred more hands to scratch at them.

They took inventory. Seven packages of beef jerky, three bags of potato chips, a packet of Tang, and eighteen bottles of water. Zack poured gas on the mosquito eggs but didn't flush them down the drain, thinking that if it really came to it, they could eat the eggs. A list was made of things they could eat if it came down to it.

Insect eggs, nail clippings, toothpaste, notebook pages, ink, couch stuffing, and cockroaches.

"How many is that?" Katy asked. She didn't even look up to see who would answer.

"Seven," Zack answered.

"What the hell happened to all the food?" Chris tried to shout, but his voice was too thin to carry anger. "I counted thirty bags of beef jerky and now we only have seven!" His face was worn, strained from the nights of drinking and snorting Adderall. Counting things while grinding his teeth had toned every muscle in his jaw, adding years to him.

He looked to Zack, hoping he would respond with some kind of plan. Zack, who ran ten miles a day and used to play football. The hipster jock merely looked at the ground and gave a shameful sigh.

"It's only been three weeks," Chris cried out. "And we're almost out of food."

"I guess," Katy said, exhausted by the situation, "I guess we ate it all."

"It is weird," Zack mumbled.

"We have to make it a month," Chris said.

After that day they started bottling their piss.

They ran out of food and water. Zack took to eating his fingernails and the dead skin that callused his palms. He eyed the bottles of piss they had collected, wondering when his desperation would grow strong enough. There was no more alcohol, no more drugs. Katy stared at her dead iPad, trailing her finger over it while lying in a pile of dirty laundry she had pushed into a corner of the living room. Chris watched Girard Ave from his bedroom, counting. Their numbers only grew, going from thirty to a hundred to a thousand.

It was week five.

He walked into the living room.

"We need to make a list. All three of us."

"Um, I don't know Chris," Zack said, wiping his gnawed hand across his face. "I don't know if I'm really up for a top ten right about now."

"What's the list?" Katy asked, pressing the ON button on her iPad. The screen remained blank.

"Someone needs to go and find food and water."

"So…make a grocery list?" Zack asked.

"Everyone needs to write down the top ten reasons they should be the one to go. And one reason why they shouldn't."

Katy looked up from her dead iPad. Zack bit at his nails and shrugged.

They sat down at the table with pens and papers. Zack wrote slowly, but consistently, starting first with the ten reasons it would be best for him to risk his life. When he reached the second question, he paused, unsure of what reason would be most compelling, reading over his first list to make sure he didn't contradict himself.

Katy wrote nothing. She stared at the paper, occasionally glancing at the other two as they wrote. Chris had written his in a furious pace, finishing the whole thing before Zack had even written half. When they finished and Katy still hadn't jotted down a word, Zack held her hand. She turned away, sniffling. Zack stared at Chris, who waited with his hands folded over one another.

"Why don't we leave her out of this?"

"Okay," Chris said. He looked over his list, then slid it towards Katy. "Then she should read them. Out loud."

Zack's face remained still, thinking it over. His list remained in his hands and he thought about whether or not he should rip up the whole thing in hopes of delaying the decision. But Chris's list was already under Katy's hands. It seemed too late, like there was no turning back from the decision they were going to have to make.

He slid his list next to Chris's.

"Read."

Katy looked them both over, not really reading any sentences, only seeing the words themselves. She settled on Zack's first.

"Ten reasons I should be the one to go. One, I'm the strongest and the fastest. Two, I know Philadelphia really well. Three, I don't have any family that will miss me. Four, I'm not really..." She covered her mouth.

"I'm not really afraid of dying," Zack finished for her.

She nodded, sniffling. After clearing her throat, she continued. "Five, I can handle myself in a fight. Six, I have a high tolerance for pain. Seven, I'm emotionally invested in coming back for Katy." She started to cry again. Zack finished the list based on memory.

"Eight, I'll hurt other people to get food if I have to. Nine, I don't have any injuries or health issues." He pointed at Katy. "She walks with a slight limp and you have asthma."

Chris nodded.

"And ten, I wasn't invited to stay here in the first place. So...in a way, it's my fault we ran out of food so quickly."

Chris sat there, silent, running over the list in his head. He asked Zack why he shouldn't go.

"I don't trust you alone with her."

"Zack," Katy cried out.

Chris remained still, but his toes dug into his shoes. "It's okay," he said. "We all need to be honest."

"Doesn't make sense not to be."

"Then I'll read my list," Chris said, yanking it out from Katy's hands. "Top ten reasons I should be the one to go. One, I'm smart. Two, I'm small and it would be easy for me to hide. Three, I don't know if my parents are alive or not, so I don't know if there's anyone worth living for. Four, you have a relationship with Katy and I don't, so I'm expendable. Five, I don't know Philadelphia very well, but I do live on this street and know the surrounding blocks. Six, I have a high metabolism, so I'm partially responsible for how quickly the food supply was used up. Seven, I'm afraid of dying and believe that if we don't get food and water soon, we'll starve to death. Eight, it was my decision to stay here and you two went along with it. I didn't plan to wait longer than a month, and it's been five weeks. Nine, Katy would resent me if something happened to you and I don't know if I could live with that. And ten... I want to help."

"And your reason not to go?"

The scribbled words were clear in his mind, but he looked down and read them off the page anyway. "I don't think I'd make it back."

When Katy stopped crying, Zack grabbed a knife and left.

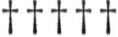

Days passed them by and their stomachs groaned like the rusty gears of a clock. Katy started looking at the loose fat on her arms and legs, making a list in her head of what she would try to eat if she really had to. She would start with the fat on her ass first, cauterizing the wounds after, then move on to her left arm, starting with a few of her fingers before moving down her wrist. She lay in a pile of dirty laundry, thinking of each body part as something separate from herself, like a piece of clothing she could remove whenever she felt like it. The longer they went without food, the more real this separation felt.

Chris watched her sink into this daze. When Zack had left, he approached her, caressing her arm. She had shrugged him off and turned her head inward, wanting nothing to do with him.

A week passed. Zack never returned. Across the street, the naked man stood at his window, his ribs extending past his sunken stomach. Chris kept the blinds shut, not wanting to see him or the infected. Moments after shutting the blind, a gunshot went off. When he looked back outside, he saw the man slumped halfway out the window, a hole in his head pouring out blood onto the street.

"Drink," Katy mumbled, laughing.

Another three days passed. Katy's eyes watched Chris as he walked into the room, the rest of her body lying still in a heap of dirty clothing. Her body was becoming as collapsed as an old pair of jeans. The tips of her fingers were gone, bitten off and bloody.

"Katy," he said. Eyes flinched to the sound of her name. A hand passed before her, keeping her attention. "Katy," he said her name again.

A chair was pulled into the center of the living room. He stood on it and pushed one of the ceiling tiles aside. A dozen packages of beef jerky fell past his face, smacking the ground. Three water bottles bounced and rolled away.

Katy continued staring and her lips slowly parted. She wanted to speak but couldn't. There wasn't enough energy. Chris sat in front of her.

"I had to make it last," he said. "There was no way...no way to make it last if I didn't."

Snotty looking tears filled her eyes. A piece of beef jerky was placed into her hand. She took it wordlessly, chewing the meat, moaning on occasion. The click, click, click sound spit out of her jaw as she ate. A bottle of water was opened and after Chris drank half, he placed it in Katy's hands. He leaned in and kissed her.

"I...I like you, Katy."

She smiled at him. He blushed and leaned in, kissing her again. Then again.

"I'll take care of you," he said, sucking her lips.

She opened her mouth, pulling him closer. The frayed wire thoughts ceased in

Chris's mind. The numbers, the infected, the lake of fire. A warmth came off of her body, feeling like the solar light he had once used to clear his skin up.

"Forget about him…" Another kiss and he grabbed her chest. Without waiting to feel if her body would give to his caress, he slid a hand down her pants. "Forget about Zack."

Teeth locked over his lips. She bit down.

"Ahhhh! What the fuck!" He ripped himself away from her clenched teeth. Blood spilled down his chin. Katy chewed, giggling with her mouth closed. She wiped the blood off on her shirt and drank the rest of the bottled water, swallowing his lower lip like a thick chunk of fat.

"Why did you do that?" he shouted, placing both hands over his mouth. Blood poured out through his fingers and there was an empty space where his bottom lip should have been. He rushed into the bathroom, looking at the mirror.

"My mouth!" A perpetual smile sat in the hunk of bloody flesh where his bottom lip once was. He took a rag and pressed it over the wound, sopping the blood up. Already, dizziness started to take hold. "Damn it."

The bathroom lights flickered. The stereo came on from the living room and Velvet Underground's "White Light, White Heat" started playing. Looking about at the light, hearing the music, Chris's eyes tried to jump out of their sockets.

"The power!" he shouted. "Katy! The power is back on!" Blood continued to spit from his lips as he talked. "They're gonna come for us!" He rushed out into the living room.

"We're gonna be okay!"

She was gone, along with her IPad and the bottle of water. All that remained was an imprint of her body in the dirty pile of laundry.

"Katy?"

The front door was open. A series of soft groans left the stairs as Katy descended. There was the sound of metal scraping against metal for all the deadbolts that kept the door locked.

"Katy?" The rag was lifted away, letting the blood flow freely from his endless smile. It felt warm over his chest. He rushed back to the bathroom and looked in the mirror, seeing if there was a way he could make it stop.

"Damn it." He pressed a rag back on the open wound, holding it tight. "Come on, come on, come on…"

As "The Gift" started, a moan came from the stairwell. Chris poked his head out from the bathroom, seeing a group of shadows spilling out over the wall of the stairwell. He slammed the bathroom door shut, turning the lock on the knob.

The moaning grew louder, closer. Something scratched at the wood of the bathroom door. Between "Lady Godiva's Operation" and "Here She Comes Now", they started pushing. The door creaked and cracked. He could spot unpainted wood under one of the hinges as it shifted off the frame. Something behind the door was the sound of a person chewing on the fat of his lip. Listening close, he could almost swear he heard a girl laughing.

click, click, click

He picked the rag back up, holding it over his lip. The bleeding started to stop and he sat down on the toilet, watching the door. Numbers ran through his head again. He figured on twenty minutes. Maybe more. Worst case he'd at least make it through half of "Sister Ray" before the door gave in.

MY MOTHER-IN-LAW IS A ZOMBIE

by Anna Sykora

When I married my Tony
I got more than I bargained for:
I got Rosangela Michelangela Antonelli
as my mother-in-law.
Born in Catania (that's in Sicily),
she has always viewed me
as an inconvenience
to her love for her youngest son,
and treated me like an ingrown toenail.

She never stopped cooking him
his favorite pasta alla Norma or zuppa di pesce,
and rolling them steaming and fragrant
through the streets of Brooklyn in a wire cart.
She never stopped turning up her nose
at my cooking, tossed together
from supermarket stuff
when I happen to have the time.

So—God forgive me—when I heard
That a gas line explosion had buried her alive,
I got down on my knees and wished Rosi-mama
(which is what her seven children call her)
a safe trip to Heaven, and a pleasant stay—
if that is where she's supposed to go.

But then, three weeks after the funeral,
Rosi-mama called me up
with plans for Antonio's birthday—
surprise!
Built like a linebacker,
stubborn as a mobster,
and with all of her original teeth,
my mother-in-law
could not accept the public fact
that she had died:

"Why, if it makes no difference?
My sweet Antonio is still my son,
And I want to bake him a birthday cake,
Karen. I'll bring it over on Saturday."
And she hung up the phone.

Though Tony the doctor didn't believe me,
and told me to take two aspirin,
on Saturday his mama the zombie rang our bell,
her skin peeling grey, and her hair clumping out,
And the cake in a box in her rolling cart.

Delighted as ever to see his old mama,
Even though she smelled like a homeless vagrant,
Tony fussed over her, and propped her on the sofa,
and scolded me softly in the kitchen:

"I'm sorry, honey, but at her age
she's not going to change
a hair on her head
in order to please you."

"Then what am I supposed to do?" I cried.
"I can't believe that she's alive;
and she can't understand that she's dead;
and I cannot stand her stink in my house,
and the body parts dropping off on the carpet.
Tony, there are toes near the television."

"There's only one thing we can do,"
he said sadly. "Send her home."

"In a taxi, to Carroll Gardens?
The building there is still a ruin, Tony."

"No, all the way back to Sicily,
And I will make the arrangements myself.
That is my duty as her son."

So yesterday we got a postcard
Of sunset over a turquoise sea:
"Children, Catania is bellisima.
Now you must come and visit me
In Crypt Number Three.
There is space here for Tony too."

by Nu Yang

She remembered flesh.

Her hand caressed a patch of warm skin as her heart struggled to beat again. Once, flesh was meant to offer comfort through touch. It still had that same effect to her.

The body shuddered beneath her with each stroke of her finger. A man with hair the color of night and eyes as wide as the full moon. There used to be another man. She didn't remember his name.

All she remembered was flesh. She dipped her head into the trembling man's neck. Her teeth grazed his pulse. She salivated with each rapid beat. The man cried out, begging for mercy. She granted it for him by closing her mouth over the center of his throat. She tore at flesh, chewed on soft skin, and licked the red blood gushing from the man. Her hands clutched the back of his head, tilting it to the side so more skin was exposed. The liquid was heavy and sweet on her rough tongue.

More. I want more.

She held the man down by his shoulders; her long fingernails dug into his skin. Sweat trickled down from his jaw to where she fed from his neck. The salty droplets added a kick to the hot piece of bloody flesh. She sank her teeth into his throat again and came away with a mouthful of soft skin and warm blood.

The man went limp under her.

She studied the man's vacant eyes—now a black hole of lost memories—and her heart whimpered.

Whenever there was light out, she hid. There were groups that haunted her. They called her kind the living dead.

Am I dead?

Her silent heart told her yes. Her empty stomach told her no.

She only traveled when it was dark out, wandering through trees and long streets that went nowhere. Sometimes she looked up to the sky. The stars triggered memories—names like Ursa Major, Ursa Minor, the Big and Little Dipper.

She didn't remember her name.

Although she preferred to be alone, it wasn't hard to stumble upon groups of her kind. They littered cities, fields, buildings. Their faces were frozen in sadness. They groaned from a pain that they could not stop. It was that never-ending, cold hunger she also felt, twisting and piercing her inside. It demanded to be fed and it would not be satisfied until she was drowning in the warm sea of flesh and blood.

Tonight, she walked among the rest of the living dead. She bumped into another body. The man's flesh was wasted—dry and brittle falling from his face in curly wisps. He mumbled, but she understood. They needed to repair themselves. The only way to do that was to find more flesh.

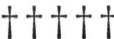

The growl deep inside her took control. She made a mistake and stepped out to where there was light. It didn't take long for the ones that hunted her kind to find her.

Three men cornered her in an abandoned warehouse. Their skin radiated in the sunlight. Her stomach clenched as the hunger grew. The men spoke words to her, but she had forgotten their meanings when the taste for flesh became her language. They had weapons, and she knew what kind of damage could happen. The men meant to kill her like she had seen with others.

A loud bang. Bullet hole in the head.

The weapons took away the memories, shut them down again. That was how her kind died and never came back.

She snarled at the men. They didn't lower their weapons. They moved closer and with each step they took, the sweet smell of flesh made her insides itch. She twitched, bit down on her bottom dry lip, and charged towards the men.

She swung her arm at one, knocking him to his knees. She grabbed him and twisted his neck, snapping the bone. Guns fired. Something hard slammed into her back, not the head. She advanced at the other men.

The second took a hold of her long hair and pushed her against the wall. He reached under his jacket and removed a large knife. His chest rose, fell, and with each breath he took, her body prickled with anticipation. He raised the knife. She grabbed his hand and rotated his wrist until it cracked. She slammed the blade into the man's stomach and shoved it up; his guts spilled out in thick pink coils. He gurgled with his last pathetic gasp for life. Her mouth latched into his warm neck, tearing at his flesh. Hot blood splattered on her face. Her knees went weak as the hunger inside her screamed for more.

The last man stood in place, shaking and crying. She had tasted plenty of tears since her craving for flesh started—the salt with the coppery tang of blood. She licked her lips—now wet and stained.

The last man pointed the gun to his head.

Take away the memories, take away the person.

Before he could fire his weapon, she was on him, teeth ripping into his throat. She licked his torn flesh, then ran her tongue up over his neck, leaving behind a trail of her saliva and the blood of his fallen companion. She stopped where the tears were still fresh on his cheeks. The taste of his terror was like seeing the first bolt of lightning streak across the sky before a storm. Her body hummed with electricity, making her feel alive even though her heart made no sound.

She bathed the men's bodies in the sunlight streaming in from the open glass windows and then covered them in their own blood. It only added to the appeal of their flesh.

When she was through, she stood back up; the hunger inside her quiet for now. She walked out of the building just as the three bodies rustled behind her. They groaned as they returned. She remembered waking up with the dull ache pulsating inside from her head to her toes, her ashy mouth, and knowing the only way to quench that thirst was to find flesh and fill herself with it.

That was a long time ago, when the virus had only affected a few select individuals, before it became an epidemic. She had stopped to help the bleeding man only to have him sink his teeth into her arm. The disease quickly spread inside her.

In turn, she spread it because that was all she knew, all that she could remember.

There was a little girl and her mother on the side of the road. They were like her.

She watched as the two of them knelt next to the fresh bodies. The mother let the child feed first. With her small hands, the girl took a hold of the limp arm attached to the young man. Her mouth ripped into flesh. The mother stroked the girl's stringy hair with a faint smile on her face.

She continued to watch the two of them and her mouth went dry with a strange taste. It filled her lungs like smoke, almost suffocating her.

Memory.

She decided to go home because she remembered.

His name is Todd.

She remembered why she had the ring on her left hand. She remembered a little boy with the same dark hair and eyes as Todd.

They were her family.

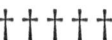

She traveled all through the night, hiding from the ones who haunted her and keeping her distance from the others like her. She only stopped to feed and search the stars.

When she made it home, her heart struggled to work, but it no longer knew its purpose.

She stood at the door, but no one came.

Maybe they no longer remembered her.

But she remembered them, and that was enough fuel to drive her fist through the wooden door. She did it again and again until the door burst open for her. She stepped into her home. As soon as she did, the memories flooded her mind. So many images hurtled to the front of her eyes that she had to lean against the wall.

She saw herself—alive with a beating heart—holding a child. *Her* child. He had a name for her.

"Mommy."

She saw Todd's muscled body draped over her slimmer one as they molded as one. She remembered how warm his flesh had been on top of hers.

The memories caused her chest to tighten. It was too much.

She continued inside the home. In each room, another memory threw itself forward. Spicy smells from steaming pots and pans. The sweet tang of berries in her mouth. The kaleidoscope of colors from the vase full of fresh flowers. The touch of Todd's hand securely on her waist. The joy of hearing her son's laughter as she held him on her lap.

When she made it to the end of the hallway, she stopped. There was nowhere else to go.

Something clicked behind her.

She turned to find a man holding a weapon. A little boy lingered behind the man's tall legs.

I know who you are.

They were her memories come to life.

She wanted to smile, but the muscles in her face didn't know how to move in that way anymore. She could only groan and move slowly to her family with her hands extended. She wanted to touch them again and feel comfort from the warmth of their flesh.

Todd fired the gun.

Loud bang.

Bullet hole in the head.

He missed as another groan filled the room.

It was the last man. His stiff neck was an open crevice of muscle and skin tissue. She could still taste his salty tears on her swollen tongue. Gone was his weapon. Gone were the two other men. But she still circled him as though he was a danger. She knew why he was there—for flesh, for her family.

She screeched and grunted with urgency as her fists collided with the last man's jaw. His head whipped back, but he remained unfazed with her attack. He shoved her and she pulled him down with her; their legs became entangled. He bit into her arm and she cried out as he pulled away with a piece of skin in his mouth. She pushed him aside, jumping on top of him. She tore into his neck again, but instead of tasting the sweetness of his flesh, she coughed up ash. He rolled her on her back and sat on her chest. Looking down at her, he gave her a rusty smile.

Loud bang.

Bullet hole in the head.

The last man went slack and collapsed to his side on the wooden floor. He didn't move after that.

She sat up. Todd still held the gun. Their son huddled behind Todd with his small arms wrapped his father's legs. He buried his face into the back of Todd's thighs.

Don't be afraid. It's Mommy.

As she stood, there was another loud explosion. The bullet struck her shoulder. The impact made her spin around and hit a wall. She slid back down to the floor.

Todd towered over her. The barrel of the gun was aimed at her face. A face her husband and son no longer recognized. With a silent plea, she asked for them to remember her.

Remember me like I remember you.

She blinked and found her eyes wet. The liquid rolled down her face until they touched her lips. It was the familiar taste of tears, but this time, they were hers.

Then, she remembered.

My name is—

Loud bang.

Bullet hole in the head.

LUCKY 43

by Joriah Wood

Erich and Vanessa met at a thrift shop while he was looking for a bargain on clothes and she was searching for film for an old Polaroid camera. He liked the look of mischief behind her smile, and she liked his easygoing demeanor. Before long, the two of them were caught up in a whirlwind romance. At 32, he was a bit older than her 21 years, but he didn't care—it wasn't like she was a kid. She claimed that fate brought the two of them together. They were soul mates.

Vanessa's family didn't see it that way. It was on a balmy Saturday night when Erich and Vanessa finally hit their breaking point. They were tired of her family's constant grief about their relationship, and their frustration boiled over after a family dinner. The lovers decided to take to the road and leave everything behind. Vanessa snapped some pictures with her folks and little brother, then the two stepped out the door and hit the road.

Erich and Vanessa talked about going to Vegas to get married, but after that night at her parents' house, they changed their plans. Instead of getting married right away, they decided to tour the countryside first, letting Vanessa collect some pictures while they enjoyed the journey. Her mother always said she wouldn't amount to anything, but Vanessa had decided to become a famous artist.

From a generation that was practically raised digital, Vanessa took solace in older things, though she refused to use the word "vintage." She decided to take the "selfie" craze to new levels with old technology. She had been considering a pet art project, and the way they left that night cemented her resolve. She would photograph herself with people they met on their journey using that old camera, and her name would be known far and wide.

They had only been on the road for a few weeks when things started to get weird. Erich and Vanessa were a few hundred miles away from home when they heard the first in a series of strange stories: a truck driver biting into a school teacher down in Florida. They laughed and figured it was just more drug addicts going crazy for bath salts or something. All the real nut jobs seemed to live in Florida.

They saw more incidents like that on the news while getting dinner at a truck stop that evening. It wasn't just Florida. A few planes leaving Orlando had gone down. Whatever this was, it was spreading fast, and people were starting to panic.

Vanessa talked almost nonstop about how her art project was going to make them famous. She wanted to be on TV, she wanted to be interviewed on the radio—she had big dreams and wanted people to know who she was. She planned to be the topic of household conversations, and Erich remembered her complaining about how, whatever this insanity was, it would make getting noticed impossible. In a matter of days, the United States of America went from mild panic to full-blown apocalypse.

Unsure of where to go, they tried to stay on the freeways, finding shelter at rest-stops and pull-offs at night. They met up with other survivors who gave them some supplies and some encouraging news of a clean-camp a few hundred miles north. One of the survivors was a radio hobbyist, and he told them about his contact with the camp via short-wave radio. The camp's radio operator told him they had food and medical supplies and were welcoming all survivors. The radio hobbyist, a large-framed chubby kid of about Vanessa's age, was so intense and driven in his quest to survive that Vanessa took a liking to him. She thought he was cute and insisted on taking a picture with him, much to his discomfort.

Erich squatted low, peering out from beneath the brim of his weathered baseball cap into the parking lot of the tiny store. The building was ransacked and gutted. Broken shards of plate-glass lined the aisles, where they had fallen inward and been scattered by the shuffling horde of zombies that laid waste to this Mom 'n Pop hardware.

His brow furrowed as he counted them in the parking lot—three, four, five at least and who knew how many others lurked in the darkness. His gaze stopped on the truck. There were two or three of the undead shuffling around the passenger door, but that was OK. Erich could wait.

In one hand, he clutched the Polaroid camera that Vanessa treasured so much. They had started with a small cache of expired film, but it was running out fast, and Erich didn't think he would be finding more of it.

In his other hand, Erich held three photos he had just taken. They hadn't developed yet, but he wouldn't look at them until he was back in the truck and ready to put them into Vanessa's album. He couldn't get distracted now.

The zombies didn't know he was there, and he wanted to keep it that way. Erich didn't want to bend the photos, so he slipped the camera around his neck and quietly removed an engineer's hammer from the rack next to him. It never hurt to be armed. It didn't take much for these things to turn people into ravenous, mindless beasts like them. His plan was always to avoid them completely, but sometimes they didn't make that easy.

Erich saw his chance—the zombies closest to the passenger door of the white box truck stumbled away from it, their backs to each other, creating a tunnel of opportunity for his escape. He had seen enough in the last few weeks to know that while their hunger and stamina made them formidable threats, they didn't react quickly to things that surprised them. He had to go now.

Erich launched himself through the windowless pane at the front of the shop and his shoes thumped out a rhythmic cadence on the asphalt as he ran. In his peripheral vision, he saw the two zombies nearest the truck raise their heads to listen, curious about the new sound. He didn't dare lose his focus. Erich concentrated on that passenger door, pushing himself to close as much distance as he could with every step. Slowing down meant being eaten alive.

By the time he grabbed the door handle, he could hear their feeding groans as the monsters shuffled toward him. He trusted his senses, the ones that told him that he still had time.

He quickly yanked the door open and slipped inside. Slamming it shut behind him, Erich didn't realize he was holding his breath until he finally exhaled with relief.

His smile of satisfaction was short lived. Glassy eyes peered at him through the open driver's window. Erich had yet to see one of these things open any kind of door or latch, but he knew they could climb; this once-young woman must have been trying to climb into the cab. The driver's side window was broken out, and it offered no protection whatsoever.

The monster's fetid breath filled the truck's cabin as she groaned, reaching her rotting hands toward him, blocking his access to the truck's ignition and his escape.

Erich braced himself against the passenger door, brought his foot back, and kicked as hard as he could. His boot landed in the center of the zombie-girl's chest, and he felt her hands clawing at his jeans as she fell backwards with a startled howl. Erich tossed the pictures into the glove compartment and fumbled through his pocket for the keys.

With measured action to avoid mistakes, Erich got the key into the ignition and turned it. The truck's starter surged. The engine turned over and over, but refused to catch.

"Come on…" Erich said out loud, releasing the key and trying again. He turned his attention to the open window as more blood-encrusted hands stretched through it. The sound of the engine turning over once more drowned out the zombies hungry groaning, and he swatted at their hands with the hammer.

The engine finally caught and roared to life. Erich put the big truck in gear and hit the gas just as one of the undead reached through the open window and got a hand on the steering wheel. The truck turned hard to the left and threatened to tip. Erich smashed at the fingers with the hammer, trying to get them to release the wheel.

The undead felt no pain, but Erich felt rotten flesh and brittle bone falling away with every desperate swing. The truck jolted hard as it hit a parking block. Erich threw his weight against the door, hoping to keep the big truck from rolling. As the vehicle crashed down on all four wheels once again, Erich yanked the dirty sleeve and pulled on the arm with all his might. He felt it release and pushed it out the window. The thumping of the zombie's body falling away and rolling behind the truck was music to his ears.

The crisp night air flowing through the broken driver's window felt good as he took the truck back to the freeway. Erich reached behind the seat for a bag of stale pretzels he had been rationing. With his adrenaline fading, exhaustion suddenly tugged at his eyelids. He figured he could make the clean camp by daybreak if he pushed through the night. Eating would help him stay awake, even though he'd been afraid to eat anything for a few days and he didn't have much of an appetite now.

Just before daybreak, Erich saw lights illuminating the horizon. Light pollution had been so prevalent before that a city didn't stand out against the night sky, but over the last few weeks, the sky had become darker and darker as generators and independent power plants had been shutting down. Lights on the horizon meant that he had to be close to a large camp, the clean camp. He felt a surge of energy as the adrenaline returned to his system.

He saw it just off the freeway, and it was a lot larger than he expected. From his elevated view from the highway, it looked like a small town. Sturdy makeshift walls kept the undead out, and Erich could see the stiff-legged gait of some of the undead milling about outside, the tempting smell of the human flesh packed inside luring them close.

He smiled. He was almost there. Soon, he and Vanessa could realize their dream.

The gate to the camp was at the end of an exit ramp, and Erich could see guards on the wall pointing at his truck and yelling. He was already taking it easy through the curve of the exit ramp when he saw it—a great mass of undead, standing on the pavement, beating on the gate, trying to push through the metal sheets on the wall to get to the meat inside. Erich slammed on the brakes, bringing the truck to a screeching halt about two-hundred feet from the gate.

Guards on top of the wall were still shouting at him, and Erich leaned his head out the window.

"How many do you have?" he heard one of the guards ask.

"Just me!" Erich yelled back. He hated being so noisy with so many undead nearby, but they seemed pretty well distracted.

The guards conferred amongst themselves. They were all wearing white hazard suits and carried rifles of some sort; maybe AK-47's? Erich didn't know much about guns outside of what he had seen in the movies. He nervously checked the rear-view mirrors; undead were sneaky and he didn't like sitting still on the road. Getting back to the freeway in a hurry would mean driving the truck in reverse up a winding exit ramp, and he didn't like that idea either. Erich drummed his fingers on the steering wheel anxiously and wondered what was taking so long.

The guard waved to him again and he stuck his head out of the truck.

"When you see the gate open, floor it! As soon as there's room, don't stop until you're through!"

Erich waved in acknowledgment and tapped the accelerator on the truck. The surge of the engine reassured him.

The mass of zombies grew more agitated as the great metal front-wall started to roll aside. Erich saw something large and yellow behind the gate. Whatever it was, it was blocking his way through.

The gate opened fully, and men in white hazard suits held shields and wielded clubs to keep the undead at bay while a giant yellow front-end loader rumbled forward. The scoop was raised to about waist-height, and the shovel plowed through the zombies with ease. It cut a swath through the mass, rolling out and turning to provide a lane into the compound. Erich saw his chance and he dropped the truck into gear.

There were too many undead on the road to avoid them all. Erich felt the truck lose stability as he hit and drove over the rotting bodies, the big vehicle lurching side-to-side as the zombies were crushed under his tires. The guards on top of the wall were waving frantically, urging him on. As he passed through the gate, he glanced at the front-end loader. Zombies clung to the sides of it, trying to climb to the driver's cab, but men hanging on either side of the driver were fighting them off with a makeshift spear and a rumbling chainsaw. The noise was deafening, but the men seemed so calm and collected, like it was just another day on the job for them.

Once safely inside the compound, he hit the brakes hard. A guard ran up to the driver's window.

"You have anything back there?" he said, motioning toward the cargo area of the freight truck.

"Sorry, it's empty," Erich said. "I picked this up a few towns back and emptied the back for better fuel economy."

The guard looked disappointed and waved toward the back of the camp. "We have a vehicle graveyard back there. That truck belongs to the community now—price of entry, I'm afraid—but at least you'll be safe here. We're clean inside, and no flesh-eater could ever get in." Erich nodded. "Get that thing parked, then head over to registration. Until you register, mess hall won't give you any food."

"It'll be good to get out of this truck and eat something that's not stale pretzels," Erich said, giving an easy smile. He glanced into the rear view mirror again.

The front-end loader was backing through the gate, and the guards were holding off the zombies with practiced ease. This place really was impenetrable.

Erich drove the truck to the back of the camp. There were rows upon rows of vehicles in various states of disrepair; many had been stripped down completely, their parts used either for making town materials or perhaps taken to fix other vehicles. He pulled into an empty spot near the edge of the lot and shut the engine off.

He didn't have many personal belongings to remove from the cab, but what he did have was precious. He slid over to the passenger seat and reached under it for Vanessa's photo book, the one that contained the pictures of everyone they had met on their journey.

Erich felt emotion pulling tears to his eyes as he cracked the book open. This project meant so much to her. He missed her company; the sound of her voice, even the way she'd sound when she was upset with him. He missed her terribly. Still, Erich thought that he might have figured out a way to make her dream come true, even in this apocalyptic wasteland—a final gift to his soul mate.

He pulled the last three photos out of the glove compartment and set them on the seat next to him. He flipped to the end of the book, to the first blank page. Each page was hand-numbered in Vanessa's flourished, bubbly style. The last photo was on page 39, the one of Vanessa with the radio hobbyist. Vanessa had numbered the pages to 100, and Erich wished they could have made it that far. He put the latest photos in place lovingly, just like Vanessa would have done.

Erich opened the passenger door and dropped to the ground, carrying the photo book and the Polaroid camera. He walked around to the back of the truck and slowly unlatched the freight door.

He heard a growl from inside and smiled.

The sun was a little higher in the morning sky, and light spilled into the back of the truck. Erich saw her beautiful face, pale and weak—she hadn't eaten for days. Her bloodshot eyes looked at him longingly, but not with the love they once had. She didn't desire his attention or his gifts—she desired his flesh, his blood. The chains he found in an automotive garage held her fast. He recently gave her the last of the sedatives they had obtained from a friendly EMT, number 31, a few days ago, but the drugs had worn off. She was awake, active and hungry.

"I got three more, baby," he said cheerfully, trying to focus on the positive. "And hey, we've got one picture left, and I thought…" he paused, hoping to see some recognition in her eyes, any lucidity at all, but her gaze remained hollow. "Well, I thought it could be of me. Of us." He fought back the tears as he spoke, but she just stared at him.

When she got infected, she turned pretty quickly—it only took about ten minutes. From talking to other survivors, seven to ten minutes seemed average. He sighed and smiled at her again.

"Let's get this done, hon. It's been a good run."

Vanessa started to get excited as Erich inched closer. She groaned and pulled against her restraints. Erich slowly rolled up his shirt sleeve, exposing bare skin.

"Not yet," he said as she snapped her teeth at him. He produced the key to the padlock that held the chains in place, and with a click, the lock released. All that held the chains now was Erich's own grip. Every time Vanessa tugged, he felt the chain trying to pull away from him.

Erich edged closer to Vanessa, careful not to lose his grip on the chain as she struggled against it. Now was the time. He had thought about this for many miles, and the moment of truth was here.

Erich extended his arm to her.

Without hesitation, Vanessa's head snapped forward and she sank her teeth into his flesh.

The pain was excruciating. Erich bit his tongue hard, trying to keep from screaming, and the iron taste of blood filled his mouth. He yanked his arm away from her, leaving a large chunk of flesh in her mouth. Stinging tears tried to blind him, but he blinked them away. Seven minutes, that's all the time he could count on. The fire was already crawling up his arm.

The sound of Vanessa chewing on his flesh filled the truck. He hadn't thought this through, and he momentarily panicked—how could he expect to hold her in place and still take the picture? He quickly looped the padlock through the chain again to hold it in place while he got the camera. He couldn't afford to waste any time now!

Holding the Polaroid in front of him, Erich carefully aimed the camera and snapped his picture. The camera spit out the little white square, and he grabbed it with his blood-slick hand.

"I'm just gonna finish this album, babe" he mumbled, the fever already clawing at his mind, trying to cloud his thoughts. The picture was slick with blood and hard to hold on to, but he finally got it seated on the final page—page 43. It still hadn't fully developed yet.

"You wanna look through it one last time?" he asked Vanessa, who only offered a wet growl in return. Erich smiled and closed his eyes. She was going to be famous for this, someday. He had trouble keeping his balance, so Erich seated himself as close to her as he dared, lifting the book so she could see it. He turned back to page one.

"Here we are," he said, feeling the burning spread into his shoulder and chest. "Day one, page one. The night we left." Erich coughed. "Remember that night? Here you are with your mom." Erich admired Vanessa's beautiful, smiling face, standing next to her mother, who was propped up in her favorite chair and wearing her "Kiss-The-Cook" apron. The red spilled from her open neck contrasted sharply against the white of the apron. "Your mom said I was bad for you, that you'd never realize your dreams with me, but what did she know?" Erich started to laugh, but it turned into a hoarse, choking cough.

He turned the page. "And look, here's you with your dad and little brother," he said. Her father was face-down on the kitchen table, a dark pool having spread from his face to surround the plates and serving dishes. Vanessa smiled big for the camera, holding the claw hammer triumphantly over her head.

Erich continued turning the pages, providing narrative for each and every one of their victims. There was the friendly EMT, post-surgery, Vanessa holding the kitchen knives she had worked him over with. He paused at the radio hobbyist that Vanessa liked so much, which was also the last picture she was in. She was smiling, so full of vigor and life, pretending to give the boy an exaggerated kiss on the cheek while he tried to hold his intestines in with scraps of his shredded shirt and skin. Erich and Vanessa had so much promise, but the zombie thing had just ruined all of it.

Erich felt his mind slipping away. He crawled over to the lock that held Vanessa in place.

"We coulda really been famous, babe," he mumbled. "Coulda been on TV and everything, I bet."

With his last conscious thought, Erich let Vanessa's chain slip. Moments later, two zombies staggered out of the back of the truck toward the mess hall, following the delicious scent of fresh meat. They would be famous yet.

IN REYNOLDS

by J. Boone Dryden

In Reynolds—as I imagine it to be elsewhere in the world—traveling alone is the safest way to go. And if you can't, you keep one hand on your gun. People live by the day. They used to call it survival; now it's just life.

Having lost Rita to the Spread, I decided to take my chances and leave the relative comfort of the old Warehouse District and cross the river into Downtown, where there was a buffer between you and the creepers. I gathered what little I possessed, carrying only the essentials, and left the rest for the squatters I called my neighbors.

I carried one pack: it held some food, enough for at least a week, a hand-drawn map of the city, a blanket, two canteens of water, bandages, and my grandfather's old German Luger. On my hip, I carried my .45 in a holster with no clasp. It was better to have ease of access than to worry about gun safety. I rummaged through my things, perhaps hoping there was something of use I didn't know about, and decided on carrying a book with me. It was extra weight but not much, and it would give some small bit of entertainment on the journey—provided I could find the time and the light to read at night.

There is no good time to travel in the city—the creepers are always there—but daylight gives you the benefit of being able to see more than two feet in front of your face.

I slipped out of the warehouse compound I'd called home for nine months and headed west down Peterson Boulevard. It had once been one of the main thoroughfares through town; now it was barely recognizable as a street: the pavement was cracked and blackened where it wasn't littered with cars or bodies.

When you travel outside, caution is an understatement. The diseased bastards we call creepers aren't altogether smart and their senses are all but dead but if you run into one, then you've run into a small army of them. Stealth is something you learn real quick. I crept parallel to Peterson, slipping into an empty alley that ran eight blocks, hoping to use it without notice. Creepers liked the main roads; they could travel in packs and could see further. Alleys allowed for hiding spots and while they seemed to have a strange ability to smell blood, it was easy to hide if you found a solid spot.

I made it three blocks—ducking from one blessed shadow to the next, when I could—before I nearly ran headlong into a halfway dead walker shambling after a pack of rats.

Now there's a strange sense of morality that washes over me at times like that. The creepers are dead as can be, completely taken over by whatever the Spread is, and they deserve peace if nothing else. Walkers, on the other hand, seemed strangely aware, of that I knew because of my poor Rita; it almost seemed amoral to shoot them instead of finding them help. No one quite knew the cause of the Spread, but there was a consensus that if you were bitten or spit on or exposed some other way, you could take a chemical shower—like they do in science labs— and more often than not you'd be fine. Walkers were those poor fools unfortunate enough to not have anyone around to get them help.

I looked at the walker, contemplating my options. From a secure vantage point, I waited to see if it would wander off and let me slip away. Such was not my luck, though. As I ducked out of my hiding spot, the creature turned around and looked right at me. There was an awkward moment, like when you see an ex-girlfriend at a party, and we stared at one another. My hand went to my gun, but the walker didn't move toward me. I walked slowly around the thing, its eyes fixed on me as I did so, but it still made no move. There was a flash of human in its gaze as I looked at it, and then it vanished in a guttural moan. I drew my gun and fired: you don't waste bullets in Reynolds—either learn to shoot or die trying. I hit the walker between the eyes and ran, not stopping to see if I'd killed it.

Creepers may not be intelligent, but they know that unexpected noise means activity, and activity means fresh blood. The alley further down was littered with refuse—old food, broken furniture, decaying parts—and I navigated as quickly and deftly as possible.

I held the gun tightly in my hand as I ran, knowing that I might have to use it soon enough. When I reached the end of the alley, which ended at Roosevelt Street, I turned right without looking and bolted for Plan B—the Chinoque River ferry: one of only two passages across the river. It was closer but more dangerous, taking me through what had once been the projects. But it would be nearly impossible to make it all the way to the bridge at this point, having no doubt raised the suspicions of nearby creepers to my presence.

In the distance, I could hear the collective moan of a group of creepers and hoped it was behind me. Eight bullets certainly wouldn't get me through their ranks if it was a group of any size—which it tended to be.

After four blocks, I turned down a side street toward the river and picked up speed to make it to the river walk. Once along the river, it would be much easier to defend myself and if it came down to it I knew the creepers wouldn't be able to catch me in the water; unable to truly control their motor functions, they had the habit of sinking to the bottom and staying there until they could somehow manage to climb out.

I could see the river ahead when a loping group of the undead came around the corner of the building at the end of the next block. I fired three rounds ahead of me, bringing down two of them before more joined behind their fallen comrades. I stopped in the street, looking for an exit when I felt a hand on my arm, and then I was being pulled bodily into an open doorway. The door slammed behind me, and we were thrown into blackness. I heard the heavy grinding of metal on metal followed by a brief silence before I heard groaning on the other side of the door.

When the lights finally came on, I was staring dumbly at the door I'd come through. I turned around to see a woman milling about what looked like an old workshop of some kind.

"Thanks for the help," I said.

"Sure thing," the woman said without turning around. "I was on the second floor—crossing in here from the old foundry next door—and it didn't look pretty. There's probably eight dozen of those bastards out there."

"Again," I said, "thanks."

I began to look around the room, as well, rummaging through open cabinets and nearly-empty shelving units. There was very little—most places like this had long-ago been picked through—but I managed to find a few cans of beans, which I stashed in my pack.

"Headed across river?" the woman asked.

I turned to look at her. She had stopped her search and was staring at me. For a refugee (which is what we all were), she looked good: her face was washed, her hair mostly clean, even her teeth looked good. She must have felt uncomfortable with my unintentional inspection, because she shifted her feet and looked down, adjusting her clothes.

"Yeah," I finally said. "I had to detour to the ferry, because I had to shoot a walker."

She looked up. "The bridge is out anyway. And the ferry isn't a great option at this point either."

"Then how the hell am I supposed to get there?" I asked. If Plan B was a no-go, my frustration came out in a way that I immediately regretted. "Sorry—not your fault."

"Damn right it's not."

The woman turned to look through some of the remaining shelving and shouted. I looked at her with curiosity, and she turned back toward me with a broad grin, shaking a small box in her hand.

"What kind are those?" I asked.

She grinned wider. I pursed my lips. When Rita and I had first fled from the Spread, we had been forced to barter and trade—sometimes giving up most of our food, other times for things we never thought could be so important—but I hadn't had to deal with it much in my time in the Warehouse District. Communal property was common, and nobody wanted for too much.

"What do you want," I asked.

The woman looked at my left hand—to the wedding ring I'd never parted with—and then back up to my face. I took a deep breath and lowered my gaze. I looked back at her after a moment.

"They better be .45's."

She tossed the compact box over to me in an arc and after I'd confirmed they were what I needed, I looked up at her. She had drawn a weapon in my distraction, but it wasn't pointed at me; it was merely drawn as a warning.

"Ok," I said, "what do you want?"

Before she said anything, I set the box down and began to remove my wedding ring. Rita would have been sad, but these were reasonable sacrifices in times like this. It was better to keep myself alive than hold onto a trinket.

"I don't want your damn ring," she said.

I paused, the fingers of my right hand still on the ring. My brow arched in question, and she started to chuckle.

"You're alone," she said. "I just wanted to see if that thing was sentimental or valuable. Seeing as it's the former, I'll let you keep it."

I was confused, and it must have shown on my face.

"It gets lonely traveling solo," she said.

I nodded slowly in understanding. I supposed it was lonely in the Warehouse District, too, with only the elderly and the families to keep me company, but I'd never really taken much notice of it.

"Then you'll get me across the river," I said.

She nodded. Then she lowered her weapon.

"Come on," she said, "we need to get to higher ground and behind steel preferably."

In the morning, I awoke naked in a bed—the first time that had happened in more than six months. The woman was still asleep beside me, and I wondered in some small way if I should have asked for her name. Perhaps now, though, it wouldn't really matter.

She must have sensed me looking at her, because she stirred to life and opened one eye to look at me. She grinned, but I wasn't quite sure why: because she was satisfied, because I'd enjoyed myself, because she had actually coaxed me into it—I wasn't certain.

We both rose and dressed quickly after that, facing away from one another. We gathered our things and I followed her, not knowing where she was taking me.

Our trip took us through three old factories, crossing from one to the other by way of walkways built from window to window. Then we began to descend, only ducking out into the streets once to cross a narrow road—Old Water Street—I think—to enter a pump house that had been left to disuse even before the Spread.

My guide bolted the door with a makeshift steel girder and sighed a deep breath.

"Only one-way traffic at any time," she said as explanation.

I nodded. She walked over and turned a large wheel on top of an access hatch into the station's basement and the pumping mechanisms. I closed and secured the hatch behind me—as instructed—and descended the ladder into dimly-lit darkness.

We reached the bottom and a light flared. My guide held a halogen lantern up to illuminate her face. She smiled wickedly at me, like there was something funny about to happen, but said nothing.

A door was set into the stone and brick; it was round and solid steel. There was no bolt on this one, and we quickly found ourselves in a muggy, dark tunnel.

"Are we under the river?" I asked.

"Precisely," she replied.

I had rarely dealt directly with a creeper, and generally from afar as we took them out from the Warehouse when they got too close. Walkers were another story, but they seemed easier to cope with. Creepers were not quick, by any means, but they had the tendency to be quiet, having such a strong predatory sense that they'd learned to be stealthy. So I felt the looming, strong hand on my shoulder before I heard the thing and cried in surprise as well as horror. I spun around, swinging my fist around and struck the thing in some soft, fleshy area. My guide spun around with the lamp, and the creature's grizzly features loomed in the light right in front of me.

Before I could pull the pistol out of my belt, the thing had lunged at me. I tripped over my own feet and went over backwards. The woman leapt over my prone form, a glint of metal in her hand. There was a gurgle, and I knew she was struggling with the creature. I clambered to my feet and pulled out the .45 from the holster.

The lantern had been cast aside, but it still gave some light. I could make out two shapes. My guide screamed, and then the creature emerged from the murkiness. I reacted with two gunshots: the first buried into the things neck; the second entered through the eye. Then it fell lifeless to the tunnel floor. I heard a sickening gurgle and thought for a moment that I might retch, but I held it back.

I quickly retrieved the lantern and held it to see where my guide was. She lay against the click tunnel wall with a hand pressed firmly to a wound on her upper arm. I bound over to her, stepping quickly over the prostrate form of the creeper.

"I'll be fine," she said, before I could protest.

"How did that thing get in here," I asked.

"Maybe someone from the other side got bit and knew not to continue on," she replied. "There's not much other option. There's no other tunnels leading into this one."

I slid my arm under her shoulder and helped her to her feet. She struggled, groaning with the pain in her arm, but rose steadily. When I started toward the direction we had been headed, though, she pulled on me to stop.

"We can't," she said.

"There ought to be baths there," I said.

"Those chemical baths?" she asked. "You think those things work?" She paused to wince as I tried to get her moving, and she pushed against me. "They only slow the Spread—whatever it is."

And that explained everything. Rita and I had been fine coming out of Tollson, a town roughly fifteen miles west, and survived for a while in the Warehouse District. We'd been ambushed on a run outside town, though, and Rita had been scratched pretty good. We had rushed to a barn where we'd been told there was a shower. The wounds had healed quickly after that, and everyone thought that was the answer.

Then one day I found Rita staring out a window in the warehouse, and when I touched her, she turned around and struck me. There was a lost—but not completely gone—look in her eyes, and I truly knew fear then. She came to a second later, but we both knew what was going on.

To us, there was only one option. I used my last bullet the next day and spent the next week with the others in the warehouse keeping an eye on everyone else, me included.

"Then what do we do," I asked.

"Give me your gun," she said. Then, before I could protest, she continued, "or do it yourself. Just leave me one—that's all I ask."

With a heavy sigh, I let go of my guide and slipped the pack off one shoulder. Opening the top, I pulled out the German Luger. I handed it to her, holding onto it for one sentimental moment.

"It was my grandfather's," I said.

"Does it work?"

"It's killed plenty," I replied. "And there should be three rounds."

She opened the gun and checked it. Then she turned to me and nodded. She held the gun tightly to her chest; I inadvertently looked, and I heard her chuckle.

"At least we had one good night."

I only chuckled in response. I held the lantern out to her, but she pushed it away.

"It would be a waste," she said. "Plus, it's not too far back to the ladder. I can make my way in the dark."

"What do I do when I get there?" I asked.

"Same setup as here," she said. "I will keep this side sealed. Just be quick about going to the old state bank. That's where most everyone lives. Anyone new would be a shock—especially without an escort."

She pushed me then. I grabbed her good arm and pulled her toward me, embracing her gently.

"I'm sorry," I said.

"Don't be. The world is what it is."

"I didn't protect you," I said. It was stupid, but it was the only thing that came out.

"I'm not your wife," she said.

I turned, holding the lantern in front of me, and grabbed my pistol in case any other creepers were still down in the tunnel. I made it about one hundred feet when I heard my guide shout from the darkness behind me:

"My name is Diane!"

I won't ever be able to drown out the gunshot that echoed around me after that. I nearly ran to the other end of the tunnel, trying to escape the thought of her dead and bleeding next to that damn creeper. And I couldn't help but picture Rita. I'd been able to save her—in some way—but not Diane.

The days that followed—and perhaps the weeks, too—were quiet. I certainly wasn't welcome in my new home with food already being scarce, but I wasn't outcast either. I did my part along with everyone else, and I did my best to explain the loss of their friend. Mostly, we just went along getting by as best we could.

Perhaps there's an answer out there; maybe there's a cure for the Spread. But who knows, and at this point, who cares?

AMERICAN REFUGEES

by D. Jason Cooper

Toby breathed on his hands, which was worse than useless. He stuffed them back into his armpits. He cursed whoever stole his gloves.

Soldiers were nearby, saying the zombies were too close, civilians were too weak, supplies were running low. It was always the same three points and it was just a matter of which one came out on top this time. The soldiers decided to camp, figuring they'd finally get the civilians to Akron tomorrow. Toby watched them argue until they spotted him.

"What are you doing?"

"Freezing."

They moved him along. Four soldiers armed and watchful and playfully hitting him about the head when he couldn't keep up. They gave Toby a shovel from some dead soldier's back pack, telling him he had an important task to do. Toby felt like an enslaved ditch digger.

They walked on an old dirt road on the side of a hill just north of the old Governor Dewey Thruway. Thruways and roads were where zombies ruled. They checked through binoculars and if they thought the zombies were too close they traveled quiet.

"Here. Good enough. Dig while we keep watch. Zombies set ambushes: they stand for months if they have to, waiting for us to come by."

Nice excuse to make Toby do the work. There was a foot of snow, but when he got rid of that they wanted him to dig a hole in the frozen ground.

"Are you kidding? That ground is frozen. I'm a science student, not a body builder."

Toby knew he was stating the obvious and that never convinced anyone of anything. He began chipping away at hard frozen clay, making no real progress at all. After an hour he had a small, shallow hole that might hold a dump.

Three more soldiers came up, bringing one of the civilians with them. Toby couldn't remember her name, but he'd seen her around. She was usually sitting or lying down, exhausted by the day's march. There was always a cloud of people around her making certain she got her food, that she was warm enough, or to comfort her when she made noises in her sleep.

"What's she doing here?"

"Shut up."

They brought her up to the hole, but it wasn't until she spoke that Toby understood.

"Please. No. I've done nothing wrong."

Suddenly, Toby was grabbed and thrown to the hard ground. A hand was over his mouth.

"Shut up. If you say a word, I will kill you."

He shuddered, felt his head pressed into the snow, blinding him. But before everything went white, he saw the shambling figures much of the world had come to fear.

He breathed out heavy, trying to blow the snow away but it was to solid for that. The soldier pressed into his neck and Toby gave up that idea.

The old woman, though, would not be quiet. She found her anger and asked how the soldiers dared…but she got no further than that. A sudden punch, to judge from the sound.

Toby listened, not sure how many zombies were walking at the bottom of the hill. It could be a few, it could be thousands. He expected to hear 'must eat brains,' 'brains,' or some other slogan the press had reported that they mouthed. Instead he heard a different tune from them.

'Freedom. Freedom.'

They did not all say it at once. It came out at random moments, said by random figures. And once one voice said the word, it was never the one to say it next.

Everyone held their breath. Toby could not move, so he just watched as puffs of breath slowly melted the snow in front of his face. He thought how once again the soldiers who protected him did so by imprisoning him.

Eventually eternity passed by. Moving more slowly than time, eventually the zombies did, too. There was no silence, just the sounds of shuffling becoming thinner, and then further away and then the soldier got off Toby's neck.

"How many of them were there?" Toby asked. It seemed to be good way to blend in; show concern for what concerned the soldiers.

"Too many for us to handle. That's how zombies work. A few go out. If they get hurt, thousands more come. That lot were probably heading to where some idiot thought they'd got a little victory for humans. Explains why they weren't concerned with the noises we made."

Then attention came back to the old lady. They woke her up by slapping her. She was afraid again.

"I've done nothing wrong…"

"You just nearly got us killed, so don't think we're going to fall for your help-less old lady act."

But nobody was convinced by the obvious.

"Listen, you figure you'll get to Akron tomorrow. It's not a big town, but sure-ly they can protect her."

"If she makes noises like that again, we may not get there. Akron used to have less than three thousand people. Since the zombies showed up they've tripled its size and built a city wall. It's the story across the country. Little towns get bigger because our cities are being wiped out."

Just then, Toby noticed her hands.

"Hey, those are my gloves."

"No, they're not," said the old woman. "They're mine."

"I recognize them. You'll find my initials inside them in black permanent marker."

"Those are my initials," she said,

"What is the other mark in the gloves? Hint, you have to turn them inside out to see it."

She froze. She could try to call his bluff, but that was a very long odds bet.

"I've done nothing wrong."

The other mark was a green heart with an arrow through it and a face on it. The message was 'I'm better than your hand.' His girlfriend had put it on after a long evening of talking dirty, telling each other about family genetic deficiencies, and thinking of names. It was why he had taken the gloves off when he slept. He hadn't wanted to ruin them after she died.

They took the gloves from her, punching her when she tried to bite them.

"Get that," said the sergeant, pointing at the hole. They widened it and deep-ened it, far more quickly than Toby had.

"Please," said the old woman.

"Can she stay in Akron?" asked Toby.

"It's too late for that," said the sergeant. He was gray haired and slim. He had the sinewy arms of somebody who was moving and working all the time. And he had the attitude of somebody who had been in the army since the year dot.

There was only one day to go. There were seven of them, armed and strong and with the experience of combat on their side. And the old woman had endan-gered them all, and stolen from him.

"Freedom! Freedom!"

She was a lot louder than Toby would have thought possible, but not for long. One of the soldiers hit her with a shovel. She fell, cushioned a little by the snow. It didn't matter because a couple soldiers took their shovels and beat her like she was a cockroach. Then they changed the neck so the shovels had their blades at a ninety degree angle from the handle. Wielded like pick axes, they broke her collar bone, chopped her body, and eventually they cut her throat and she died. They'd taken their time.

They continued to cut her to pieces. Arms off first. Then legs. Then head. They made him put the pieces into the hole he'd helped dig.

Her blood steamed in the cold. It quickly froze on the ground. As it did the soldiers tried to shovel it into the hole as well. Soon it was overfilled with blood stained snow and dirt and pieces of the old woman's body. Toby suddenly remembered her name had been Olivia.

"God, did she mess herself?"

"Yeah. Everybody does when they die. The muscles can't clench any more. It's people who haven't seen death who try to find dignity in it."

"So, she died for making too much noise?"

"And stealing stuff. And Akron's told us no more feeble old people. They don't do enough work, they want instant respect…"

He went on for some time. Toby wondered if the explanation wasn't just a list of his excuses for what he did.

The old woman's head had landed face up. The eyes were open, blue, and cold. Her face was less wrinkled than it had been in life. Toby realized she had been scrunching up her face the whole time she had been on the march.

They'd started covering her up when one of the soldiers signaled. In the distance was the sound of groaning and the moan of 'freedom' from those who would simply destroy things and call the gaps freedom.

Toby followed the soldiers as they retreated. Even if they could destroy this group, it would just call others. He hefted the shovel they'd given him, putting the blade forward like a pick ax to make it some kind of weapon. One of the soldiers noticed what he was doing and gave him a sidearm.

Toby nodded his gratitude and looked at it. The safety was off so he put it on because he didn't know guns. At the small click the soldiers froze, fear on their faces. Somewhere in the distance the groans of zombies stopped and they called out 'freedom.' But instead of the usual random moan, they all said it at once. The soldiers pinched their lips and drummed the air in frustration.

They grabbed Toby and pushed him along. They made more noise, now, to get extra speed. They still didn't speak, but they didn't care if they stepped on a branch.

Toby wondered if they were going to head back to the main party. There would be more soldiers. But the zombies would find out where they were.

They came to a ridge, stopped and turned. The sergeant looked through binoculars and headed a sigh of relief.

"It's OK. They've stopped to eat the old woman." He was still whispering. He breathed deep. "There's only about twenty of them. Still, we better get back while we have the chance."

"We left footprints," said Toby, pointing at the trail.

"Zombies are too stupid to follow a trail."

The sergeant sniggered, safe in his superiority. His men did the same. Toby swallowed.

"The…when I put the safety on…why was that a problem?"

"Because zombies hear any click of a gun and they all head towards it. What kind of science do you even study? Enough talk, move out."

Toby followed, certain they were going a different way from the route they used to come out—there was no trail of footsteps this way. They took the gun back but let him keep the shovel. He hefted it a few times. It was short and would be almost useless in a fight. And he studied astronomy. Nobody cared about stars any more, but he did.

They came around a bend in the dirt track to face thirty-some standing corpses. They stood covered in snow without a single footprint to or from any of them. It hadn't snowed for several days.

The soldiers froze. The last two men turned so all angles were watched. The zombies did not move. They were like really creepy statutes.

One of the soldiers let out a breath. Suddenly all the zombies shifted their heads and stared at the thick cloud of steam. Another soldier swore, their eyes turned to him. Then they started coming forward.

"They'll still be cold. Their blood's probably frozen. Take them out."

Soldiers shouldered their assault rifles and as soon as they did the zombies started moving.

'Freedom!'

They all said it again and again, none of them caring if anyone else was speaking. Living people wind up saying the same thing in unison, all shouting or all taking a breath at once. The zombies were not that orderly. They ran on instinct rather than rules.

They came in a wave, and like a wave of the ocean bullets didn't do a lot to stop them. Soldiers fired and pieces of flesh flew away. But it did little to stop things that didn't feel pain. There were puffs of flesh, sometimes blood, but chest and arm or leg kept going.

"Head shots!"

The sergeant followed his own order. But it's harder to hit a smaller target. Bullets missed, people screamed, and the zombies were on them.

Toby swung his shovel. The blade hit the neck of a zombie, slicing deep into its neck. Muscles were cut and the zombie lost control of part of itself. It turned and grabbed him. Trying to bite.

Toby chopped and heard metal hit bone. He swung again and again and the soldier suddenly pushed him out of the way.

There was yelling and Toby saw the soldiers giving away bullets and using their rifles as clubs, slashing with bayonets, and using shovels like battle axes.

They weren't trying to kill, that wasn't good enough. They were trying to dismember. Toby backed up. His glove was half pulled off and his hand was cut.

He pulled the glove back on, it must have been the soldier who pulled the shovel off him.

The wave went around the soldiers. Toby backed away.

"Keep going keep going!"

Toby ran as fast as he could. The zombies followed him.

"Freedom! Freedom! Free us…"

And then they began to fall. The soldiers took their flank, and now they could get clear, easy shots at the head. Zombies fell. So did a soldier. But the zombies fell. And still they came. Another group from the other direction, where they'd eaten the old lady.

Toby ran and picked up the first shovel he saw. He was exhausted and he didn't want to die. He didn't want to be in the ground, surrounded by the judgment of others. He looked to the soldiers.

"Grab equipment."

"What?"

"Move or we'll leave you behind. More are coming."

Toby could hear the voices calling for freedom. The soldiers grabbed him and pulled him along and then he was carrying a backpack of equipment and they kept pushing. They gave him one order after another. They doubled back, shifted around, went one way and then the other to throw the zombies off the trail. Eventually it was dark and they were at the camp.

People around him were talking and leaving gaps in the conversation. Soldiers patrolled, keeping zombies out and keeping people in, always giving orders. Toby was just another unfree face in the crowd obeying orders.

THE NOT TOM

by Ian Welke

It wasn't Tom. Tom was dead. He had been dead for a week before his body staggered into the Old Dive on Anaheim in Long Beach. I dropped my drink. The two men at the table in the back corner got up and left. Joe Harris stood in line at the bar. He looked over at the corpse standing to his right. He looked down at the Social Security check he'd come in to cash. He looked across the bar to me, shook his head, and left.

"Tom?" Martha said. She was the only regular cool enough to speak to it. She said his name once more, and downed the gimlet she held steady in her right hand.

Tom's body just stood there. The stench of death hung in the air around it. The folks in the bar at that hour in the morning weren't the freshest specimens, but they weren't in the same league as a rotting corpse. His pale skin glistened with some clear fluid. The fluid shimmered in the dim light it caught from the crack between the Budweiser posters covering the windows. The rest of the light, from the electric beer signs, cast him in a strange pink glow.

Jack McCready planted a palm on the table in front of him to steady himself as he stood. "He'll eat our brains," he said, backing away.

Martha glared at Jack. "Oh, hush. You don't have brains enough to make but a light snack. Tom? You aren't gonna eat any brains in here, are you?"

Tom still stood there, right over the stain on the carpet where Tim Drake had puked his guts out last September. Drool dripped from Tom's mouth. It wasn't the first time I'd seen him drool in the bar.

I reached behind me and judged the seat of my pants. Relieved that I hadn't literally lost my shit, I poured two double shots of Old Granddad, which had been Tom's regular bourbon. I put one glass on the edge of the bar closest to him, and backed away, cradling the other. "Got a shot for you, Tom."

His jowls shivered, and a low sad moan came out of his mouth accompanied by more drool.

"If this doesn't take the damned cake," Jack said.

Tom continued to shake. More fluid came out of his mouth.

"Jesus, Tom. That stuff coming out of your mouth reeks." Jack craned and turned his head like a confused dog. "Tom? Do you hear me, Tom?"

"Tom?" Tom's body said in a garbled and choked voice. More of the foul smelling, viscous fluid followed the word out of its mouth. Jack fell over. One of the old men sitting next to the Pull Tabs area spat out his drink. "Tom?" the body said again. Less drool spilled out and the sound was clearer.

"I think it's learning to talk from our words." Jack stood up, peanut shells and dust clung to his blue jeans.

"Words. We know these." Each time it spoke, less fluid dribbled down its chin from the previous effort. "How to make the mouth move them... how to force air in and out...This is diffic..." More fluid. "Diffic...Hard."

"What do you mean 'we'? Are there more of our dead friends out there in the parking lot?" Martha asked.

I had the rag in my hand wiping down the bar before I realized I was doing it. My nervous reflex. For some reason, I found my compulsion to clean funny. Funny enough that I decided I deserved another shot of Old Granddad. "Maybe it's more like the royal we." I licked my lips after downing the shot. "Once you come back from the dead, you may have delusions of grandeur." I took my rag over to the old man's table and wiped up the spat drink. "Get you another?"

"No thanks, I'm good." He threw down a couple of bills, got up, and left, all the while not taking his eyes off Tom's corpse.

I picked up the empty glass, and headed back to the bar, running my fingers over the soggy felt of the pool table on the way. Remembering the dead man standing between me and my station, I quickened my pace, eager to put the bar between myself and it.

"We are not dead. We are not Tom."

"Very well, Not Tom, I'm Martha. Now who the hell are you and what are you doing in the body of our dead friend?"

"We are not from your world."

"Oh, brother," I said, back behind the safety of the bar. "Tom, did you fake your own death just so you could pull this joke?" Even as I said it, I knew there was no way that could be true. The smell was too authentic, and Tom had never been capable of pulling off something elaborate. Sure he was a jokester, but his jokes were usually lame and you could see them coming from a mile off.

"We are here to make first contact."

"And you've chosen a dive bar?" Martha raised both eyebrows.

"Yeah. Why not the state's capitol in San Francisco?" Jack asked.

"State's capitol is in Sacramento, Jack." Martha looked back at Not Tom. "But he has a point. Why here? Why not D.C.? Or the U.N.?"

"We have monitored your broadcasts." A bit more fluid came out on the bigger words, but it had mastered the smaller ones. "These are the sorts of places you are less to be afraid. Most welcoming. 'Sometimes you want to go where everybody knows your name.'"

Martha laughed. "Pour me another gimlet. I'm going to need it. What you're telling us, is that you planned your alien invasion by watching 'Cheers' reruns?" She and Jack, the only remaining patrons, both started laughing. For a moment their pony tails, hers red and bushy, his brown and oily, bobbed in unison.

"Invasion is incorrect. We mean to make contact. To be partners."

"And you came to a dive bar because that's what you saw on the T.V. Why come here in our friend's body?" Martha asked.

"We are too small in ourselves for you to acknowledge. We needed a host. We considered using a mecha...mecha...mechan...mechani..." It stopped, wiped its drool, and seemed to reset itself. "You would say robot. But we thought a more familiar vessel would be less alarming."

"Less alarming?" Jack flung his hands in the air, still shaking more than usual. "You can start your Earth lessons with the fact that walking around in a corpse is likely to upset folks. Especially the ones that knew him."

"And lesson two," Martha said, raising two fingers. "If you want to talk to Earth's leaders, a bar before lunch isn't the right place."

"Don't be harsh, Martha."

"She's right, Jack." I eyed my empty glass and decided to remedy its sad condition.

"But..." the Not Tom stammered.

"It's all right. You're welcome here," I said. "Come sit down at the bar."

"Just like that? You're not going to kick him out?"

"Jack, if anyone's getting eighty-sixed today, it's you. Come over to the bar, Not Tom. This was Tom's favorite drink." I pointed to the double shot still sitting on the edge.

Not Tom shuffled towards the bar. I could see it now. The delay in his limbs working together. I wondered how many of them there were inside working the controls. Together they could make him move, but it was far from seamless. It seemed to stop and contemplate how to sit on the stool. I had to admit it wasn't the first one to experience difficulty with that task in this establishment.

"Inebriation does sound tempting," Not Tom said.

"There you go," Martha said. She took the stool next to him. Jack sat two stools away, with Martha between him and the Not Tom.

It struggled to raise the glass to its lips, but its hands didn't shake as much as some of our customers.

"Can you even get drunk on Earth booze?" Jack asked.

Not Tom set the empty shot on the bar and nodded. There was a jerky motion to the nod, like they couldn't quite get the rhythm right. "Yes. I can confirm that our processing of the Earth liquor matches our simulations. We process nutrients much the same as you do. When this body consumes something, the nutrients—or in this case the welcome poison—is divided between each of us. Speaking of poison, can we have another?" It reached into Tom's coat pocket and pulled out a hunk of silver metal and set it on the bar. "We do not have your currency, but we understand that silver is valuable. Can we buy a drink for each of you?"

Jack licked his lips. "Well, you know how to win friends, I'll give you that."

"It goes a long way to make up for the strange entrance," I agreed.

"We are glad. We need to practice making the meat move. Better accuracy is required."

"For that, might I suggest the Earth game, pool?" Jack said and stood up, taking a step towards the pool table.

"Yes. We remember seeing this game played in many of the transmissions of your televised mythologies."

"Y'all go ahead." I tossed Martha the keys to the pool table so they wouldn't need quarters. "I'll meet you over there with drinks. A gimlet for you, Martha?" I fixed the cocktail, opened another Bud for Jack, and I brought the bottle of Old Granddad with me for myself and the Not Tom.

The Not Tom stared down the cue stick when I got to the table. "Our calculations…" It paused. "Are we mistaken, or is this stick not straight?"

"You're not mistaken," Martha said. "It's all part of what makes this a great trainer for you. Now as you look down the warped cue, you see how the table's not level?"

"We see, but we do not understand."

"Well, have another drink. It will make sense soon."

We stopped to down our drinks. The bourbon either started to mask Not Tom's smell or it deadened my senses sufficiently.

Not Tom readied its first pool break.

"Now just smack the cue ball dead center," Martha said.

The cue clacked off the ball. Not Tom shanked it.

"No problem." Martha repositioned the cue ball. "Try again. Just remember the center. You're feeling the booze now? Each part of you? Now use that boozy feeling. Use it to line up the bent stick and the wavy table and hit the ball in its center."

Not Tom's next shot missed the ball altogether.

"Actually, better than the shank," Martha said. "Now one more."

It wasn't the best break I'd ever seen, but there was a solid smack as the balls collided and spread out across the table.

"Good." Martha smiled.

"That was good advice. Are you an educator?"

Jack laughed. "Martha? She's no teacher. She used to be a spot welder, but she don't even do that no more."

"Jack, can I see you over at the bar." I retreated back behind the bar and made sure Jack took a seat before I spoke. "Now Jack, don't make fun of Martha in front of the Not Tom."

"Or what?"

"Or she might just kick your scrawny ass."

Martha and Not Tom returned to their seats at the bar. I poured drinks so that their glasses awaited their arrival.

"Do you have bars like this on your world?" Martha asked.

"Not like this." Not Tom stopped talking. It's face was hard to read when it stopped to think. The aliens inside assigned cohorts to work its mouth, but not to make expressions. "It is different being here than we thought."

"You have nothing to worry about," Martha said. "That's the good thing about L.A. Most people aren't really from here. My folks moved here from Kentucky when I was in high school. That mangy man tending bar is from Texas. Jack's the only one that was born here, and he's the one that doesn't fit in."

"You are very nice." It was hard to tell with the lack of expressions and no tonal changes to its voice, but it seemed sad.

"What's wrong?" I asked.

"We came all this way and we came to the wrong place. Not a good start to the mission."

"Well, this might not be the right place for meeting our leaders," Martha said.

"Or for scientific exchange," I added.

Martha pointed a finger at me, crediting me with the observation. She said, "But if you're feeling down about one of life's mistakes, you're in the perfect place. This is exactly where you need to be to take a moment for yourself."

"We are torn. We want to drink to consider this error, but we suspect this will soon lead to more errors."

"See? You've come to the right place after all." I refilled Not Tom's glass. We drank our drinks and let the day slip away into an error-filled night.

INHUMAN RESOURCES

by Brenda Kezar

"What the hell were you thinking, bringing that zombie into my house?" Lola peeked through the kitchen door and watched Larry plop down beside Gran at the dining room table.

"Ma, I'm sorry, but I'm his sponsor—"

"That doesn't mean you have to bring him home for Thanksgiving." She let the door flap shut.

"He didn't have any place else to go. The church group relocated him here, and he doesn't know anyone."

"Doesn't he have family of his own?"

"No. His wife left him because he's…you know…"

Lola crossed her arms. "Dead?"

He winced. "Ma. Keep your voice down."

"What? Like he doesn't know he's a zombie?"

"Of course he knows he's a zombie. Have you taken a good look at him? There's no way anyone couldn't know." He peeked into the dining room. Gran studied Larry's face, smiling politely. Larry smiled and studied her back. "And they prefer the term 'alternately existing.'"

"They?" She peered into the dining room again, her eyes wide. "There's more like him?"

"I don't know, ma. Probably."

She shoved a bowl of mashed potatoes into his hands. "Put these on the table. And if that thing eats your grandma, it's your fault." She grabbed a bowl of stuffing and Andy followed her to the table.

"Your friend doesn't look so good," Gran said. She put a hand daintily over her nose. "Doesn't smell too good, either. What's that aftershave, lighter fluid?"

"Mother!" Lola snapped.

"He doesn't have swine flu, does he? I can't get sick and miss my senior center

Christmas cruise. They make you pay up front on account of so many passengers croaking before they set sail. It doesn't pay to plan ahead when you're a senior."

Larry smiled and nodded sympathetically.

"Don't talk much, do you?" Gran asked.

"Mother," Lola sighed. "Maybe you haven't noticed, but Andy's friend here is a zombie."

Andy threw his hands in the air. "Ma! We talked about this! He's 'alternately existing'!"

"Alternately what?" Gran eyed Larry.

"He's dead, mother," Lola said.

Gran leaned toward Larry and squinted. "Oh. Well, I guess that explains a lot." She chuckled. "But why would Low-Low-Mart want to hire a…what do you call yourself, again, dear?"

"Alternately existing," Andy answered for him.

"Yes, that." She patted Larry's leg. "Although I'm sure you're a nice enough young man."

"Because they're having problems finding employees." Andy tore off a drumstick.

"So what's it like," Gran asked, "being one of the undead?"

Larry shrugged and slapped a spoonful of potatoes onto his plate. "Um ayz etter udders."

"Come again?" Gran's brow furrowed.

"Some days are better than others," Andy repeated for him.

"I didn't know you spoke Zombinese," Gran said.

Andy rolled his eyes. "English, Gran. He speaks English."

"So how long have you worked with Andy?" Gran asked.

Larry didn't look up from the corn cob he chewed but held up two fingers.

"I'm his sponsor," Andy said. He dropped the turkey bone onto his plate.

Larry's eyes lit up. He reached across the table with his free hand and made 'gimme' gestures until Andy passed the bone to him.

"I'm responsible for training him and turning him into a valuable Low-Low-Mart employee," Andy said.

Larry popped the turkey bone into his mouth, and it sounded like he was chewing rocks.

Gran watched Larry chew. "Isn't that hard on your teeth, dear?"

Larry shook his head and swallowed, then reached into his mouth and pulled out his teeth.

"Sweet Jesus," Lola cried.

"Wow." Gran reached out. "Can I see them?" Larry nodded, and Gran took the dentures. "Holy Moly! These suckers are heavy!"

Andy sighed and dragged his fork through his potatoes. "They're titanium. The church group got them for him when his teeth fell out. He needed them for his…uh…special dietary needs."

"Wow. That church group is something else. I wonder if they can set me up with a pair of these." She removed her teeth and held them up. "All I got were crappy plastic ones." She batted her eyes at Larry. "Can I take them for test drive?"

"Mother!" Lola leapt to her feet.

Larry nodded, and Gran slid the teeth into her own mouth. She grinned, and the oversize metal choppers stretched her smile into a bling-filled, Cheshire cat grin.

"Whaddya think?" She clicked them together twice. "Should I get me a set?"

Andy sighed and shook his head. Thank God Thanksgiving only came once a year.

"Aren't you going to stay for the game?" Lola handed Andy his coat.

"Nah. I want to get home before the turkey-coma kicks in." He slid his arms into his coat. "Besides, Larry and I have to work tonight. It's his first Black Friday at Low-Low-Mart."

"You poor dears." Gran rushed to the table and returned with the pumpkin pie. "Take the rest with you. You boys can share it tonight."

Larry took the pie. "Ank oo, Gran."

"And don't be a stranger. Lola's an excellent cook, and I know single men don't eat very well."

The color drained from Lola's face. "Mother!"

"What?" Gran shrugged. "You're not getting any younger, and Andy's out on his own, now. You want to spend the rest of your days alone?"

Andy shook his head. "Gran, I don't think—"

"At least he's got a job. You could do worse."

Andy opened the door. "Let's go, Larry. Before Gran fits you for a tux."

Larry grinned. "Ank oo for food. Appy Anksgive." He wiggled his eyebrows at Lola. "See oo soon!"

She rolled her eyes in return.

The usual course of business for Low-Low-Mart's busiest day was to get grocery stocked first, as quickly as possible. The rest of the evening would be spent concentrating on the merchandise side of the store—where the action would really be.

"So how's the new guy doing?" Mark leaned against a shelf of fabric softener.

"Okay, I guess. He's over in paper goods." Andy slid another jug of Tide onto the shelf and checked his watch. "Speaking of which, I'd better check on him. He should be done by now."

Andy rounded the corner of the paper goods aisle and froze. Larry stood in the middle of the aisle, a case of paper towels tucked under one arm, staring at his free hand. Two fingers lay in a black puddle on the gleaming white tiles.

"Dude! What the hell!" Andy grabbed an orange caution cone and slid it to Larry. "Put this on the floor while I call maintenance." He ran to the meat cooler and punched the page button. "I need maintenance to aisle ten for…" For what? An amputation? Black ooze mop up? He sighed. "Maintenance to aisle ten for a wet spill."

He hung up the phone and rushed back to Larry. "Are you all right? Does it hurt?"

Larry held his hand up and wiggled his fingers. With each wiggle, black spray squirted from the stumps.

Andy's stomach fluttered.

"Heh-heh-heh." Larry wiggled his fingers again, and the fresh bursts of black spray sent him into hysterics.

"Dude! Knock it off! You're making a mess."

Jasper rounded the corner with a mop and bucket. He gave Larry and Andy a sharp glare, pulled the mop from the water, and set to work on the spill. "I'll mop up this black gunk, but I ain't picking up those fingers," he growled.

On the way to the first aid station, Andy and Larry passed five associates watching a safety-team member change the number on the "accident-free days" board to zero. The associates turned and glared.

"Way to go, deadhead," one of them said. "There goes our ice cream party!"

Larry shook his head and groaned.

"Don't let it get you down." Andy clapped him on the back. "It happens to the best of us."

† † † † †

At lunchtime, Andy rushed to the break room for a piece of Gran's pie. He threw the door open and ran into a wall of stink. "Oh! What the hell is that?" He threw his hand over his nose and glared at Hoang. "Did your balut go bad?"

Hoang shook his head and jabbed his finger Larry's direction. "It's not me. It's whatever your friend is cooking."

The microwave dinged and Larry shuffled over and opened the door. Gray and black spatter covered the inside walls of the microwave. One pink, ropey string dangled from the top, then dropped into the bowl.

"Oh, my god." Sara wrinkled her nose. "What is that?"

"If you put a paper towel over the bowl, it won't splatter so much." Andy peered at the mess in the microwave. "I hope you're planning on cleaning that up."

Larry grunted, set his bowl on the counter, and grabbed a few paper towels.

"Is that noodle soup?" Andy peeked in the bowl. "Did you check the expiration date?"

Larry gave the inside of the microwave a few cursory swipes, then slammed the door shut and tossed the towels away. "No soop. Ains." He picked up the bowl and carried it to the nearest table.

"Ains?" Andy asked. He pulled out a chair and sat next to Larry.

Larry patted the top of his head. "Ains."

Andy frowned. "What?"

Larry swirled the spoon around the bowl and scooped something out. "Ains!" He shook the spoon, and the contents fell onto the table with a spat.

Andy leapt to his feet. "Brains? You're eating brains?"

Sara rushed from the room, her hand over her mouth. Hoang shook his head. "I better not hear anybody complain about my balut again."

After lunch, Hoang, Sara, and Andy were called to the management office. Assistant manager Paul shook his head in disappointment. "Who wants to tell me what went on at lunch?"

Sara crossed her arms. "He was eating brains, Paul. Brains! Cooked them right in our microwave."

"That's enough." Paul held up his hand. "We have to be sensitive to other cultures—"

"Cultures?" Sara shrieked. "The guy's a freakin' zombie, cooking brains in the microwave where I cook my chicken tenders!"

"I'm never using the microwave again," Hoang said.

"Hoang!" Paul said. "Of all people, I thought you'd be more sensitive. Remember when people freaked out about your balut?"

"Yeah, but balut is food. Brains aren't food."

"Don't some Asian cultures consider monkey brains a delicacy?" Paul asked.

"Only the weird ones." Hoang shuddered.

"But that's how we felt about your balut. An egg with a half-developed baby duck inside doesn't sound like food to us, but we accept it as part of your culture. We all have to be sensitive to the needs and habits of others. A diversified work force is important."

"Bullshit," Sara said. "It's just freaking weird."

"What about your Lutefisk? Gelatinous fish soaked in poisonous lye? That's not weird?" Paul asked.

"Well…"

"Now, I expect you guys to embrace the Low-Low-Mart commitment to diversity and be sensitive to Larry's special needs."

"Whatever." Sara stood. "I swear to god, the first time he tries to eat my brain,

I quit." She stomped off. Hoang shook his head and followed her.

"Where do you think he got those brains?" Andy asked.

Paul shrugged. "Probably the foreign foods market. They have all kinds of weird crap."

Andy left Paul's office and paused inside the stockroom doors, bracing himself for what waited outside, in the store. As he did, Paul's voice blared over the intercom. "Attention Low-Low-Mart Associates: please move through the pallets and ask our guests to step back three feet. Customers, please abide by these rules. And, as always, thank you for shopping Low-Low-Mart."

Andy took a deep breath and pushed open the doors. On the other side, in toys, Larry stood in front of a display of "Monster High" dolls, grinning from ear to ear.

He looked at Andy, still grinning, and pointed at the dolls. "HHHHOT!"

"Forget the dolls, man. We've got work to do." Andy said. "Let's start in electronics."

They approached the first pallet, a pallet of printers, where most customers had complied and stood back. Larry approached a large woman in sweat pants who still held one hand on the pallet. She swung her arm at Larry, he dodged it and snarled.

Andy rushed over. "What's up?"

The woman turned on Andy. "Lurch here seems to think I'm going to give up my spot."

"No, ma'am. We don't want anyone to give up their spot. We just need everyone to step back."

"I ain't stepping back."

Larry stepped forward, snapped his teeth and growled.

She rolled her eyes. "You don't scare me, Lurch. If you want me to move, you'll have to pick me up and move me. My son wants one of these for Christmas, and he's getting one. No minimum wage slacker is going to mess up my boy's Christmas."

Larry narrowed his eyes and growled again. Andy put his hand against Larry's chest. "Forget it. It's not worth it." He pulled Larry to the side. "These people will trample little old ladies and beat each other half to death so their kids can have this year's hot toy. Let them act like animals; the important thing is to keep yourself safe. This job isn't worth dying over."

Larry arched an eyebrow.

"Sorry, man." He glanced at Larry's bandaged hand. "It isn't worth…losing… more body parts. Just let it go."

Larry nodded, but narrowed his eyes at the woman again. She narrowed her eyes back.

"I know. I'd like to bite her, too." Andy said.

By the time they reached the last pallet, it was almost time to open them.

"All right. I need everyone to step back," Andy shouted. The crowd grumbled and held their ground. "I can't open it if I can't get to it, people." More grumbling, but the crowd stepped back. As soon as Andy and Larry were next to the pallet, the crowd closed in around them again.

"Okay," Andy said to Larry. "Now the fun really begins. When they make the announcement, we start cutting away the plastic so people can get to the merchandise. One quick swipe with your box-cutter and step out of the way. I'll take this side, you take the other. When we both zip through it, it'll fall away in two pieces, and then we'll get out of the way and let the customers handle the rest. We'll move to the next pallet in line. If we come to a pallet people are already tearing into and it looks too dangerous for us to get in there, we'll skip it and move on to the next. You got it?"

Larry nodded.

"All right, people. Let him around to the other side." The crowd parted enough to let Larry through, and he disappeared around the pallet. A few moments later, Paul's voice came over the intercom: it was time. Andy stepped forward and opened the pallet with one quick zip. After less than a second's pause, the plastic fell away in two pieces, smooth as silk. Andy smiled, and backpedaled as the crowd surged. He stepped to the next pallet, but customers were already tearing it apart.

"We'll skip this one," he yelled, but Larry wasn't mirroring him on the other side of the aisle.

He pushed through the crowd between the pallets and looked up and down the far side of the aisle. No sign of Larry, and the pallet they had just opened was almost empty. A large woman with her sweat pants stuck in her butt-crack stepped back from where she'd been leaning over the pallet, reaching for one of the last GPS units, and he finally spotted Larry, spread-eagled on the floor.

"Holy hell!" Andy rushed to Larry. "Are you all right?" The woman in sweatpants glanced up from the GPS in her hand, then down at Larry, and then shrugged and walked away.

Larry shook his head and sat up, his eyes glazed. Andy gave him a quick once-over: dusty footprints peppered his shirt and his pocket dangled loose, and he had a dent in the side of his head in the perfect shape of the pallet corner.

"Damn, dude. You've got a dent in your head."

Larry's fingers explored the divot. He groaned.

"Does it hurt?"

Larry sighed and shook his head.

Andy thought a minute. "We should go to automotive and grab one of those pop-a-dent things; pop it back out."

Larry narrowed his eyes.

"I'm just kidding." Andy helped Larry to his feet.

The paging system crackled and called all backup cashiers to the front.

"Shit," Andy said. "I have to go cashier. Do you think you'll be okay opening the rest of the pallets in this aisle?"

Larry groaned.

Andy clapped him on the shoulder. "You can do it! The worst is almost over."

Andy had been cashiering about an hour when the security alarms went off for the thousandth time. He glanced up from the items he was scanning.

Norman, one of the door greeters, approached a man with a cart full of big-ticket merchandise: a small flat screen TV, a computer, a Blu-ray player, assorted toys. Sweat rolled down the man's face. Norman put his hand on the front of the cart, but the man yanked the cart away. Lynette, the other door greeter, started over to help. The man spotted her, rolled his cart out of Norman's reach, and pulled a gun from inside his coat.

"Back off!" He held the gun high for everyone to see. "I don't want to hurt anyone."

Lynette and Norman both froze, and the entire front of the store fell silent and still.

Andy hesitated. He shouldn't intervene, but he was good with people and might have a chance at talking the gunman down. He stepped from behind his register. "Hey, man, be cool," he said.

"No, you be cool." He jabbed the gun Andy's direction. "Stay back."

"I just want to talk. Do you really want to spend Christmas in jail?"

"It's worth the risk. My kids deserve a Christmas."

"There must be a better way."

"If there was any other way, you think I'd be doing this? I lost my job. Nobody's hiring. Our savings ran out so fast." He swallowed hard and his eyes welled with tears. "My kids are going to have nothing…nothing for Christmas."

"I understand," Andy said calmly.

"No, you don't," the gunman shouted. "You don't know what it's like to not have any money."

"Take a look around you," Andy said. "We work at Low-Low-Mart, dude!"

Lynette and Norman nodded in consensus.

"Okay. I see your point," the gunman said.

The exit doors hissed open. A police officer peered over a row of shopping carts and another peeked from behind the pop machine.

"Drop the gun," the officer behind the carts said.

The gunman's eyes bugged. He looked at Andy, at Norman and Lynette, and then his gaze settled on a customer nearby with a baby clutched to her chest. His eyes rolled in desperation, and he grabbed for the baby. The woman screamed and turned away, and they struggled.

The police dashed from their protective cover and rushed the doors, but the gunman spun around, with the baby clutched to his chest. The police froze as the mother crumpled to the floor, sobbing.

"Back off!" He pointed the gun at the baby.

Larry shambled past Andy. Andy reached for him but missed. "Larry, don't be a hero," he yelled.

Larry curled his lip, gave Andy a thumbs-up, and shuffled closer to the gunman.

"Back off. I mean it!" He pointed the gun at Larry. "Don't make me do it."

Larry shambled closer and the gunman fired two shots. Employees and customers dropped to the floor, screaming. Two dark holes in Larry's chest oozed black ichor, but he didn't slow down.

The gunman shook his head in disbelief. The gun slid out of his hand and hit the floor with a metallic clatter. Larry slipped the baby out of the gunman's grasp and handed it to its mother. He turned back to the gunman and grinned.

"I shot you. You're dead." The gunman took a step back.

Larry narrowed his eyes. "No sit, serwock." He grabbed the gunman, sunk his teeth into his throat, and yanked. Arterial spray spattered everyone within a ten foot radius and the gunman's eyes rolled up into his head. The police rushed in. One rushed the gunman; the other kept his gun trained on Larry.

"Hands in the air," the cop shouted at Larry. Larry raised his hands and chewed merrily.

"Don't shoot!" Andy yelled. "He's one of us!"

The next evening, Larry received the Low-Low-Mart "Hometown Heroes" award at their nightly meeting.

"Congratulations, Larry. Low-Low-Mart is proud to have you on our team." Store Manager Jacob turned to the rest of the associates. "I'd also like to introduce the newest member of our team. Rick, come on in here and say hi."

Rick rounded the corner, and several associates gasped.

"Really?" Andy asked.

Jacob held up his hand. "I know what you're going to say, but everyone deserves a second chance. Right, Rick?"

"Ennnnnhhh," Rick grinned. The grin stretched the skin on his face and caused the neck wound Larry had given him to ooze a fresh trickle of black.

"I'm assigning you as his sponsor, Andy. I trust you'll do just as good with him as you did with Larry."

Andy shook his head. "Maybe Larry should be his sponsor. He's more in tune with the needs of the 'alternately existing.'"

Larry grinned and shook his head.

"That's not possible." Jacob said. "Larry's leaving the stocking team. He's been promoted to security."

THE ZOMBIE MIKE CHRISTMAS SPECIAL

by Terry Alexander

Derrick McKnight stepped through the curtains to thunderous applause and walked to a small center-stage podium. The hem of his blood red Santa coat dragged the floor, a heavy goody-bag slung over his shoulder. Harsh overhead lighting reflected on his ebony forehead. He waved to the audience and lifted the microphone to his lips. "Ladies and Gentlemen, welcome to the Zombie Mike Christmas Special. In keeping with the season, we have a very special event for you tonight." His deep voice resonated through the small theater.

The applause echoed in the auditorium.

Four large screens dominated the stage behind him. They crackled to life at a wave of his hand. "We've upgraded the monitors for this extravaganza. These screens will give the studio audience the highest resolution and clearest picture possible, and the state-of-the-art cameras we've placed inside our location will provide the television viewer the best experience possible."

"Christmas is the season for giving. Do you remember the excitement of opening presents on Christmas morning?" Derrick reached into the gift bag and withdrew a stack of greenbacks. "Tonight three players will challenge Zombie Mike for a one million dollar payday."

Derrick pulled a yellow tablet from the gift bag. "Let's meet our players." The applause echoed from the concrete walls. "This fine looking lady has sent ten zombies straight to hell. Before the war she was a school teacher from Oklahoma. Welcome, Cathy Sasnett."

A tall, dark-haired woman walked on stage, a spotlight circled her and followed her every movement. She waved to the audience and blew the grizzled veterans crowding the front row a kiss. The screen flashed to a grainy photo of Cathy, holding a severed head by the hair.

The seniors in the front row jumped to their feet. "Damn, she's a looker. Wouldn't you like to find that gift wrapped under the tree? She looks like a million bucks and kills zombies. What more could a man want?"

A blush crept up her face. She nodded to her admirers and stood at Derrick's side.

"He's a small man with a big desire to kill zombies, his favorite weapon is a roofing hatchet to the head. Welcome Zipper Hayes." Derrick gestured to the curtain.

A sandy-haired man, barely five-four with a small mustache, raced onstage, the spotlight operator having a tough time tracking his speed and movements. A jagged scar ran the length of his face. He yanked the microphone from Derrick's hand. "I'm Zipper Hayes," he shouted. "I'm here for the green. I'm a zombie killing motherfucker and when I kill Mike, that'll be the icing on my birthday cake. The only thing I like more than killing these carrion eaters is pussy." His eyes settled on Cathy, he licked his lips suggestively. "When this is over, why don't you and me hook up? You can help me spend my cash."

Cathy's eyes narrowed. "I only mess around with humans."

"Uppity bitch, ain't you."

Derrick yanked the mic from Zipper's grasp. "Hope you fight as well as you talk." He turned to the camera, a wide smile plastered on his face. "A friend of mine is playing tonight. Before the outbreak, he was an MMA fighter with a professional record of 16 wins and 4 losses. From The City of Angels, put your hands together for my old running buddy, Carl 'Bazooka' Runnels."

A tall man stepped through the curtains. The light reflected on his ebony skin. He ripped his shirt off, and poised for the crowd, flexing his bulging muscles. "Mike's gonna have a bad day. He ain't ready for this ass whipping." He did a standing back-flip and threw several shadow punches. Carl and Derrick fist bumped and mugged for the camera. He settled in next to Zipper.

Derrick pointed to the center monitor. "Here's the star of the show, Zombie Mike."

The image of a walking corpse filled the large center screen. His cheeks bloodless and pale, a yellow tint circled his eyes and mouth. Clear fluid drained from several facial wounds. A line of drool hung from his bottom lip, sticking to the red and white costume.

"In keeping with the Christmas spirit, all of our players will be dressed like that jolly old elf, Saint Nick. Believe me; it wasn't easy getting Mike in that costume." Derrick turned to the contestants. "We're bringing back an old Christmas tradition, but with a twist. In the center of the Peterson Brothers Slaughter House is a gift bag. Each contestant must get a chunk of coal from the bag and give it to a crew member when they exit the building, to qualify for the grand prize."

Derrick paused to draw a breath. "To maintain the holiday spirit, Christmas songs will be played in the background." He turned to the contestants. "After you change into your outfits, each of you will be taken to separate entrance points. We'll give you a map showing the location of the sack and an exit."

The players followed a scantily clad young woman off stage to heavy applause. Derrick held up his hands for silence. The uproar slowly died to scattered claps. "As usual, there are weapons hidden inside for the players to use against Zombie Mike, but as always there are pitfalls, booby-traps to snare the unwary. Now, Ladies and Gentlemen, place your bets. You can't win if you don't wager." A wide toothy grin split Derrick's face. "Before the action starts, let's pause for a moment, for a word from one of our sponsors, The Acme Food Company of Peoria, Illinois. There's nothing better than an Acme burger, they use real meat, not meat substitute."

Snow collected in Cathy's hair. She brushed it from her eyes and wiped her palms on the red pants. The flannel outfit chaffed her skin. She stood in the cattle pens, studying the crude map, her entry point a rusty metal door marked with an X. The stunner and the killing room lay inside. She moved forward, her bare hands touched the cold metal door, and chills raced up her arm. "Jingle Bells" played softy through the overhead speakers. Rusty hinges creaked as she forced her way inside. The lingering odor of death and old blood filled her nostrils. She passed a stainless steel table, piled high with the tools of the trade.

A two pound kill hammer caught her attention, one end flat, the other end tapering to a narrow point. Dark stains colored the hickory handle.

She remembered the old stories from her great grandfather about hog slaughter days. On a cold November day, all the neighbors would gather together to lay in their winter meat. Ten to twenty hogs would be killed before sunset. Great Granddad would regale her with stories of Ned Whitehall, a Cherokee Indian who favored an eight pound sledgehammer. A single hard swat between the eyes and the hog went down, waiting for the knife to sever the jugular.

Her trembling hand circled the handle. The weight surprised her, two pounds of guaranteed killing power, if what Great Grandpa said was true. She jammed the handle in her wide belt, the metal head riding against her hip.

Cathy glanced at the map. A bold line led through the double doors at the far end of the kill floor, then up the stairs to the second floor. A large smiley face marked the location of the gift bag. Her footsteps echoed from the walls. "Silent Night" began.

"Run up the stairs, grab the coal and run like hell for the exit," she whispered. "That's all I have to do."

"Well, Miss Sasnett is making progress. Can she win the million dollars? It's certainly possible, but Zombie Mike won't make things easy. We'll check on her and our other players in a moment, but first let's visit the star of the show." The screen flashed to a close-up of Mike's face, his milky eyes glared into the camera. A large rat stood on his back legs nibbling at a chunk of flesh dangling from Mike's hand.

Bony fingers circled the rodent. Mike's mouth stretched to accommodate the animal's size. Sharp claws tore at his hand and wrists, shredding the dead flesh. Chisel teeth bit at his rotten nose. Jagged teeth closed on the rodent. Rat blood squished from Mike's lipless mouth, and dribbled down his chin.

"Mike is enjoying a snack. I hope he doesn't ruin his appetite. Let's check on Zipper Hayes. The short man may suffer from a Napoleon complex, but I want to see if he can live up to his boasts." Static and snow filled the third screen. "We're having problems with the camera." A flustered Derrick stared at the monitor. "We'll take a commercial break, as our technical staff resolves this situation. Now, a word from the Double D Bullets, stock up now before the next attack. Try the new splatter round, guaranteed to kill with a single headshot."

Derrick walked to the rear of the stage. He switched the microphone off and glared at the tech crew. "What in the hell is going on? I thought you guys had the bugs ironed out."

"Mr. McKnight, we checked the system three times. It was working great. I can't understand what happened." A pudgy man in coveralls answered.

"I don't want excuses. I want the damned thing fixed. We're putting on a show here. We've got millions of viewers waiting for action. The audience wants action. If we want the big wagers we have to provide the audience action." Derrick switched the mic on and turned to the audience, his trademark smile on his face. "While my staff is dealing with the present difficulties, we'll check in on Bazooka Runnels."

Zipper crouched in the shadows of an empty supply closet off the main hallway. He watched as Cathy walked by and hesitated at the stairs. After a moment of indecision, her hand closed on the metal handrail. She gazed into the darkness as she took the first step.

"Sorry," Zipper whispered into the thumb sized microphone. "One of the other players was too close. Had to wait until she passed. Where is the neutralizer?"

"Second floor in the Santa bag." A distorted voice answered. "It'll shut down the feeding receptors in Mike's brain and render him harmless. Whatever you do, protect him at all costs. Once we kidnap him on live national television, it'll ruin Derrick McKnight's career. Then the government will be forced to listen to our demands for zombie rights. No more radio use, until you're on the roof and ready for pickup."

"We'll be there." Zipper broke the connection.

Carl Runnels gazed down the dark hallway, a shiver ran the length of his spine. A single light glowed over the doors at the far end. "Silent Night" ended, and switched to "Deck the Halls." He jammed the crumpled map in his pocket. The patter of tiny feet across the concrete floor caught his attention.

"What the shit was that?" He side-stepped and peered into the darkness. Something moved on the floor. "Fucking rats." He jumped forward and hurried toward the light. Nervous perspiration dotted his forehead. He sleeved the moisture away, remembering the early days of the outbreak.

California was a hellhole. The contagion decimated ninety per cent of the population within the first week. No one knew how to deal with the creatures during the first days. Everyone made the same mistake, thinking they could reason with, or capture the re-animated dead. Humane tactics failed miserably. The survivors discovered that gem of information the hard way. He lost Shelia and Julie during the third week. They tried to escape from the city to the less populated rural areas. The major highways were jammed with thousands of abandoned vehicles. They joined a large group, and walked the interstate for three days. Then the horde attacked. No one was prepared.

The herd closed in on all sides, hundreds of the rotten cadavers, hungry for fresh meat. He grabbed Shelia's hand and ran, desperately searching for a hiding place. Shelia clutched Julie to her chest, straining to keep pace. A pickup with an extended camper caught his eye. It wasn't the perfect hiding spot, but it would serve. Carl raced toward the vehicle, pulling Shelia forward. She fell to the hard concrete, Julie slipped from her hands. The baby squalled, drawing the herd closer.

"Get up." Carl bounced on his feet, glancing from his family to the oversized camper. "Come on, damn it, get up."

"Carl, help me." Shelia struggled to her feet, a round dot of blood discolored her pants at the knee. The circle grew steadily larger. She grabbed Julie and cradled the squalling infant in her arms.

The zombies shambled closer. An ice cold hand closed on Carl's wrist, hot drool landed in the crook of his elbow. Unreasoning terror clawed at his heart. He jerked his hand away and ran.

"Carl, don't leave us. Please, Carl. Don't leave us."

The terrified cries of his wife and daughter rang in his ears. He crawled to the roof of the camper. Tears filled his eyes as he listened to the screams of the dying, the crack of breaking bones and the slurping of blood. He lived with those sounds for the last five years. They haunted him every day. He had an opportunity to save his family, but chose to save himself.

Wiping tears from his eyes, he shook his head to banish the memories. Derrick offered him a chance to make it right, a chance to kill Zombie Mike. The stench hit him, as he shouldered through the door, the heavy odor of rot and corruption. It's Mike. Carl stared into the darkness.

Unable to pierce the thick shadows, he eased forward. A metal tray clattered on the floor. A chill tingled up Carl's spine. He turned to run, an unvoiced scream lodged in his throat. A row of lights came on showing him a path to a second doorway.

Zombie Mike shuffled into the dim light, blood covered his chin. He threw the rat to the floor, his white eyes focusing on Carl. His awkward gait propelled him toward the fighter.

Carl ran, heart beating like a trip-hammer. He circled Mike easily and raced down the lighted path. There should be stairs on the other side of these doors. He slammed into a solid unyielding door. Something crunched in his shoulder. Carl fell to the floor, his squinting eyes focused on Zombie Mike.

"Bazooka's really in a jam." Derrick gestured to the screen. "Can he escape Mike and make it to the gift bag, or will he be the first victim?" He glanced to the technician standing off stage and received a thumbs up from the portly man. "I've just been informed Zipper Hayes' camera is now working. We'll check on him after this break."

He flashed a mouthful of even white teeth. "Don't forget to place your bets. First contact betters that picked Carl are cashing in. Place your bets. Who will live and who will die? Place your bets." Derrick faced the center camera. "Now, a word from our newest sponsor, Rotrell Cigarettes, voted number one by the Seventh Colorado Militia."

"O Christmas Tree" drifted from hidden speakers.

Zipper moved cautiously toward the stairs. He had to find Mike. The ZRC wanted to make a political statement and rub Derrick McKnight's nose in shit; kidnapping the most famous zombie on earth seemed to fit the bill. The problem was getting Mike out of the slaughterhouse in one piece. Zipper had no intention of dying to further the agenda of the ZRC. He'd taken this job for the long green they promised.

A blood curdling scream prickled the flesh along his arms. "Oh God, someone help me."

Zipper ran toward the sound. "Carl, where are you?"

"Over here. The fucking door's blocked. I can't get out," Carl shouted. "Mike's in here. Get me out, man."

"I'm nearly there. Keep dodging him." Zipper rounded a corner. A metal door vibrated from Runnels' pounding. A rusted latch held it closed.

"Easy for you to say." Carl's screamed, hysteria heavy in his voice. "You ain't the one in here."

"Give me a second. The latch is stiff." Zipper strained against the knobby handle, rust flakes rained to the floor as he moved the bolt back and forth. "Keep running. I'll have it open in a second."

"Hurry up, damn it."

"We have a Good Samaritan in tonight's episode." Derrick gestured to Zipper's frozen image. "This offers a unique gambling opportunity, Ladies and Gentlemen. Can Zipper Hayes save Carl before Zombie Mike enjoys a bite of human flesh? And why is Zipper doing this? What is his motive? Place your bets. You can't win if you don't wager. Be one of the lucky few to win cash and prizes. Let's take a quick glance at Carl."

Zombie Mike slapped the steel table, reaching for Carl. A wet growl came from his inhuman throat. "Zipper, quit fucking around and get the door open." Carl pressed his back to the wall. Mike's reaching hand caught in the red velvet sleeve and ripped it from the Santa suit. An involuntary shudder raced through Carl.

"Hang on a few more seconds. It's coming loose." Zipper worked the rusted latch back and forth.

"If he bites me, put a bullet in my brain. I don't want to change into one of these things," Carl shouted. "Promise me, you won't let me turn."

With a clack, the bolt slid free. Carl glimpsed a shaft of light through the open door and the face of Zipper Hayes.

He braced his feet against the wall, and shoved the table violently. It skidded across the concrete floor and slammed Mike's stomach. The zombie fell to the floor clawing at air, as Carl raced past.

"Get the hell out of my way." He shoulder blocked Zipper, sending him sprawling.

"Carl Runnels escaped. Everyone who bet on Bazooka's survival is counting their winnings." Derrick slapped the podium with a resounding thud. "Come on, people, place those bets. Who will be the first to fall and who will live? Chose a side wager: What is Zipper Hayes' secret agenda? What's he up to? Who is he working for? Place your bets and find out."

Derrick turned to the side camera. "Before we go to a commercial break, Double D Bullets has sweetened the pot. They're giving a thousand rounds of ammunition to the first at-home viewer that correctly names the first victim. Place those bets now."

The wild screams bouncing from the concrete walls made Cathy flinch. She quickened her step. Knowing Mike was busy dealing with one of the other contestants gave her a surge of hope.

A single light hung from an electric wire above her prize. The gift bag, blood red with white trim, sat in the middle of the floor. Cathy's heart thumped wildly in her chest. One million dollars, she drew in a deep breath. A high-pitched squeal came from the darkness. She gazed into the shadows. Small close set red eyes returned her stare. A dead weight settled in her stomach. "Twelve Days of Christmas" played in the background.

Rats, fucking rats. She raced toward the bag, squashing two slow moving females under her boots. The others scattered, running to the far corners of the room. The temptation of fresh blood and meat proved to be too great, the starving vermin scampered across the floor and fell on their dead.

Cathy's footsteps echoed in the empty space. Rats scurried in her path, circling her feet. She failed to see the trip wire near the floor. Her boot caught on the slender strand. After a second of resistance, the line snapped. A weighted pendulum dropped from the ceiling, and slammed her thigh.

An explosion of pain radiated through her leg, bone snapped like a dried stick. She fell to the floor in agony. "Shit." Tears filled Cathy's eyes. "Shit, shit, shit." She gritted her teeth against the pain. *Should have taken my time, I knew about the traps.*

Cathy crawled along the floor, determined to get the Christmas sack. Waves of pain shot through her leg with each movement.

Hungry rats circled just out of reach. Crimson eyes fastened on her as the vermin lost their fear and drew closer.

"Miss Sasnett is certainly in a jam. What do you think, ladies and gentlemen? Will she live or is she toast?" Derrick gestured toward the screen. "Place those bets, now. Be one of the lucky ones to win big money." He turned a solemn face to camera one. "Before we return to our program, I'd like for you to see this short message from Rotrell Cigarettes."

Carl bounded up the stairs. Nervous sweat ran down his face and dripped onto his shirt. His heart hammered against his ribs.

He sprinted past Cathy, as she crawled across the concrete floor, swinging the kill hammer at the rats. Two lay within reach, several devoured the dead and injured animals, as they kicked their life away.

"Carl," she screamed. "Damn it, Carl, help me."

Bazooka Runnels ignored her pleas. The vermin scattered as he passed, scurrying to the far walls. Sweaty palms closed on the cloth bag. A smile of triumph curled his lips, as he reached inside. His excitement turned to terror in an instant.

"Shit." He threw the bag in the air. It dropped to the floor spilling the contents. A small box-shaped device shattered on the concrete floor. "Damn it." A large rodent clung to Carl's hand, chisel teeth buried in his palm. Blood threaded from the wound and dripped to the floor.

"Son of a bitch," Carl shook his hand violently. The rat's clawed feet raked his wrist and forearm. The starving rodent tore chunks from his hand and swallowed them whole. "Let go, mutha fucker." He grabbed the tail and peeled the animal away. Carl slammed the female on the hard floor and crushed the body under his feet. A dozen of its brethren jumped on the bloody smear, devouring the remains.

"Sorry, fucker." Carl's blood splattered to the cold floor. The overpowering scent drove the remaining vermin berserk. The squealing mass leaped on his legs, biting the red pants seeking the flesh beneath. The song ended. "We Three Kings" immediately began.

"Bazooka's in a jam again. Can he and Miss Sasnett survive the rats?" Derrick's voice rang through the auditorium. He mopped his forehead with a white hanky. "Place your bets. Will they live through the rodent attack or fall victim to Zombie Mike? Maybe they'll claim the big prize? And what about Zipper? What is he up to? When we last looked in on him, he was in grave danger. Is he alive or dead? Place those bets, now."

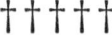

Mike crawled through the open door. Zipper rolled from his outstretched hands. Gray rotting fingers closed on the cuff of his Santa suit. The pants ripped at the outer seam all the way to his thigh. He kicked the monster's face, dislodging one of the monster's few remaining teeth.

Zipper rolled away from Mike's flailing hands and climbed to his feet. "Come on, you bastard. Get up. Come on, don't you want a taste of Zipper." He stomped

Mike's fingers, snapping the bones.

"You're going to have to do better than that, if you want to get me." He kicked Mike and danced away, staying out of his reach. "Come on. Get on your feet. We need to get to the roof."

Mike struggled to rise. After several attempts, he awkwardly gained his feet. Clear ooze drained from his nose cavity. Broken teeth dangled from his split gums.

Zipper backed toward the staircase, placing each foot carefully. "Come on, you ugly fucker," he taunted. "The ZRC is paying good money for you."

Mike stumbled after his elusive quarry. Zipper's hand circled the metal hand-rail. He thumped the step with his boot heel. Got to do this in stages. Zombies don't do stairs well.

Zipper bounded up three steps. "Come on, Ugly. Keep coming."

"Help!" A high pitched shriek came from the second floor. "Somebody help me."

"That's Cathy," Zipper whispered. "What the hell is going on?"

Carl raced down the staircase, a blood-covered piece of coal gripped in his hand. "Get out of my way." He shoved Zipper to the side.

"Carl, wait! Mike is…" Zipper shouted.

"Oh, Fuck." Carl's dying scream echoed through the abandoned building.

"Joy to the World" played in the background.

"Carl Runnels is Mike's first victim. Told him to keep a cool head, but he didn't listen. Everyone who chose Carl is collecting their winnings right now." Derrick gazed at Carl's bloodstained image. Zombie Mike knelt over the body, tearing huge chunks of his flesh and neck. "He was so close, too. But there are two more players in this contest. Can one of them get a piece of coal and escape? And what is Zipper's agenda? Will we discover what he is after? We'll get back to the show after this message."

Zipper stared in awe as Mike tore chunks of flesh from Carl's corpse and swallowed it whole.

"Come on, Mike," he mumbled. "It's time to shove off. We need to get to the roof." Zipper blundered onto the second floor, unprepared for the swarming rats.

Cathy sat under the weak light, the Christmas sack at her back, the broken suppressor scattered on the floor. A red smear covered the head of the kill ham-mer. The rats circled just out of reach, darting in to bite her fingers and hands.

"Zipper, help me," she screamed. "There's too many of them. I can't fight them off."

"Great, zombies and fucking rats." Zipper kicked the starving rodents from his path, mashing several under his boots. "We need Mike up here. Maybe he'll forget about us when he sees all these rats."

"I don't need a lecture on zombie feeding habits. Get me out of here." The hammer descended on a skinny rodent with a solid thump.

"Mike's on the stairs. He killed Carl." He offered her his hand. "Come on, get up. We'll hide on the far side of the door and hope he focuses on the rats. When he gets here, we'll duck down the stairs."

"I can't walk, dumbass. My leg's broken."

"This just keeps getting better and better." He lifted her from the floor. Struggling with her weight, he staggered toward the door. "Hopefully he'll chase the rats. After he passes, we'll get downstairs and out of this hell hole."

"What about the coal? You need to get a piece of coal."

"McKnight won't be giving me any money." His cheeks puffed out, as he repositioned her weight.

Cathy's drawn pale face crinkled in agony. "Why are you here?"

"The Zombie Rights Coalition hired me. They wanted to make a political statement. They believe humans and zombies can co-exist. After what I've seen tonight, I think their plan is fucked." He leaned against the wall, easing the strain on his shoulders and back. He kept his feet moving, hoping to keep the starving rats at bay.

The song switched to "O Come, All Ye Faithful."

"I wish they'd turn off that fucking music," Zipper grunted. He watched as the hungry rodents devoured the dead and injured, hoping Zombie Mike would reach the second floor before they finished their meal.

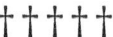

"There you have it, Ladies and Gentlemen. Zipper Hayes is a ZRC spy. Those of you who made the right choice can cash in now." Derrick smiled for the studio audience. "As a special incentive to our at-home audience, The Dundee Brothers Coffee Company has promised a year's supply of their fine brew to the first hundred people in our TV audience who select the winner of tonight's event."

Derrick wiped his face with the damp hanky. "We're nearing the end of this game, but before we discover who will claim the big prize, listen to these words from The Dundee Brothers."

Blood dripped from Mike's chin. He shambled up the stairs, bouncing from wall to wall, and through the open door. Sensing his approach, the rats scrambled to escape.

Zipper peered from the gap on the hinge side. *Come on, just a few more steps, just a few more.* The muscles screamed in his back and shoulders, Cathy slipped in his grasp. He struggled to readjust his grip. Sweat beaded his forehead. Zipper bit his lower lip, offering a silent prayer that Mike would move away from the door.

A fleeing rat darted between Mike's legs. It circled the door and leaped into the air. Sharp claws caught in Zipper's pants. The panicked rodent dashed up his leg and jumped onto Cathy's chest.

"Get this fucking thing off me. Get it off." She slapped at the terrified rodent.

Zipper shoved the door, tried to force his way past Mike to the stairway. The zombie's hands closed on his shoulder. Zipper took the first step, hoping to pull away from Mike's grasp. Cathy's weight shifted. Zipper's ankle turned, his weight pitched forward, carrying him down the stairs. Cathy slipped from his arms, rolling down the steps. A rotting hand closed in his hair. Zipper twisted. He fell down the stairs; his momentum carried Mike along.

Zipper lay on the concrete floor. His body burned with pain. He lifted his head to check on Cathy. A low moan escaped her lips. He groaned, and rolled to a sitting position. A hot numbness radiated through his left arm. Jagged bone jabbed through the forearm, the limb flopped uselessly at his side.

Mike rolled to his belly and struggled to stand, purple intestines drooping from a gaping hole in his stomach. He moved forward on unsteady legs.

Mike's hand closed in Cathy's hair. Zipper slowly gained his feet and lashed out in desperation. "Leave her alone, Mother Fucker!" His fist smashed the zombie's face. His knuckles slammed the open mouth. Mike's jagged teeth tore the flesh. The zombie staggered from the blow, waving his arms like a drunk.

Zipper grabbed Cathy's arm, and dragged her toward the exit. A burning sensation centered in his bleeding hand.

Mike stumbled forward. He dropped to his knees, his feet tangled in his intestines.

The overhead music switched to "Go Tell it on the Mountain." Zipper slammed the panic bar, he struggled to move Cathy's limp body beyond the threshold. The closing door caught on her boots. Zipper pushed her feet aside and stepped inside the slaughter house.

"Okay, you son of a bitch. We've got things to settle."

Mike's outstretched arms reached for Zipper's throat.

"And there you have it, another exciting episode of The Zombie Mike Show. Congratulations to Cathy Sasnett, as the winner and sole survivor of tonight's contest. Our at-home viewers and studio audience who made the correct bets are cashing in right now. If you are one of the lucky gamblers, go claim your prize." Derrick stopped for a moment listening to a backstage voice through the small device in his ear.

"Ladies and Gentlemen, it appears that Miss Sasnett lost the lump of coal she was required to bring with her. She is disqualified. Since she's the only living contestant, the prize money will roll over and the next payout will be two million dollars." He gazed at the image on the screen of Zipper and Mike battling near the door.

"The ZRC gave it a good shot, but they can't stop Zombie Mike. Zipper Hayes will be delivered to their headquarters tomorrow. I trust Ryan Clark and his cronies will use his remains for scientific research. Bazooka Runnels will be humanely dispatched. His remains will be burned at a private ceremony."

Derrick smiled for the audience. "I know this has been a stressful few years, but we are slowly winning the world back. I want everyone to enjoy the Christmas season. Be sure to join us after the holidays for the next exciting installment of The Zombie Mike Show."

BITTER
INHERITANCE

by Jason S. Ridler

Tasteless Uzbek coffee burned Ludris's tongue. In the stadium seats of the Compound, hard currency thugs gulped expensive liquor in plastic cups, made bets, and talked too loud. Ludris sat front row for the troll fight. Would Bogdan demand anything less, he wondered, even if the rest of the seats were empty?

"Hope you enjoy it, Sideshow," Bogdan said, fanning himself with his gold betting sheet, dressed like a sparkling Christmas present. "And afterward, I have prepared some dessert." He cackled, as if the plan he'd hatched was genius.

"Great," Ludris said. It could be only one thing. A fight with some Dullas street samurai, one that earned Bogdan the satisfaction of making the civilians of this world dance to his tune, meanwhile Father's debt remained tight around Ludris's neck. Ludris sipped slowly.

"Hey," Bogdan said, "it's my birthday. Try not to look like such a beaten troll." He cackled more, knowing damn well that few things were as trollish as what Bogdan referred to as Ludris's Latvian smile of mashed teeth, mangled lip. Face only a troll could love.

"Yes, boss," Ludris said. But if tonight was like any other, after the fight, he'd win the chance have his face used as a punching bag against whatever Moscow thug with a fistful of judo and a lifetime of beatings had to offer. As much a puppet as a re-animated troll.

"Wait," Bogdan said. "Here it comes. You'll love him!"

The Compound gave a sour roar as the first troll lumbered toward the cage, barbed wire wrapped around his forearm, limping to the steel octagon like a rusty Soviet tractor. A klaxon voice screamed in pale imitation of American ring announcers. "He's back from a Baltic grave and craves glory. Shout out for the Riga Mangler!"

Boos rained down heavy on the lurking giant. Ludris sipped. How far we've fallen from Rome and Greece, he thought. These trolls were zombies at the gate.

Moscow was believed to be the third Rome, once upon a time. How fitting.

"He a cousin of yours, Sideshow?" Bogdan asks, plucking a new coca leaf from its case and shoving into his big mouth.

"Yes. He has father's eyes. He never gave them back."

Bogdan laughed with a full, wet mouth, and slapped Ludris' torn jean jacket. After spitting a dark wad onto the concrete floor covered with peanuts and teeth, he gasped. "If he was your Dad, they'd sell out this place every night! Ha! For a bodyguard, you've got a twisted wit." He chewed and adjusted his wide collar and jacket, worth half a month worth of debt. "Are you sure you don't want some leaf?"

Ludris nodded. "Not good for my Latvian smile."

Bogdan laughed again, as if it was the first and best joke he had ever heard. Chewing, spitting, chewing, spitting, eyes starting to shine. The Friday night ritual. Ludris knew Bogdan would soon bore of the fights, and look for his own. But what then? How many Fridays until father's debt was paid? A thousand…he'd lost track. It was too depressing. Not that you can pay back the horrors Dad had unleashed, all of them without Bogdan's father's approval, all of them getting publicity the crime family did not want. Off the deep end, they'd shot him at a distance, too scared to get near his killing hands. Father had chained his son for the crimes he committed against Bogdan's family. Forever.

Ludris sipped.

The Riga Mauler stood in the ring, green skin freshly reanimated and almost shiny. The computer jammed in his neck like a single Frankenstein bolt. Hello, cousin, Ludris thought. I hope whoever made your chip was not drunk on Balsam.

"His opponent," said the announcer, "From Siberia. With a perfect record—"

"Uncle Joe! Uncle Joe!" Bogdan chanted, and the crowd followed. The troll was an anabolic nightmare, a brush mustache stitched above his lips, a dull hammer and rusty sickle where his hands had been. What was next, Ludris thought, Zombie Trotsky vs. Undead Lenin with Vampire Marx as the referee?

Bogdan was out of his seat. "Go Joe! Eat his head!"

Others took up the chant, on their feet.

Ludris sipped and let his eyes wander, and found beauty. Around the front row sat a catalog of glamorous women. Soft, lithe, faces painted to opulent extremes that gave them a quality you'd never encounter on the Metro, a kind of beauty he'd dreamed of long ago in Jelgava, reading comic book pornography in his father's old chest. So much tender beauty. Soft and lush and close—

He bit the inside of his cheek with a jagged tooth until they blurred and the bell rang.

Don't play with fire. Don't open that box. Or you'll end up as he did, far worse than chained with debt. When they finally stopped shooting them there was only a stain.

Bogdan screamed as Uncle Joe slashed and crunched the Riga Mangler to meat and bone. And Ludris relapsed toward beauty, then picked at a scar on his hand while the words of Rilke ran through him like ice. "For beauty is nothing but the beginning of terror which we are barely able to endure, and it amazes us so, because it serenely disdains to destroy us."

As Uncle Joe shambled to the locker room, green chest wearing jelly blood stains, Ludris wondered if father had ever read Rilke. And if he had, would it have stopped him from mutilating all those women?

The rest of the night was clockwork. Bogdan chewed leaves, made brash claims, then bumped into a pale-skinned kid outside the Compound and started mouthing off. "Do you know who I am?"

And they all did. And they did not care. And that was when Bogdan said. "Ludris. Go to work."

Thankfully, not one of the bruisers knew a wrist lock from a wrist watch. A busted knee cap, cracked elbow, and guillotine choke and it was finally over. All traces of beauty had been lost in the parking lot melee.

"They didn't even touch you!" Bogdan said, raising his hand. "This is the real Riga Mangler!"

Ludris was from Jelgava. It also made no difference. He huffed as their ride came, and tried to summon the beauty of the front row. Instead he saw his Latvian smile in the tinted window of the Humvee.

While that Cossack Semyon drove, Bogdan and Ludris faced each other in the wide passenger hold, bigger than Ludris's apartment. Bogdan smiled beneath his razor thin mustache. "Hungry for dessert, Sideshow? Or do you live on coffee and jujitsu alone?"

Outside, Electric Moscow glittered against May rain. "Depends on dessert."

"How about freedom?"

Ludris moved very, very slowly. Bogdan could be a shit, a fucking Uzbek of a boss, but he'd never dangled that word in front of him before. Now, a five-leaf smile pasted on his face, he looked like a grinning god. "As of tonight, you've worked off your father's debts to my family."

"Impossible—"

"Do you want the math? Five dead whores, each would make us a collective value of about a hundred grand a year, right? And most are burned out in a year or two, so, that's a million hard right there. But I've been betting against the odds with you for five years. Five years! And you've destroyed the competition every time, even when I tossed whole gangs of thugs at you, or ex-Spetznaz assholes, or whatever. You had the odds against you every time and I came up big! And, hell, you've been a good partner in crime. Even though you act like a fucking monk." He laughed. "A funny monk, but a monk none the less." He opened the centre drawer and pulled out a bottle. Ludris assumed it was expensive champagne. "See? I don't throw you to the jackals just for the fun of it. You'd never be free on a bodyguard's salary. And you've made me feared on the street." His grin was twisted. "I wish father was more feared, you know? That the name Lechies would make me bullet proof. But the truth is, Daddy is old school. Old fart even remembers communism. And he's not half the man I'm going to be." He unwrapped the cork. "And you are much more than your father ever was, fighting skills be damned. He never would have survived the shit I threw at you. And you don't suffer from his... appetites. Amazing that, since such things do run in families."

Ludris breathed.

"But we are better than those who trained us, Sideshow. We deserve better than they provide. For me, that means the growth of the Lechies empire. For you, the freedom to chose your fate. And if you want, that fate can still be with me. And instead of killing debt, you'll earn hard currency." He popped the cork.

Ludris caught it before it hit his throat.

Bogdan howled. "I have my own Jedi Knight! I am a fool for letting you go. But you've earned it. Give me the cork and take a glass." He did, and Bogdan poured. "Let us toast this last night as master and servant. Tomorrow, we meet again as free men."

They clinked glasses. Bogdan downed it in single shot, not savouring the taste, but wanting the feeling hidden in those bubbles. Ludris tapped the glass with his scarred finger, the thick cut on the index from the knife fight Bogdan had tossed him in with some Muscovite on angel dust...then there was the arm he broke blocking a pipe shot in a club when the trolls got out of their poke cages...the bullet that just missed his lung during a drug hand off on the outskirts of Central Moscow...Each time, Bogdan healed him with boiler room doctors. Never adding the expense to the old man's debt.

For a scoundrel, Bogdan had a rogue's honour.

So, for the first time since being tazed and dragged into the family Lechies' service, Ludris took a long, deep pull of liquor. "Thank you."

Bogdan poured another glass. "My pleasure."

One taste was all he could handle as memory raced and the hummer slowed outside of a concrete bunker of buildings. "What is this?"

Bogdan shoved in another leaf, resembling a bulimic squirrel. "Dessert."

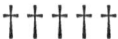

Lilacs, opium and vodka gave the pink hallways a tangy decadence. Ludris winced. But worse than that was the sound. Nothing. Soundproof. Anything could be happening behind those doors.

But he couldn't leave.

He knew how Bogdan's mind worked.

This was a gift, but also a test and power play. If he refused while still under his service, the carrot of freedom would be stomped into oblivion before his very eyes.

It was also a sick game. Bogdan knew what father had done to prostitutes. Everyone from Talinn to T'bilisi knew. Even in a world of chip-controlled cadavour fights, the human beast was still the most terrifying, and the seeds of that horror, Ludris knew, were in his blood. But he had not let them hatch—

"I don't feel very good," he said.

"Relax, Sideshow," Bogdan said, then spat at the red Persian carpet. "I know this must be difficult. To be a virgin at your age." He laughed. The majesty of the carpet design under their feet, of ancient craft Ludris would normally enjoy studying, made him dizzy. "But I would not feel right if you did not leave different than you arrived. This is a rite of manhood. And I will not have you free only to live life as a monk!" He laughed.

A warrior monk, Ludris thought. Like the Brethren of the Sword who pacified the pagans of the Baltic. Whose dedication to combat and agony kept them pure and free from sins of the flesh. But how many had monsters in their bellies? Krakens of brutality that preyed on beautiful things like acid on paper? Devouring that which they loved most? Sweat shook off his stubby, hard fingers.

They approached a braided door and Bogdan spun on his Cuban heels, gripping down his lapels. "This is it, Sideshow. Enjoy your night. And if you think of cheating, of just sitting in the corner and meditating for a half hour before you vanish, your debt will be doubled." He smiled and slapped both thin hands on Ludris's shoulders. "You came to me a boy, but you will leave a man." He jabbed Ludris's shoulder, then ran down the hallway to his own door. "Go in, go in!" he yelled.

Ludris did.

Soft light welcomed him. The room was sparse. An overly clean smell was covered up by jasmine perfumes that swallowed whatever foulness lay beneath.

The bed. The girl. Black hair, big and long. Crossed legs in stockings and feet locked in stilettos. Skin a dark green. A fresh lady troll. Wet, purple lips were pursed and inviting. Her thousand yard stare drilled him. A choker around her neck disguised whatever electronic wizardry had brought her back to life.

He remembered to breathe. "Hello."

She stood and his nerves twitched. Green beauty. An homage to desire and lust. Curves and the swell of movement as she stepped closer. What had she been when life ran in her veins? A stripper? A model? A daughter?

She stepped with the precision of a sniper between sets of heartbeats. His back hit the door. But freedom stayed his hand from embracing the knob and twisting as her breasts rested against his chest. Her head cocked to the left, the right. He expected to hear servos and gears clacking and gasping, to feel ice cold flesh.

Instead, warmth embraced his hand, and pulled him toward the bed. Her eyes never left his. The stare focused. He followed, blood like burning sand.

He sat stiffly as she undressed him. Not fighting. Not helping. Until he was cold and exposed, tight fists at his side as she pushed his chest so he finally lay down. Above him, she was more radiant, her beauty a rapture of symmetry and desire.

As his blood boiled, he shut his eyes as she mounted him. Rough, painful and slow, like being stretched in an arm bar. He saw the words of Camus like a neon sign in Moscow Square. "Beauty is unbearable, drives us to despair, offering us for a minute the glimpse of an eternity that we should like to stretch out over the whole of time."

Warm hands lay upon his chest, melting the ice on his eyes.

She stared down, mouth hitched open, hungry gasp.

He shut his eyes, body like silk on his rough skin. Panting, he listened for something other than his heart punching blood through his body, mind gripped in a kumate with itself. Will pleasure burn through me, eat all that was stable, and release the beast of sin Father had hid in my blood?

Pleasure flooded him and he tightened every muscle, every pore, every ounce of himself as she rode him. His mind screamed in the darkness for a tether, a life line, something to distract him from the swell of rapture rising—

Pain cracked across his face as she slapped him, hard.

Eyes wide, she tried it again, and he caught her wrist as his member retreated.

She winced. Her free hand slapped him, harder. He spun her wrist behind her back, pinning her to the bed as she grunted. "Punish me."

Sweat dripped from his busted nose and ran down her body.

Pleasure evaporated into shock. He released her and stood.

"Did I do something wrong?"

He covered himself. "You're no troll."

"Some find it easier this way."

Ludris stumbled back from her, legs numb. "Why did you hit me?"

She sat, legs crossed. "That's what you paid for. Did I do it wrong? Do you just want to hurt me? You own me until dawn."

He pulled his pants up, steel in his movements. "I do not own you."

She got on her knees. "I've upset you. Please, hurt me?"

"No!" He dressed fast, but felt weak…what the hell was in that champagne? "Just tell me where he is. Which room is Bogdan Lechies, and give me the code to his room."

He ran down the silent hall feverish with anger and narcotics racing through his veins, knowing full well what lay behind the doors, knowing what Bogdan had really wanted Ludris to become. And the Slavic turd was going to get it.

He punched in the key and entered the room, door slamming shut.

She was slumped in the corner, eyes wide, crimson flower staining her chest and leaking to the bed where Bogdan stood naked. "Sideshow! Done already? Glorious! I knew it wouldn't take much. We're brothers, now. Brothers!"

The girl's ample chest was motionless. Face a frozen pulp painting of agony. "No," Ludris said. "We're not. And I quit."

Rage inflamed Bogdan's happy face. "Quit?" He dove faster than a greased bullet and tackled Ludris. A breathless moment bit through him as Ludris slipped on the blood, spraining his ankle, pain like icicles shooting through his veins. Bogdan's bloody fists dropped down, sharp and quick, powered by hate and Momma Coca. "Quit? I own you! Own you!" Bogdan scrambled to get his knees on his chest, aiming for Ludris' shoulder.

Damn, Ludris thought. He's been practicing. He wants to pin my shoulders and then, what? Shit, he's quick. The room spun.

Knee on the chest, Bogdan mashed forward onto a mount. "Dizzy yet? You Latvian fuck, do you think I'd take you into a brothel without spiking your drink?" Blood became lead as Bogdan elbowed his face. "C'mon, Sideshow. Time for the main event! I want to see your Daddy's beast in you. C'mon, fight!"

A thundering elbow made the world swim in cascades of sparks and wonder. Thoughts drowned in the tangled mess of his mind as he fought for control.

A thud, then Bogdan slumped off to the side.

Water smacked Ludris's face. When the sparks died, he stared up at a beautiful face, slightly green. In her hand was an empty glass. "Get up."

He did.

Bogdan got to his knees, a knot on his head from where she'd hit him with a blackjack in her other hand. But he was rising. "Bitch, I'm going to sell what's left of you for dog food." He lunged.

Something burst through Ludris.

He gripped Bogdan's right wrist with his left hand and spun it tight so his momentum turned him over, balancing on his good foot. But he did not let go. He dragged him from the floor, iron grip unbreakable. "Free yourself. If you can."

Bogdan snarled and pulled while throwing an awkward punch Ludris telegraphed long before it was a thought in Bogdan's head. He slapped it to the left and hammer-stuck Bogdan's nose, sending him stumbling.

But he pulled him up. "Freedom is yours. Take it."

Bogdan was gasping, wet red breaths. "You're dead. You're both dead." He pulled away, and Ludris yanked once, hard, twisting him into a hammer lock. Bogdan screamed into the sound proof room as Ludris shoved him hard against the wall, the dead woman by their feet.

"I quit! I quit!"

He let go. Bogdan slumped to the ground beside the woman he murdered and defiled. Shaking, small, broken. Pathetic.

"Get out," Ludris said. Bogdan pulled his quivering mass from the ground. "If you come back, I'll kill you. If I see you, I'll kill you. If this girl is harmed, I'll kill you. And if you ever do this again, I'll tell your father. And you will wish that I had killed you tonight. Understand?"

Slowly, handfuls of fine clothes in his crimson hands, Bogdan left. When he was gone, Ludris kneeled before the dead woman and closed her wide eyes. "Did you know her?"

The live woman shook her head. "Why did you let him live?"

Ludris stood. So, I'm a fighter, not a killer. "What little honour I have is precious. What are we to do with her?"

"We have people."

"I'm not surprised."

"What are you going to do now?"

"Are your people hiring? Coolers, I mean. Muscle."

She smiled. "No. Sorry. Would defeat the purpose of this place if they thought there were repercussions."

He shook his head. "And what about you?"

"I still have debt. Sorry." She smiled, cracking some of her green makeup.

"Me, too."

†††††

He limped ten miles back to the Compound, clothes caked in debris and grit like a second skin. In the alley, glistening with moonlight, two trashmen were tossing a large Troll body into the dump. Its arm fell outside the dumpster, covered in barbed wire.

"Hey," Ludris said.

The two trashmen turned, reaching for guns. "What the fuck do you want?"

"Work."

"Yeah," said one, "do we look like Moscow Welfare?"

"I see you lost one of your trolls."

"So?" said the other. "Why do you care? Oh, shit...that's what's his name? You know, the shitheel who hangs with Lechies' kid."

He wiped the grit off his ugly face and raised his hands in surrender. "You need a celebrity to put asses in seats. I can do that."

"Right. And who the fuck are you?"

Ludris walked into a stitch of moonlight and they backed up. "I'm Ludris Ekles. Son of Ivan Ekles."

They're eyes went wide, and the one holding the Troll dropped him. "That sick freak?"

Ludris nodded. "And if you have green paint, I'm also the new Riga Mangler."

THE LAST CIRCUS

by DeAnna Knippling

It's the end of the world and my daughter is worried that we'll be late for the circus.

"Mom. These aren't our seats. We're in the wrong section? See, Section 116, not 216. We not supposed to be this far up."

"Oh, good."

She pulls on my hand and leads me back down the concrete steps. This place gives me vertigo. I'm afraid of heights. I could never be up there, dangling from the ceiling. There are going to be acrobats. They've been working on this for months.

It's cold in the arena, and we all have dirty coats on. Nothing's clean, everyone's hungry, we're all pale—even the black people look pale—and outside there are zombies. Leadership says it's getting better. We'll be able to go out soon. But I'm afraid of Dot getting skin cancer. I have nightmares about it. So stupid.

My main act is later in the show. What I love about it is the way everyone looks at me. I know, somewhere in the audience, that a child will ask its mother: "Is she naked?" And the mother will say, "No, darling, she's wearing a body suit." And it is true, but less true than the mother thinks. The child's eyes will see me more clearly. Men? Will see me with the eyes of fantasy. Women? With the eyes of jealousy. Children? Will see me fly. I do not care. I will be seen.

"Stop sticking your tits out and get warmed up."

But it is affectionate, the insult that only love can bring. He is only an acrobat. He will catch women who are thrown to him. Any woman. But me, I am the one he teases.

I flip through the screens. Leadership has forgotten some of the cameras face onto the parking lot. Yeah. I see 'em. I want to think it's like Dune, where the giant sandworms can hear your footsteps through the ground, so you gotta walk without rhythm if you don't want them to find you. We been practicing for months, music at all hours, featuring some pretty heavy bass. But fuck, I don't know, it could just be something random. There was a flood of zombies, and it will roll downhill until it hits us.

As far as the eye can see.

Fuck it. I got a board to run.

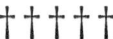

The lights go down and Dot shushes me. Nobody's got a camera or a cell phone, Leadership won't allow anybody to charge their batteries. I wish I could take a picture. Just one.

I wish there were dogs on roller skates. Or elephants.

The pulleys are silent today, is good. I swing out over the proscenium, I know it because of the marks on the track above me. Limp. I am arched backward, my heart open to the roof, to the sky. A cacophony echoes around me. Distractions. Nobody sees me—perhaps a child will see me. Once I heard the shout, in Russia, of a grown man who saw me before he was meant to see me. I found out later he was a mental defective. He saw me. I should like to perform for an audience full of mental defectives one day. Their vision is so brutally honest. I would purr for days.

Lieukov dangles. I keep an eye on it all. This is what thrills me: everything fucking going on all at once. Somebody was talking about automating it the other day. Get rid of the musicians and just use precanned shit. Saving on bodies, I guess. Put all the lighting and sound cues on a computer. Run the pulleys off a grid.

Nah. That's not theater, I told 'em. Ain't nobody's spirit going upward on the wings of full-scale karaoke. It takes everybody. A hundred hearts that don't want to beat as one. Beating as one. I'm a cynical son of a bitch, but I know that much. Have to build the electricity of synchronicity.

I should write a song for that. Pop song. Top 100 on the radio. Hah.

The zombies come out and I grab the arms of the seat.

"Ladies and gentlemen. Please be aware that the zombies you see here are not deadly threats. They are actors. Please holster all weapons. Repeat. Please holster all weapons."

Why am I here? Why are we doing this? I can't breathe.

Dot puts her skinny little arm around my back. "It's okay, Mom. It's not real."

I let the fabric roll around me. I fall. I fall a hundred feet—no, they tell me it's more like twenty feet, but it feels like a hundred. I love it every time.

Why here? Why not—New York? Or Barcelona? I would have loved to be trapped in Barcelona, surrounded by hairy, lisping men. "You are so tall. What is your name?"

But I would only smile and say nothing.

The children shriek, a woman gasps. I am twisting, fighting the red fabric, making love to it, hoping, despairing, fighting, surrendering. Below me are acrobats in costumes. He will catch me. He always catches me.

I move the spots with Lieukov. Underneath, the zombie extras try to grab her. The ribbon dances away. Every jerk, every flip, every thrust is perfectly timed. They grab, she swings—I mean, don't get me wrong. She's a fucking bitch. A whore. But goddamn, I get hard watching her up there. I think about plowing that ass every time.

And then she looks down at them, clutches her heart, and lets go. Gotta watch. For a second I see her pancaked on the stage. Every fucking time I see this.

Anton catches her, lucky prick.

Zombies swarm over her, stuff her in a zombie suit, and throw red ribbons over their shoulders. Stage is covered in blood. The cover of some old goth song is thumping through people's chests and the synths are running hot.

Intermission. Lights up. The audience can't move for a second. Then they get up to piss. Good thing the windows are blacked out with cement or blocked with steel panels.

I flip through the screens. Tyrell looks over at me from the sound board. I nod.

His bottom lip scrapes his teeth. But all I hear is the —ck.

"I want to see the stage, Mom."

So we head down when everyone else goes up. Blessed with big bladders, both of us. Ever since the rest stop in Topeka. There are foldout chairs on the floor, and I see they have no cushions.

I wish there were clowns. I want to laugh.

Dot takes one step onto one of the sets of stairs up to the stage, and the ushers flock toward her. They were watching her. Seeing so many people coming toward her at once, I pull my knife, run in front of her, and crouch low and wide, just like Danny taught me. The ushers pull back. "It's all right, ma'am. She just can't go on stage like that."

I'm shaking. We should just go.

In spring, they promise me, there will be flowers in the dressing rooms again. Now they are bare, I see them for what they are. Plain cement boxes, with bright, naked lights and mirrors. Racks of clothes. Makeup. When we traveled, I did not care. Dublin! Moscow! Detroit! No matter how shabby the room, how ruined the city, it was still romantic. But here, staying still like this. Ohhhh, I am dying.

I will sit over the audience instead of here, dangling my feet over the catwalk. Leadership will not like it.

But Leadership will not look up.

"We can't just lock the door, man."

"You want this placed packed with people? How many do you think we could fucking pack in here? A hundred? Some fucker would be bit, too. And then where would we be? Sardines in a can. Yum."

I lock the door to the booth.

Tyrell looks like he wants to be noble. But fuck it, the noble people all got thinned out from the herd.

I close my eyes. No.

Open them. Dot and I climb onto the stage. That sound. Of hush. When the lights went low and the first shadow moved on the stage. The hush before everyone started shushing each other. But we are not in our seats, and the lights are still bright, and that sound should not have come yet. We both know it.

Then screaming.

Then people rushing down the stairs.

Thank God, thank God I will not die falling down the stairs like that. There is a woman above us. I see her feet, her legs. Her feet twist as she looks toward one of the doors to the lobby. I cannot see her face.

"Help me!" I gouge my fingers into Dot's shoulder. I put away the knife and wave my other hand to get her attention.

Falling. They are pushing each other forward, they are falling down the stairs like dominoes. Some spread out into the seats, but where will they go?

Below me is a mother and a girl in a dirty purple jacket. The girl sees me, the mother sees me and screams for help. The red fabric is gone, but the pulley is bringing it back toward me.

The girl catches the fabric in her hand.

She is still looking up at me.

I put my fists together, then I spread them around my waist in a circle, and then I wave them in front of me to make a knot.

It is not falling that is hard. You have the fabric wound where you want it, and you hook a leg around the spin of it to stop. It is climbing that is hard. I climbed mountains, I climbed trees as a girl. This one, what does she have to climb? But the walls?

She is done. Her mother kisses her.

They are coming.

The mother looks away from her daughter. I start pulling, winding the fabric around my legs together, so I don't cut off too much blood flow. If I faint she will fall.

Falling is easy, but you shouldn't do it if you are not ready.

The kid's halfway up. I don't say a fucking word. Mags has the pulley board. Not my call.

They shove me off the stage, I fall, I roll toward the bottom of the stage and cover my head. I want to watch her but I can't. All I can see is her falling. And being ripped to pieces. I could look straight at her and not see her being lifted to safety.

I know I couldn't let them lift me.

I look for trap doors. Stages have trap doors. But they're usually on top of the stage. Not at the bottom. We're all so dirty I don't think they can smell me.

"Mom! Mom!" The girl is screaming. Who wouldn't scream for their mother at a time like this? I shouted for my mother, but of course she must be dead by now, for a long time. I haven't shouted for her for a long time. Blood is everywhere in ribbons, just like in the show, but the colors are not the same and do not shimmer under the spotlight.

This is what the Leadership wanted. Did they know? I think they did. So I send up a prayer for them, to say thank you. Thank you, you let me perform one last time. If we could have done the whole show, there would have been hope, too. It was that kind of show.

People beating on the door. Tyrell wants to open it, but it's the wrong kind of fucking sound. Ain't nobody knocking and sobbing for fucking help. I ain't cold. Not that cold. It's just they're fucking up here already.

"What are we going to do? We're going to die up here, aren't we? What are we going to do?"

Mags.

"There's food and water behind the servers," I say. "Not much but some."

Tyrell gives me a look, but fuck him.

"Ain't for me." I cough up phlegm and spit on the floor. Fuck civilization, man. "I just wanted to see her do her shit one last time."

I untie the ribbon from her waist. It is tied tight, good girl, but my fingers are like steel bars. She's done yelling for her mother. I know. There is a part of us that leaves an open hole that says, "What if she is still alive? What if some miracle occurred?" That is all we have, until we have something better. I wish I had something better to give her. Than a catwalk over chaos. I will not make her say it, I will not make her acknowledge her grief for as long as I live. I wipe my face with the fabric but my tears will not stop.

"You are so brave."

Did I say it, or did she?

Lieukov looks into the booth, wiping her face with her ribbon, almost dropping it over the side of the catwalk, then leaving it on top of the grillwork instead.

The girl walks up there like she was born to it.

Lieukov takes her hand and starts walking towards us.

The only way into the booth now is to break a window.

Tyrell beats on the glass and shouts. "No! No! Go the other way!" There's a gate between the zombies and the catwalk, but guess who didn't fucking lock it.

I am walking toward the door when Mags tackles me.

"You ain't going nowhere, sugar," she says. I hear a gun cock behind my fucking head. Then she gets off me.

"You want to save your girlfriend, just keep running the show."

"What?"

"You heard me."

I lift up my head, get on all fours. I could take her. I look at Tyrell. He's got a cold motherfucking face now. And a gun.

I think that definitely Leadership knew about this.

They're fighting in the booth. The girl says, "What are they doing?" She sees. I love that in all of this, she sees.

"It's political," I say. I sniff hard and wipe my hand on my face. "That means when one person tries to take power from someone else."

"Should we help him?"

"I do not know. Sometimes power should be taken away from people. I do not know."

The lights dim.

The show goes on. No performers. But the lights and the sound cues, they go on. No music. The musicians are gone. We sit, our legs dangling over the catwalk. The little girl drops a dirty tennis shoe on a zombie's head. We laugh; it's an old one and part of its face slides off. She drops her other shoe but it misses.

"What are those?" she asks. Pointing.

They look like spotlights but they never turn on.

"We should get out of here," I say.

She nods. I can hear the zombies on the other side of the catwalk cage door; we are very lucky they are not so smart. Where will we go, the roof? I touch the fabric fondly as we walk. I cannot get it loose if I try, that is good for performances, but not for here, and now.

The girl touches my hand, then pulls it close to touch the handle of a knife. Of course.

She has pockets.

Lieukov wraps herself in red ribbon.

She looks like a fucking queen.

We look into the parking lot. Cars, trucks, all still. I can barely see at first. I'm not used to daylight. There's a bracket on the side of the roof, sturdy, I cannot shake it, pulling with all my weigh.

"You see that truck?" I point to the trailer where the circus carries equipment while we are on tour.

She nods.

I hand her the knife and it disappears inside her dirty purple coat. She climbs down, hands wrapped in her dirty socks, sliding fast but not too fast. The noise in the building is so loud now, even out here it shakes my breath.

I curl up the fabric. I will fall with style.

"Doors locked," Mags says.

"We're a go." Tyrell takes off his headset.

They look at me.

"What?"

"Those extra spots you asked about," Mags says.

"Yeah?"

"Turn 'em on, sweetie."

Now she screams.

The glass in the window shatters, but the fabric protects me, it has always protected me. Of course I saved it.

For myself.

For anyone who wants to know what it was like, the circus.

We are traveling, we steal a car and I teach her how to drive. I am lying when I say I know how, but I have been in more cars than she has, I say with a smile. So she has to listen to me anyway. It is the same with guns. I tell her, you will just have to take my word for it.

For a long time, nothing.

And then the radio, on our fifth car, an orange Mustang with half a tank of gas, we hear:

—tonight we can confirm the last of the zombie hoards is dead, drawn in by hundreds of noble people in -----, who were hiding in a local arena. They invited the entire hoard inside, using the loud music and bright lights of a circus—

I am weeping. We have not spoken for two days. I am thinking of killing myself this morning.

"How was it supposed to end, the circus? What was the rest of it going to be like?"

It is sunset.

—lights back on. The following security precautions remain in place—

They are bright, so bright, ahead of us.

This morning I wished to die. But now, now I tell her.

IN THE AGE OF RESURRECTION : A ZOMBIE LOVE STORY

by Deborah Walker

When I brushed my hair this morning, a few strands fell out and stuck to the hairbrush. They were adhered to a piece of skin and flesh around the size of an antique pound coin. I picked this coin of flesh off the hairbrush and held it to the light. I stared at it—as if I could see the fragmentation of my DNA in that small lump of tissue.

I threw it into the moleculator bin at the side of the sink. Then I carefully brushed my hair to hide the already scabbing wound.

I stared into the bathroom mirror. That was that, then.

I would pod into the space-station today to visit a doctor. Then I would put my affairs in order: I would make two long-overdue visits, one to my brother Peter, and one to my darling Marla.

And after that...

"Ms. Petrovitz, I am sorry to inform you that you have entered the first stage of transformation."

The first stage. The point of no return. Stellar radiation had caused irrevocable damage within my body and within my mind. My DNA was on the long, slow escalator of deterioration. In a few weeks my mind would be gone but my body would live on.

There had been no real doubt in my mind, but I needed to have a doctor confirm the diagnosis.

"Have you entered it onto my medical records?" I asked.

"Yes, Ma'am." The doctor's face was professional stone. I wondered how many times he had delivered this diagnosis.

"I can arrange a counseling session for you, and I can also recommend a very active self-help group."

"No thanks, Doctor. That's not my style." I stood up and held out my hand. "I intended to get euthanized and my chip activated as quickly as possible."

I had no intention of enduring the long, slow process of dissolution.

"Well, that's your choice, Ms. Petrovitz, but I would caution you against making any hasty decisions."

"Doctor, I knew what the score was when I came to this part of space. I made my decision a long time ago."

"As you wish."

A zombie was entering data into a processor at the front desk. They can be trained for simple tasks. It looked like a women, a small frame encased in a flexible silver metal-rub suit holding her body together. I gave her a wave as I left the doctor's office. There's no stigma here, as there is on Earth. We cherish our zombies. They're part of our life.

Why wouldn't we, when we know that we will become them?

I've worked as a miner for the last ten years. I have my own asteroid and a snug living space carved out of the rock. Now that I had the official diagnosis, I hooked up to the net and willed my home and mining rights over to Cassidy Sung. That would give her a shock. Before I met Marla, me and Cass had an on-off relationship for years. You know the type of thing.

Still, I hoped that me passing on the asteroid to her would mean something to Cass. I didn't vid her, nothing much to say. Actions speak louder than words, in my opinion. I hoped she'd get some enjoyment out of the money my asteroid would bring her.

I was in a thoughtful mood as I walked the space station High Street along to the Church of the Resurrected Flesh. As I looked around the street I could see normals and zombies all mixed up together. We've built a fine place out here in this corner of space. We're tolerant here.

And I've seen things that the human eye was never built to see. I've seen the sun rise and set on a dozen worlds; I've marveled at the slow dance of strange lights over the over the ruins of ancient worlds; I've met people, weird people who have blown my mind with their alien philosophies. I have no regrets.

"Sister."

The voice of a priest called out from a balcony on the Church. He was dressed in the garments of one of the resurrected, although he was a normal. He wouldn't be able to talk otherwise.

"It's later than you think. Come into the Church and prepare yourself."

That made me stop for a minute. He was looking at me like he could tell, but by my reckoning, I had a couple of weeks to go before my mind went. Perhaps the priests develop some sort of sense about these things.

"I'm coming in, anyway," I shouted.

"Hallelujah, Sister."

"I'm just here to see my brother," I said.

I was sorry to disappoint him. I've never been one to be into religion, much. I imagine it's a comfort to some. That flake of flesh this morning hadn't changed my perspective.

The priest on the balcony looked at me properly for the first time, seeing not a potential soul to be saved, but a person. "Ah, yes. You're Brother Peter's sister, aren't you? Come in and be welcome. I saw him working in his cell half an hour ago."

I walked into the church and past the rows of pews that were filled with the resurrected. Their hands moved over church beads, as they made their prayers to God. Rich folk buy their contracts and set them here, saying prayers for their souls.

A light blinked at the back of each of the zombies' necks, the electronic pulse that bathed their damaged brains in hormones. That flash of light kept us safe, turned them into supplicants and stopped them from becoming what was their nature—flesh-eating, mindless creatures.

I walked to Peter's cell and knocked on the open door.

"Hey, Peter."

My brother was dressed in a metal-rub suit, too, but he'd pushed down the face covering mask.

He was engrossed in his work, as usual. "Have you heard what the scientists are saying?"

He almost spat out the word "scientists." As if science wasn't the thing that bought us here and had gifted us with this spectacular life in the stars.

I peered over his shoulder trying to read the paper upside down. "What are they saying this time?" I asked.

"They say that they're on the verge of a cure for transformation." He jabbed his finger angrily at the article.

My heart beat wildly for a foolish moment.

A cure?

But reality quickly reasserted itself. If there was a cure—and that was doubtful —it was too late for me. I was already walking along the dark tunnel. I felt glad that someone was waiting at the end for me.

"There's no cure, Peter. They've been on the verge of a cure for the last fifty years."

"They say that there's a new way of blocking out the stellar radiation." He stood up and walked to the window of his cell, looking out on the rows of zombie supplicants in the nave. "As if we want a cure. Look at the supplicants out there. Everything that made them human is gone, they're brain dead. Here in the heavens His rays delete the old self, but they live on. They're in a state of innocence. They are incapable of sin. Even though their bodies continue to degrade, the power of

His love has bestowed a miraculous regeneration on the limbs."

I didn't say if it weren't for that pulse in the back of their necks, bathing the supplicants in calming hormones those innocents would be tearing us limb from limb. I didn't want to argue with him, not now. So I said, "It's a miracle alright."

He smiled at me. "Have you found the light, Pat?"

He was kidding. Peter knew that I didn't share his faith, that I thought the church was just a crutch for those who couldn't accept the reality of living in space.

If you live here, radiation causes incremental damage to your DNA. Eventually you reach the transformation point, and your mind dies. What happens afterwards—the continuation of the body—didn't seem like a miracle to me. It was just a trick of biology. The same stellar radiation that killed your mind activated an older simpler part of the brain that allowed you to keep on moving. These multiple layers of our brains were just a consequence of our stroll through the long slow path of evolution.

"What's wrong, Pat?"

He was my brother—he knew me.

"I've got something to tell you, Peter."

He stopped reading the article and looked at me.

"My transformation's started."

"Oh, Pat." He reached out and took my hand. I could see that he was conflicted. As a priest, it was wonderful news, another soul was about to enter the resurrected afterlife, but as a brother the news was not so good.

"And have you changed your mind about the Church?"

"No, Peter, I'm sorry."

It crossed my mind that I should lie to him, just to make him happy. It would mean an awful lot to him. But that wouldn't have been right.

"What are you going to do?"

"I don't want to linger."

Some people hid their transformation, putting off the inevitable for as long as possible, but not me. I wanted to make my goodbyes today. Tomorrow I would go to the bureau, and get the final dose of radiation.

"That's what I would have expected of you." We hugged. "You've had a good life, Pat."

"Will you promise me something, Peter?"

"Whatever you want."

"Promise me that you won't make me into a supplicant when I'm dead."

"Of course not. I respect your wishes."

I breathed a sigh of relief; that was the thing I feared most.

Because when I'm dead, I wanted to spend the rest of my existence with my girl.

I went to see my love.

I hadn't been to see her for a few weeks. You know how it is when somebody dies, at first you visit them every day, and then little by little the visits begin to diminish. You start to get on with your life again. But some things don't diminish, I missed her every day, every minute. She was still my lovely girl.

She worked in the hydroponics factory. She'd always loved growing things. The living space in my asteroid had born testimony to her obsession. I smiled. I only hoped that she was more successful here than she had been in our home. I was forever throwing out her dead ferns and whatnot.

I waited for her shift to finish, watching the silver suited zombies completing their simple tasks. Their unhurried, deliberate movements were replicated throughout the factory. They reminded me of a shoal of silver fish swimming through the ocean of their afterlife. They were…cohesive. I felt an inkling of what my brother had been trying to teach me all these years.

At the end of the shift they bought Marla to me and guided her to a chair.

"Marla, my love."

I took her hand and felt her skin through the silver of the suit. I stared into her eyes looking for recognition but there was nothing there.

It's unknown how much the zombies remember. It's a matter of research or a matter of faith, depending on your point of view. The Church argues that zombies have entered a state of purity, that their minds are lodged in heaven, while their bodies fall back into the clay.

Others, those who don't understand, are less generous. They say that the zombies are automatons, or even monsters like the zombies of old, inhabited by malevolence.

They would not say that if they could look into the eyes of my love. I believe that she can hear me.

"It has been a long time, since you left me, Marla. I've been lonely without you. But I have good news. I will be joining you tomorrow."

I scan her eyes.

"You've gone ahead, but I'm expecting you to show me the ropes, just like you always did. You always looked out for me."

I'm crying now, willing for some reaction in her eyes.

But there is none.

It is too much for me. I do not want to linger. I leave her sitting in the chair. Looking forward to the morrow when I will enter the bureau.

I will complete the process that started when I first came here. They will bathe my head in radiation, my mind will slip away, my relentless brain will stop. The chip on the back of my neck will activate and I will step into the underworld.

Where I will be with my love Marla; as I was in life, so I will be in death.

by Jim Cort

Trick arrived in Lunaport on the shuttle from Phobos, two steps ahead of a warrant. The whole Martian district had become too hot for him, and he decided it was time to slip away and lay low for a while. On the platform, a re-am shambled up to take his luggage. Trick didn't have any, and ignored him. The re-am just stood there stupidly.

Re-ams gave Trick the creeps. He didn't like the way they looked—their skin was grey and blotchy, their eyes glassy and vacant, like a doll's eyes. He didn't like the way they smelled—like cabbage cooking. Mostly he didn't like that they were walking dead men.

It was only seventy-five years ago that a chemical solution that regenerated dead tissue had been discovered, and that only by accident. The solution cost a mint to produce in any kind of quantity, and reanimates, as they were called, were little more than a curiosity.

The major drive came about fifty years ago, when re-ams were put forth as saviors of the space program. It had grown increasingly expensive to send living humans into space and bring them back safely. The Space Administration had seen its funding cut year after year. Forced to do more with less, Space Admin had lent a sympathetic ear to proposals for sending dead men into space to perform the more menial jobs, and most of the space walks. After the Tagusaki Corporation made their breakthrough with synthetics, Thanatopic Nutrient Solution was only pennies a dose. Re-ams were cheaper than robots, safety regulations could be much more lax, and there was a constant supply. It was decided that the shores of space would be populated with the dead.

Now, standing in LunaPort, Trick was surrounded by walking dead men carrying luggage, sweeping the floor, cleaning the head. He shook off his revulsion and got back to the business at hand: laying low. The first place he thought of was Clavius.

The domed city of Clavius was one of a score such places that had appeared like blisters on the lunar surface. Its claim to fame was entertainment of all types, sacred, profane, and indifferent. Theaters, holo flick centers, casinos, cabarets, supper clubs, gentlemen's clubs, and just plain cathouses—there was something for everyone. The main attraction for Trick was that in Clavius, everything was for sale. He could buy all the safety and quiet he wanted. Life, however, has a way of intruding.

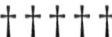

There was this citizen telling his pal about The Big Game in the coffee shop where Trick was eating breakfast.

"Fifty, sixty thousand in a pot," the guy had said, "and these guys act like it's nothing."

Trick had the habit of keeping his ears open no matter where he was. He leaned back in his booth, nibbling his sweet roll, and listened.

"They got real playing cards, some kinda replicas Alfano had special made, not this computer-simulation stuff like in the casinos," the guy went on. "My cousin, she used to be a waitress there. What do you think they bet with?"

The friend started to answer, but the citizen cut him off. "Gold. Little gold bars. You know Alfano's got a thing about gold. My cousin told me there's these little bars all over the table—you gotta have a grand just to ante up. Just imagine."

Just imagine, thought Trick.

Alfano was Fredo Alfano, the boss of Clavius. No matter where people might go, they take their bad habits with them. Soon enough they transform their new world into a replication of the old one. Every domed city had poverty; every city had slums, desperate, destitute people, crime and crime lords.

Alfano had started out as a leg-breaker for Boss Timpson back in the day, and then his lieutenant, and then his right-hand man, and finally his murderer. He operated from his headquarters in the Element 79 Club. Under his reign, the city worked as smoothly as an atomic clock, and there was nothing that went on that escaped his notice.

Professional curiosity caused Trick to pay a visit to Element 79 later that same day. On his way there he saw someone haranguing the crowd in the plaza. He was a scrawny guy with a bad complexion shouting that re-ams were an offense against the laws of God and man. In the crowd several others were handing out pamphlets. These were the Speakers for the Dead, a fringe group dedicated to the abolition of re-ams. Their protests were usually overshadowed by the immense profits re-ams brought in.

From a distance came the sound of sirens—police skimmers coming to break things up. Everyone scattered, the Speakers because they knew they'd be copped, the ones in the crowd, because they were used to doing what the one next to them did. Trick stood in a doorway until the troopers went by. When the coast was clear, he proceeded to the club.

Everywhere he looked inside Element 79, Trick saw gold—gold pillars, gold banisters, gold threads in the curtains and the skimpy costumes of the waitresses. For a hefty price you could order drinks with gold flakes in them, roasts encased in hammered gold. The word "gaudy" seemed inadequate.

Off to one side was a stage where a buxom girl took her clothes off with the aid of a re-am dressed like a circus clown. The re-am would clumsily yank one piece of clothing after another from her pale, fleshy body, while the girl pretended to be surprised each time. It got old very quickly.

Trick hung out at the bar, drinking SimBeer, and heard everything confirmed. The Big Game was the worst kept secret in Clavius. The place closed up early every Wednesday and the game started in a back room. The staff would make sandwiches and set up a bar and then leave. Players included corporate bigwigs, famous entertainers, other bosses from other cities, and politicians. The mayor of Clavius was a regular. Alfano always kept two of his bodyguards in the room.

A wrong turn on a trip to the head brought Trick to the door of the back room. It wasn't even locked. Inside it was just a big box. No odd corners. No place for anyone to stand unseen. The one door was the only door. It was tempting, very tempting, even for someone who was laying low.

Trick had mentally sketched out the broad outlines of the job in 15 minutes. Getting into the room would be about as hard as falling out of bed. If everyone stayed sensible, he'd be in and out inside of 10 minutes. Wham, bam, thank you ma'am.

The whole setup was a plum waiting for someone to shake the tree. There was only one catch: six hours, tops, after he pulled the job he'd be in a crater on the dark side with a slug in the back of his head. He'd learned enough about Alfano to know the big man could shut up the city as tight as an air lock. He owned the troopers. He owned the newsholos, the phones, the taxis, the metro. Everybody knew they could pick up some easy money being Alfano's eyes and ears. When the time came for Trick to leave, there'd be no way out.

It seemed a shame, but there was no point stealing something if you couldn't live to enjoy it. And anyway, he was supposed to be keeping a low profile. Still, there was some part of Trick that refused to let the problem go. Feeling safe had made Alfano careless. He deserved to be knocked over. Trick was convinced there was a way to work it. There was something that everyone else had overlooked. There always was.

Two weeks later, he found it.

On his way back from dinner, strolling down the back streets through the artificial night, Trick was still turning things over in his mind. A movement up ahead caught his eye. It was the figure of a man, just a silhouette in the street lights, moving across the back lot of a restaurant. The figure staggered slightly, and walked straight into a wall.

Then it backed up and did it again. And then again. Trick heard a giggle and fell back into the shadows. He crept behind a trash pod and peered around it.

"Make him go in circles," the girl giggled.

She was about sixteen, dressed in electric blue hot pants and a green plastic halter. An imitation raccoon coat, in pink, hung open down to her candy-striped high top sneakers. The colors looked even worse in the street lamp. She hung on the arm of a skinny piece of work all in denim with a multi color Mylar fringe. His silver hair stood in a line of spikes along the top of his head. He looked like a pissed-off cockatoo.

The boy hit a few keys on the PalmCom in his hand and the reanimate began shuffling in an erratic circle.

"Now make him dance," said the girl.

The re-am stopped. Its right foot slowly rose from the ground, the knee bending at a grotesque angle, and went down again—then the left foot. Then the right, then the left. Both arms slowly rose as the legs bounced up and down.

Trick had heard about this. These teeners had stolen the re-am from someplace, using the pirate signal from the PalmCom to make it move. Sometimes teeners set them on fire or made them walk off buildings or paraded them naked through shopping malls. This pair didn't seem that inventive.

"I'm tired of this," whined the girl. "Let's go to the holo flicks or something."

"Yeah, OK," said the boy, "just one more; watch this."

The re-am stopped gyrating, and walked toward the wall. It dropped to its knees with a violence that made Trick wince. Then it jerked forward and smashed its head into the bricks with a crunching noise. The re-am pulled itself back and crashed forward again.

"Oooh," squealed the girl, "headache."

The skin on the re-am's forehead had ruptured and gobbets of fluid, black under the streetlamp, seeped from the wound and dribbled down its face. It started to leave a wet patch on the bricks.

The two kids strolled away hugging each other while the re-am knelt and beat its brains out behind them. It would continue to perform the last command in its onboard buffer until it was switched off, or it bashed its own head in.

Trick waited until Young Love was out of sight, then he crept up and yanked the plug of the spinepack. The reanimate stopped moving, its face an oozing mess against the wall. Trick took a closer look. This reanimate was a black man, about as big as he was. A rental, to judge from the clothes. When the idea came, it was like someone opening a door in Trick's head.

The way to get out of the city was to be dead for a while.

The hardest thing was burning the re-am's body after he had stripped it of clothes and hardware, but that couldn't be helped. If he'd left it as it was, it would be a mystery. Burning, it was just another vandalized re-am, and no one would notice the shades and spinepack weren't there.

With this final piece, all the rest of the puzzle fell into place. He strolled through the Clavius Mall to buy the money belt, the plasma welder's mask, and the other things he'd need, making each purchase in a different store. He broke into a theater after hours and stole a curly blond wig. He also stole a Savage Model 1050 pump shotgun and a box of shells. Shotguns were the only reliable weapons out here. The behavior of high velocity rounds from a rifle, or even some handguns, in low gravity was unpredictable, and ray guns were strictly for the holo flicks. Anyway, he liked a shotgun. It was loud, it looked mean, and you didn't have to be a good shot to hit something.

Wednesday morning Trick shaved his head and then kept to his hotel room until nightfall. When the time came he pulled on the wig, and put the re-am's clothes and hardware in a knapsack and slung it on to his back. He hung the welder's mask by its strap around his neck. Over these went a long duster. In the left pocket of the duster went a plastiweave bag; in the right, his card lock scammer.

He checked the action on the Savage one last time and filled it with shells. The rest of the shells went into the right pocket of the duster. He tied a loop in a short length of rope and tied the rope around his waist. Once he hung the shotgun through the loop and buttoned the duster closed, no one would see it.

He got to Element 79 by 20:30, and waited across the street in the doorway of an abandoned sex shop where the light from the street lamp didn't reach. At 21:00, five people came out the front door. At 21:45, six more people left from the back. Some walked away; some got into compact skimmers and drove off.

At 22:06, the large skimmers arrived, some of them chauffeur driven. The passengers were mostly older men, richly dressed, with an air of wealth and power about them. Ultimately there were three of them. They passed one by one through the back door of the club.

Trick waited another two hours. Then he moved.

The scammer made short work of the lock on the back door. Trick slipped inside and eased the door shut behind him. A single dusty light burned in the narrow paneled hallway. Trick strapped on the welder's mask and slipped the shotgun from the loop in the rope.

There were murmured voices behind the door. Trick backed up, pumped the slide once and launched a kick at the lock. The plastiwood around it shattered and he burst into the room and yelled "Nobody move!"

His mind took a snapshot: four men at the card table: Alfano—a lump of a man who looked like he was made out of bricks, then some tall thin guy with gray hair, a Latin-looking guy next to him—he looked scared, a black guy with a big gut, drinks on the table, cards, half-eaten food. In the center of the table was a pile of twenty gram gold ingots, glowing like a small fire.

On the far side of the table were two of Alfano's goons. The one on the left was reaching inside his jacket. Big hero. Trying to impress the boss. Trick wanted to scream at him, "Can't you see this gun? Can't you see the freaking gun?" but there was no time for that. He swung the shotgun around and fired.

The blast caught the bodyguard high in the chest and flipped him over backwards. Trick heard his skull crack on the floor, but the guy never felt it. His piece went clattering into the corner. The room reeked of blood and gunsmoke. Trick jacked another shell into the chamber and covered the other guy.

"Easy, hot shot," he said, "don't be stupid. Take it out slow. Two fingers."

The gunman eased out his pistol, holding the butt in thumb and forefinger.

"Drop it in front of you and kick it away." Trick said and watched as he did so. "Now put your hands behind your head and keep 'em there. That goes for all of you."

Alfano stared at him. "Who the hell are you?" he said.

Trick tossed the bag to the tall guy. "Get the gold off the table and put it in here."

"What the hell is this?" said Alfano. He seemed to think he was in charge.

"What does it look like, moron?" said Trick. "You with the bag, get busy."

The tall guy moved about the table, shoveling the gold into the bag. Alfano stood there turning purple, rage and disbelief alternating on his thick face. Trick began to worry he might do something foolish, but all he did was talk.

"I don't know who you are, but I'll find out. You'll never get out of this town alive. I'll have your balls for breakfast. You hear me? "

The tall guy had finished clearing the table and stood next to it holding the bag like he didn't know what to do next.

"You," said Trick, "bring that over here."

"I swear to God, I'll kill you myself," said Alfano.

The tall guy sidled up to Trick and held the bag out at arm's length. Trick took it and motioned him back with the muzzle of the shotgun. Then he backed into the hallway.

"First one out this door gets shot," he said, and dashed away. He could hear Alfano's voice echoing down the hallway as he ran.

"You're dead, you hear me? You're a freaking dead man."

He didn't know how right he was.

An hour later, Trick was sitting in the back of a lorry skimmer with about three dozen re-ams. His head was shaved like all the others, and he had the spine-pack antenna stuck to the back of his neck. He wore the re-am's dark glasses, complete with sonar rig, but minus some crucial circuitry so the buzz wouldn't bother him. He was dressed in dark blue coveralls, just like all the others. Underneath the coveralls was a money belt stuffed with Alfano's gold.

No one could see that his brain wasn't skewered with electrodes. No one would notice that blood, not Thanatopic Nutrient Solution, flowed in his veins. No one could tell him from the walking dead man he pretended to be.

This shipment was meant for Tycho Farms, the premier hydroponics facility on the moon. Trick had slipped into this line of rentals while the minders were off getting a coffee or taking a leak or getting laid or something. When they came back, no one noticed one extra re-am in the line. They were marched into the skimmer and sat on two benches on either side of the cargo hold. In a moment they were joined by two troopers with Mossburg 790 riot guns.

The guards were there because of the Speakers for the Dead. The Speakers hadn't limited themselves to rallies or peaceful marches. Some engaged in "propaganda of the deed." They wanted to remove the profit motive from the use of re-ams and took to acts of sabotage. A few months back, one of these re-am shipments was intercepted by armed Speakers, and all the re-ams stolen. Speculation was that the Speakers cremated them by loading them into trash pods and shooting them into the sun. The facts were naturally suppressed and some story about mechanical failure was put about instead.

But the Corporations complained to Space Admin, and Space Admin provided armed guards for the shipments. This meant all cargo holds had to be pressurized, fortunately for Trick.

The skimmer vibrated as the engine fired up. Two metal bars came down, one from each side of the hold, and pressed against the re-ams seated there. Then someone outside flipped a switch, and they all went limp against it. Trick was pinned by the dead weight of them on either side. He felt a lurch and then movement.

Trick was smothering. The re-ams pressed like sacks of gravel against him. Inside the hold, the cabbage smell began to sicken him, and he was having trouble breathing. He didn't know how the guards could stand it. Trick tried to distract himself. He thought he recognized one of the re-ams across from him. He looked an awful lot like Jerry Blaustein—everybody called him Spider. It was hard to tell in the dim light of the hold, but Trick finally caught a glimpse of the spider web tattoo on his neck. It was Spider all right, poor bastard. The best burglar Trick had ever met. Bet he'd rather be in hell than here.

The skimmer heaved to a stop and Trick was almost crushed by the shifting bodies. A guard cracked the airlock and jumped down from the back. All at once all the re-ams shuddered and sat at attention. This caught Trick by surprise, but no one was there to see it. The bar lifted, and one by one the re-ams turned, stood, stepped out of the truck and lined up.

Standing in line, Trick took in as much as he could of Tycho Farms. Above him was the massive geodesic dome. Trick could see the stars glowing in the lunar sky. Off to the left, surrounded by rows of hydroponic tables, was the control shack, just a trailer set up on blocks with various antennae jutting from the roof. A minder would be in there running the programs that were beamed out to the reanimates at their various tasks. Trick knew that until they got into the work area, all the commands were being issued by the minders here with their PalmComs.

To the right he could see the skimmer they had come from and the guard, still holding his riot gun. He was a scrawny guy with a bad complexion. Trick nearly jumped when he recognized him as the Speaker in the plaza. He struggled to keep his breathing shallow as he tried to dope this out. What's this guy doing here? He didn't pull anything on the trip, so he must have something else in mind. Something's going to happen here on the farm. Trick almost smiled. This guy was going to cause some kind of disruption, and Trick could use it to his advantage to get away. It was almost too perfect. All he had to do was wait until this guy made his move, and then get out when everyone was looking the other way. He could stow away on a skimcoach to Plato or Copernicus and be gone before the rumpus was over.

The re-ams started marching, different streams breaking off to different work areas. Trick noticed Spider move off to the packing area. He saw a re-am there slice the roots from a head of lettuce with one quick stroke from a long curved blade. Another stream picked up baskets to move the produce from the tables to packing. Trick's group went down to the tables to pick the crops.

The tables were about waist high and filled with water, tinged slightly blue from the nutrients mixed in. On top of the water floated plastic foam sheets studded with holes. Bunches of green leaves poked through the holes. This crop was leaf lettuce. Trick's job was to pluck each shaggy head from the plastic sheet and drop it into the basket carried by the re-am next to him. When the basket was full, the re-am carried it to packing and was replaced by another re-am with an empty basket.

Trick watched intently from the corner of his eye to see what to do. Bend from the waist, reach down, pull the lettuce head from the hole, turn, and drop it dripping into the basket. Then begin again. The lettuce heads trailed ugly pale roots like the tendrils of a jellyfish. All the re-ams moved in unison, controlled centrally by the programs narrowcast from the control shack.

After doing this thirty times, Trick thought he was going to pass out. He couldn't believe that live people used to do it all day long. Every muscle ached from being held unnaturally stiff. His head throbbed and he was starting to sweat. He began to regret his decision to wait for the Speaker. If something didn't happen soon, a guard would be sure to notice the sweat stains and probably shoot him.

As he turned to another grow float, Trick saw the Speaker steal into the control shack. This had to be it. He bent, reached, pulled, turned and dropped again, all his senses primed.

The re-am next to him bent, grabbed a head of lettuce, and dropped it on the table with a splash. Another re-am did the same. Farther down the table, a re-am was smashing the grow floats with its fists. At the next table over one re-am picked up another and slammed him onto the table, shattering it. Water and lettuce leaves were everywhere.

Trick jerked up, tore off his shades and looked around. All over the reanimates were going berserk, stumbling in all directions spasmodically destroying everything around them. On every side the destruction was universal, random and completely silent. The Speaker must have screwed around with the control programs. Trick stared, dumbstruck, just a little too long and a re-am overturned the table he was standing by. The table landed on him heavily and Trick felt his left thigh bone snap. The pain was beyond imagining, and Trick bit his hand to keep from screaming.

Trick struggled to keep himself under control. He rolled out the way and crawled through blue puddles and soggy greenery, dodging falling bodies and tables. He pulled himself to his feet on a broken table. The airlock door was about twenty-five meters away. He heaved himself to a crouching stand and started a staggering, limping run, pain stabbing him at every step.

Just ahead a re-am hopped from one foot to another, waving its arms. Trick bent low and shoved and the re-am went down, writhing on the floor like a squashed bug. On the other side of the dome he saw the workers from packing shambling toward the mob, still carrying their long knives. Guards and minders were wading into the crowd, vainly trying to restore order.

Every muscle in his body begged him to stop, but he couldn't stop. On the other side of the airlock door was a corridor. If he could get to that, he could make his way to the crew's living quarters, steal a change of clothes and hide out until the skimcoach arrived. His leg was shrieking at him to stop, but he couldn't stop.

Fifteen meters to the airlock.

From out of nowhere, a re-am appeared, whirling like an insane dervish, its arms raised. One of its fists collided with Trick's temple and he went down, cracking his head on a table leg. A moment later, another re-am landed on top of him. This time he did cry out. A firestorm of pain ran up and down his spine. He pushed himself up slowly with his left hand and reached around with his right to roll the body off him. He was groggy from the blow. His head was pounding. The agony in his leg was making him sick. He thought for a moment he was going to lose it, but he forced things back into focus and started crawling toward the airlock.

Try to concentrate on something other than the pain. The gold, all that gold. Never seen so much gold.

A reanimate staggered past him, tripped on a head of lettuce and fell forward, splitting its head open on a shattered table. Purple liquid spurted from the wound.

Ten meters to the airlock.

You could live like a goddamn maharajah anywhere with that much gold.

His left leg hated him. It was trying to kill him. No, that's crazy. He shook his head, trying to keep it clear.

Six meters to the airlock.

The sweat streamed into his eyes. It grew harder and harder to catch his breath. His head was splitting. He could barely drag himself along. The row of tables was coming to an end. He'd have to pass into the open. It took more strength than he thought he had to wrestle himself to a standing position and lurch toward the airlock, trailing his useless leg.

Two meters to the airlock.

A re-am shambled up to him and Trick, still dazed, saw it was someone he knew.

"Hey, Spider," he gasped, "I'm hurt. You gotta help me, man. I gotta get to—"

Spider grabbed the top of Trick's head and sliced it neatly from his body with one quick stroke of his curved blade.

Tycho Farms was shut down for a month. The official story was sunspots had scrambled the control signals. The Speaker who had sabotaged the computer was killed trying to escape. They dumped his body into one of the trash pods with all the re-ams and shot it off into the sun.

Back in Clavius, there was a big shakeup for a week or so. Fredo Alfano turned the whole town inside out. They said on the street he was on the warpath about some guy that ripped him off for 75 large. Six men were shot by mistake, but they never did find the guy.

NEWSFEED ZOMBIES

by Aislinn Batstone

Jack Adams didn't project a direct message to the barber shop girl's mental feed, no advance notice of his intentions battling the stream of social updates inside her skull. Regardless of his line of work, he couldn't understand why you'd want the web in your head or a camera in your eyebrow. Was her life so exciting she'd watch it over again later?

She was plump and pale with peroxided hair in two childish pigtails, arms and legs dotted with tattoos. She moved slowly, her eyes focused somewhere off in the air to her right. Typical newsfeed zombie. Her voice cracked when she spoke and her tongue had all the energy of the fat Shingleback lizards that lay so blue and glossy on the bitumen of Australia's desert roads.

"What can we do for you, sir?"

There was a hint of curiosity in her wide, brown eyes but she ruined the impression of intelligence by zoning out just as he was about to reply. He waited. Next, her eyes focused on him for long silent moments. He waited some more. He guessed she'd forgotten he had no implant and tried to message him again.

"Sorry. Have you been away? We can do your implant on the spot if you like."

Even in the mining town where he'd been stationed he could have got an implant, if he'd wanted to. "Just shave me."

Her mouth turned down and he noticed a scatter of freckles across the bridge of her nose. They reminded him of Petra, the copper-coloured birthmark on the small of her back above the swimsuit line, those sweet summer nights in Norway where they'd met.

The attendant ushered him to a lay-back chair and he eased into it, lifting his dusty boots onto the footrest. Around him other men suffered tattoos unflinchingly, anesthetized by inner entertainment. The implant itself couldn't be seen but like everything else in this brave new world it advertised itself, a brand name logo inked in behind the left ear.

Jack's attendant returned with a blade she was polishing on a bit of white cloth. She wore glossy black boots and black fishnet tights, tiny windows onto her very white calves. Petra had worn fur-lined boots in winter, and in summer, sandals and cotton dresses. She'd never followed fashion, until she'd succumbed to it.

"You'd look better with a beard, sir. Every man does."

Copper mines were too hot for beards. He indicated the girl should continue, and she worked on him in silence, lost in the trivia supplied to her by the mobile device embedded in her skull.

He left the barber shop in the cool twilight of evening. He had no fear of mugging from the newsfeed zombies populating the streets of Boston, even with months of pay on his pocket card. He hated the city, hated all cities, but it was here that Petra had promised to meet him when he came on leave.

He took the T three stops to South Station and walked two blocks to the club. He sat at the bar and ordered pizza and beer. The beer arrived first. He drank it and ordered another as the pizza arrived. He ate, closing his eyes as oil oozed rivulets down both sides of his chin.

The second beer he nursed for two hours. Apart from the missing tattoo behind his left ear he was sure he fitted right in, the way he spent the time just staring into space. Right now he couldn't claim anything much in the way of original thought. Maybe you could call it meditation. He ordered a third beer and drank it fast. The fourth beer hastened time and he found it was ten o'clock.

She wasn't coming. She'd never come any of the four other times she'd promised it. He'd lost her after bringing her here—another black mark on the workbook of his life. He hadn't believed the USA could ruin or even change her; she was Norwegian, for God's sake. She should have been beyond the hopeless fashions. He couldn't imagine her wearing anything other than sandals and cotton dresses in summer, could never have predicted her getting a tattoo, let alone an implant.

And yet she had, and rapidly retreated into 'the life of the mind', the phrase that had once, ironically, described intellectual endeavour. There was nothing intellectual about four-word headlines and brain-spam assaults from advertorial clouds that hovered like swarms of insects at bus stops and in the entryways to buildings.

Between ten and midnight he drank his final beer. Five beers, making one for every promise she'd broken. What else could you expect from a newsfeed zombie? He took his duffel from under the seat and headed for the exit. No-one noticed, not a single person nodded even a simple gesture of farewell.

He took the T to Logan airport. This time the company was sending him back to Australia. He knew deep down that Petra would never get on a plane again. Wherever she was, she was stuck there, locked in what passed for thought. He might as well find a corpse to share his bed.

Jack Adams boarded his plane and sat in his allocated seat with the soles of his dusty boots flat on the floor. He stared out the window. He'd been told he was missing out on life by not having an implant. Was he the only one who could still be moved by the beauty and lightness of the clouds in the sky?

A flight attendant arrived by his seat. "Sir?" Her eyes, wide and hazel, engaged him fully. No newsfeed occupying her attention. "Sir, would you like a drink before take-off?"

"You…you…"

"Yes sir?"

He found his voice. "Please, bring me a whisky."

She nodded and turned to leave.

He clutched at his armrests. "If…if…you have time on this flight…talk to me?"

"Of course, sir." She smiled.

Here it was, proof there were still people in the world he could connect to. If he tried to find more…How long would his pocket card last him without work? Two months? Three? Australia was the place for it, the kind of country that could fall so far behind in time that it somehow came out ahead.

He wouldn't mine copper for the implants anymore. Much as he loved the material, it was perverse to take something so supremely adaptable and turn it into something hard and cold, lifeless and stupid. He sipped his whisky and looked out the window. Soon he'd be flying high among those weightless clouds. Lighter already as he waited to join them in the sky.

You think you know zombie?

**More Tales of the Undead in
BLACK CHAOS I**
from **BIG PULP**

AUTHOR BIOGRAPHIES

Terry Alexander (*The Zombie Mike Christmas Special*) lives with his wife Phyllis on a small farm near Porum, Oklahoma. They have three children and eleven grandchildren. Terry has been published in various anthologies from Pro Se Press, Airship 27, Pulp Modern, Metahuman Press, Hazardous Press, Grinning Skull Press and May December Publications. He is a member of the Tahlequah Writers, Ozark Writers League, Oklahoma Writers Federation, and The Fictioneers.

Bo Balder (*Daddy's Home*) is a freelance writer who lives and works in the ancient Dutch city of Utrecht, close to Amsterdam. When she isn't writing, you can find her madly designing knitwear, painting, and reading anything and everything from Kate Elliott to Iain M. Banks or Jared Diamond. She will be the first Dutch author to have published a story in the famous *F&SF* (*Fantasy & Science Fiction Magazine*), forthcoming in September 2015. Her other short fiction has appeared in *Penumbra*, *Spark* (forthcoming), and quite a few anthologies. Her SF novel *The Wan* will be published in summer 2015 by Pink Narcissus Press.

Aislinn Batstone (*Newsfeed Zombies*) lives in Sydney, Australia with her family. Her science fiction, fantasy, and crime short stories have been published in magazines and anthologies in Australia, the USA, and the UK.

Steven E. Belanger (*The Zombie's Lament*) has been a high school English teacher and Decathlon coach for the past fourteen years. He loves writing, reading, playing and watching baseball, collecting really old baseball cards, viewing anything zombie-related, and hanging with his super-photogenic greyhound, Jackson. His fiction, reviews and articles have been published by *Space and Time Magazine*, *All Due Respect*, *OnThePremises.com*, *Over My Dead Body! The Mystery Magazine Online*, and Hidden Thoughts Press. He blogs at stevenebelanger.blogspot.com. Reach him at sb@stevenbelanger.com.

Thomas Canfield (*Shackles of Death*) resides in the mountains of western North Carolina. He is the author of the zombie novel *The Moon is an Arrant Thief*.

Angel Luis Colón's (*Dave Vs. the Zombie Apocalypse*) fiction has appeared in multiple online and print journals, including *Shotgun Honey*, *The Flash Fiction Offensive*, *Revolt Daily*, *Thuglit*, and *All Due Respect*. His debut novella, *The Fury of Blacky Jaguar*, is due out this summer from One Eye Press.

D. Jason Cooper (*American Refugees*) has written seven books including *Understanding Numerology*, which introduced the use of higher numbers, and *Slums of Paradise* (Twilight Times - no, not that franchise) in which the Pope attempts to use sacred relics to influence the rising of a vampire. He is also the author of *Mithras: Mysteries and Initiation Rediscovered* and the story "Mithras" for the upcoming *Modern Gods Vol III* anthology. He is a regular contributor to *Blastoffcomics.com* and has a website *djasoncooper.com*. His biggest contact with zombies, though, came from working for the bureaucracy for twenty years.

Jim Cort (*Dead Moon*) has been writing since just after the earth's crust cooled. His novel *The Lonely Impulse* is available from Smashwords: https://www.smashwords.com/books/view/337106.

James Dorr (*Cold, Lifeless Fingers*) is an Indiana writer. His book *The Tears of Isis* was a 2014 Bram Stoker Award® Fiction Collection finalist. His other books include *Strange Mistresses: Tales of Wonder and Romance*, *Darker Loves: Tales of Mystery and Regret*, and his all-poetry *Vamps (A Retrospective)*. Dorr invites readers to visit his blog at http://jamesdorrwriter.wordpress.com.

J. Boone Dryden (*In Reynolds*) is a graduate student pursuing a joint JD/MFA degree at Hamline University in Minnesota. He has previously been published on *EveryDayFiction.com*, *365Tomorrows.com*, *BigPulp.com*, and in *Left of the Lake Magazine*.

Sean Ealy (*In the Storm They Came*) is a writer and avid Red Sox fan living in Oregon. His fiction has appeared in *The Saturday Evening Post*, *Triptych Tales*, *Fiction Vortex*, and other publications. When not changing diapers or making bottles, he is hard at work on finishing his novel. He frequently blogs about life and writing at seanealyfiction.com or you can find him on Twitter @SeanEaly.

Gary Ives (*Sweet Bird of Death*) lives with his wife and two big dogs in the Ozarks where he grows apples and writes.

W.P. Johnson (*White Light, White Heat*) is a writer of horror, weird fiction, and noir. He graduated from Temple University with a degree in English Literature and has been published by *One Buck Horror*, Kraken Press, *Shroud*, Dark Moon Books, Perpetual Motion Machine Publishing, *Pulp Modern*, Fox Spirit Books, Dark House Press, and Thunderdome Press. You can follow him on social media through the moniker americantypo. He currently lives and works in Philadelphia and is working on his first novel.

Brenda Kezar (*Inhuman Resources*) is a horror and fantasy writer from North Dakota and an active member of the Horror Writers Association. Her stories have appeared in *Daily Science Fiction*, *Silverthought*, *Bonded by Blood V*, *Penumbra eMag*, *Zombidays: Festivities of the Flesheaters*, and others. Her website: www.BrendaKezar.com.

DeAnna Knippling (*The Last Circus*) went to her first Cirque du Soleil show shortly before writing "The Last Circus": she had to do something, since she couldn't possibly stand up and yell "Zombie attack!" during the packed arena show, no matter how much she wanted to. She also used to hang out with a bunch of theater geeks and found she missed being up in the booth more than she realized. She lives in Colorado and has recently been published in *Penumbra*, *Crossed Genres*, and more. Her website is at www.WonderlandPress.com.

Wayne Laufert (*The Dead of Summer*) worked for many years as a reporter and editor for a weekly community newspaper. The federal government has employed him since 2010. He has excreted a smattering of cartoons, a handful of mini-comics, and some Bugs & Cranks baseball blog posts. This story is his first published fiction since his college literary magazine, which doesn't count. He lives in Baltimore.

Jason S. Ridler (*Bitter Inheritance*) is a writer and historian. He is the author of *A Triumph for Sakura*, *Blood and Sawdust*, the Spar Battersea thrillers, the short story collection *Knockouts*, and has published over sixty stories in such magazines and anthologies as *The Big Click*, *Beneath Ceaseless Skies*, *Out of the Gutter*, numerous *Big Pulp* publications, and more. His popular non-fiction has appeared in *Clarkesworld*, *Dark Scribe*, and the *Internet Review of Science Fiction*. A former punk rock musician and cemetery groundskeeper, Mr. Ridler holds a Ph.D. in War Studies from the Royal Military College of Canada.

Anna Sykora (*My Mother-in-Law is a Zombie*) has been an attorney in NYC and teacher of English in Germany, where she resides with her patient husband and three enormous cats. To date she has placed 136 stories, mostly genre, in the small press, and one made the finals of Rosebud's 2014 Mary Shelley Competition. She has also placed 356 poems. Writing is her joy.

Gabriel Valjan's (*Zombees*) *Roma Series* is available from Winter Goose Publishing. The fourth installment, *Turning To Stone* is out in early 2015. Gabriel is the author of numerous short stories. He was short-listed for the 2010 Fish Prize, and won the inaugural ZOUCH Lit Bits Contest. He lives in Boston, Massachusetts.

Deborah Walker (*In the Age of Resurrection*) grew up in the most English town in the country, but she soon high-tailed it down to London, where she now lives with her partner, Chris, and her two young children. Find Deborah in the British Museum trawling the past for future inspiration. Her stories have appeared in *Nature's*

Futures, *Cosmos*, *The Year's Best SF 18* and in the Bram Stoker Award-winning *After Death* anthology, under her pen name Kelda Crich.

Ian Welke's (*The Not Tom*) short stories have appeared in *KZine*, *Big Pulp*, *Zombie Jesus and Other True Stories*, and the American Nightmare anthology, amongst others. His first novel, *The Whisperer in Dissonance*, was published by Omnium Gatherum Media in 2014. His second novel, *End Times at Ridgemont High*, is expected to be published in the spring of 2015. Before writing full time, Ian was lucky enough to work at Blizzard Entertainment and at Runic Games. These days, when he's not at his desk writing, Ian enjoys a variety of games. His favorites tend to be elaborate board games with many pieces and rules to confuse, though he's happiest going mad with his characters in the Call of Cthulhu RPG.

R.A. Williamson (*We Always Get Our Man*) is a software developer, reticent exhibitionist, and former child actor. Born in Canada, he now lives with his sultry little woman and their three feral children in a zombie-proof fortress nestled deep within the verdant Snoqualmie Valley, where he writes sporadically for the western horror serial *Whiskey & Wheelguns*.

A graduate of Bath Spa University in England, **Dawn Wilson** (*When It's Not Love, It's Hate*) has had the pleasure to dabble in kitsch, surrealism, and espièglerie. Her work can be found in *Gone Lawn*, *Metazen*, *New Dead Families*, and *Punchnel's*, among others, while the author herself can be found dismantling the kitchen for wearable items, or at nightdawn.wordpress.com. She has recently completed a madcap novel.

Joriah Wood (*Lucky 43*) is a pseudonym for Christopher Smith. He began writing when he realized it was less expensive than playing paintball. Preferring the short-story format, he writes for the weird west serial anthology, *Whiskey and Wheelguns*, as well as penning the occasional comic book script at Champion City Comics.

Nu Yang (*Memories*) resides in Southern California, but she is a Midwest girl at heart. Her publication credits include Three Crow Press, Hic Dragones, *JournalStone*, *Big Pulp*, *SQ Magazine*, Edge Publishing, and *Shroud Magazine*. She is a 2006 graduate of the Odyssey Writing Workshop and a June 2009 graduate of the Writing Popular Fiction Master's program at Seton Hill University. Find her online at nuyangwriter.wordpress.com.

ARTIST BIOGRAPHY

Ken Knudtsen *(cover illustration)* is a writer, artist and loyal drinking buddy. He has been fortunate to have worked on projects ranging from David Geffen (*Inventing David Geffen* - PBS), *Wolverine* (Marvel Comics), and, of course, the adventures of a little girl and a crazy monkey (*My Monkey's Name is Jennifer* from SLG Publishing). It is never a bad idea to surprise Ken with a bacon snack.

Peg, slamming something against the broken door, pushed the rotting wood hard into Susan's mask and mouthpiece. Susan fell back, mouthpiece dislodged and bubbling, the mask hanging to her knees. Instinctively, she grabbed for Peg's, but Peg fought back, swinging her fist full force between Susan's legs, then ripping away the line to Susan's tank.

excerpt from *Dead in the Water* by Janett Grady

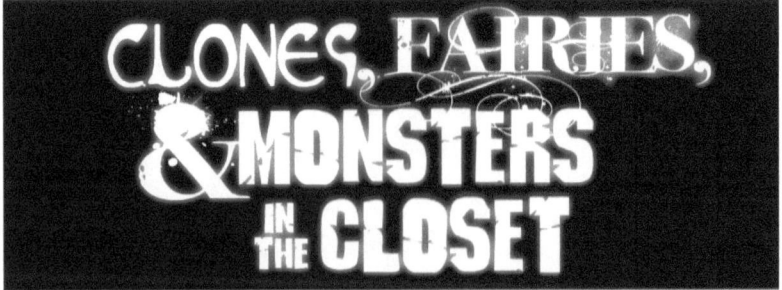

Child of Words

Science Fiction & Fantasy
from BIG PULP

THE KENNEDY CURSE

SLAIN · ACCIDENT · CANCER · PLANE CRASH · LOBOTOMIZED

The American Camelot meets Grand Guignol

Plane Crashes. Assassinations. Lobotomies. Suicide. Miscarriages.
Drug Abuse. Sex Addiction. Mental Illness. Car Wrecks. Cancer.
With a family history like that, you'd think they were *cursed*.

Political SF, Horror & Crime from **Big Pulp**
Edited by Bill Olver

M

Murder &
the Macabre
from **BIG PULP**

The gorilla started towards us, looking less and less like a gentle giant with each stomping step. Her gait was strange. I couldn't recognize a gorilla's normal gait, but it couldn't have been as jerky or as stiffly lumbering as the one advancing upon us. As she grew closer, other odd attributes also became clear: gaping wounds dripping gray ooze, broken fangs, and a sickening stench that distance had been kind enough to keep away until then. Backing away only made her move quicker, and before long, she was a mere ten feet in front of us. It was then that I noticed how much Knight's fear had increased.

"What do we do?" I asked him and he shook his head frightfully.

excerpt from *Test 17*
by Jessica McHugh

www.ingramcontent.com/pod-product-compliance
Lightning Source LLC
Chambersburg PA
CBHW030326020726
47493CB00004B/1176